The VAMPIRES of YORK TOWER

KIRSTEN MCKENZIE

ALSO BY KIRSTEN MCKENZIE

The Old Curiosity Shop Time Travel Trilogy

FIFTEEN POSTCARDS

THE LAST LETTER

TELEGRAM HOME

The Ithaca Time Travel Trilogy

ITHACA BOUND

ITHACA LOST

ITHACA FOUND

The Cheviot Hills Time Travel Series

THE DEADLY LIFE OF DIANA PENN

Standalone Paranormal Thrillers

PAINTED

DOCTOR PERRY

THE FORGER AND THE THIEF

THE VAMPIRES OF YORK TOWER

Short Story Anthologies

LANDMARKS

NOIR FROM THE BAR

REMAINS TO BE TOLD

THE VAMPIRES OF YORK TOWER

WINGSPAN EDITION

KIRSTEN MCKENZIE

SSP

This edition published August 2025 by Squabbling Sparrows Press

ISBN 978 1 991331 60 1 (Wingspan Paperback Edition)

Cover design: Germancreative

*Dedicated to my childhood friends from Royal Terrace.
Sneaking into haunted houses, reading vampire comics,
swallowing lego, and watching terrifying motorcycle gang
movies, set me up well for a lifetime of
night terrors and trust issues.
Thanks!*

Multitudes who sleep in the dust of the earth will awake:
some to everlasting life,
others to shame and everlasting contempt.

—Daniel 12:2

1

THE COURIER

T he marble lobby of York Tower had seen its share of secrets over the decades, but none quite like what was about to walk through its doors that morning.

Will Taylor leaned against the polished front desk, the creases of his uniform shirt like razor blades across his shoulders as he checked the morning's visitor log. The same names, the same times, the same routine. Except today there was something new — a memo about staff changes.

"Well, look at this," Will said, glancing at his colleague. "They've finally hired a replacement for Graeme.'

"A turnip would be an improvement," Rufus snorted, his shirt buttons straining against his girth. "At least it wouldn't talk."

"Yes! If I have to hear one more time about the key characteristics of a 1967 Chevelle SS muffler, it'll be too soon," Will said.

"Or how the engine timing on his precious Pontiac GTO needs 'just a little adjustment.'" Rufus mimicked Graeme's nasal voice. "Like any of us gave a shit."

"They're starting the new guy today," Will said, flipping through the logbook. "Or should I say, we're starting his training today."

"Today?" Rufus frowned. "Why the rush?"

"Management's worried about coverage over the festive season."

Rufus let out a dry laugh. "Since when do we take vacations?

My biggest adventure this year was taking a different route to work. What else did you hear about the new hire?"

"Young guy, saving for college, the usual story," Will said.

"Kinda wish I'd gone to college now. Maybe then I'd own one of these apartments instead of babysitting the tenants."

"You know all our tips are about to disappear into the young guy's pockets, instead of ours," Will said.

"You're still getting tips?"

"Mostly about the weather," Will replied, deadpan. "Still better than working the beat, though."

"Yeah, my knees prefer standing guard to chasing perps through alleys." Rufus shifted, his arthritis a constant reminder of those days.

"Speaking of the old days — you remember my dad?"

Rufus nodded.

"He spent his last three years in that place on the Upper East Side. Premium care, they called it." Will's voice carried an edge Rufus had rarely heard. "Died alone on a Tuesday afternoon while I was stuck in traffic. Staff didn't even notice for four hours."

"Jesus, Will. I'm sorry, I didn't know—"

"That's why I actually give a damn about the tenants here," Will continued, his eyes scanning the empty lobby. "Someone should. These rich old folks in the tower, they've got everything — money, fancy apartments, the best medical care. But half of them seem lonelier than my dad was in that state facility."

A buzz at the lobby entrance cut short their conversation.

"Your turn," Will announced, switching his attention to the monitors hidden beneath the polished mahogany countertop.

Will watched Rufus leverage himself off the stool, keys jangling as he padded across the marble floor. His partner's limp was more pronounced, the arthritis always acted up when the weather turned. The doctors had told Rufus to lose weight, but Will knew better than to bring that up again.

Behind the toughened glass stood a courier in a tailored brown uniform, as motionless as a statue. Will glanced between the monitor and the door, unsettled by how perfectly still the figure remained. No FedEx purple and orange, no Amazon blue, no harried Uber driver's casual wear. The uniform was crisp linen, with subtle brass buttons and hand-stitched company insignia he couldn't place.

The courier's stack of parcels was wrapped in thick cream paper, tied with twine — a far cry from the usual battered cardboard boxes they usually saw. His face was like a guillotine — stern features carved with the same unforgiving precision as the famous blade.

"New courier, and not one of the usual services," Rufus called as he unlocked the door. "Hey, which company are you with?"

"A private employer," the courier replied evenly.

"Never seen that uniform before," Will noted, his old detective instincts kicking in. "Must be exclusive."

"Indeed." The courier's face remained unreadable.

"We need a name for the logbook," Rufus insisted.

"Burtons," the courier said, the name slipping from his lips as if it meant nothing at all.

"Come on in already," Rufus huffed. Will recognized that tone from their days on the force — the familiar frustration of hitting a wall of non-cooperation. "It's too cold to leave the door open and I don't want to sweep up any more leaves today."

The courier crossed the threshold, his polished boots unmarred by the slurry of fall leaves and unseasonably heavy rain.

"Who're they for?" Will asked, hand poised above the call system.

"Apartment 306," the courier replied, his voice precise.

"That can't be right. Check your docket. That place has been empty since I started here."

"An elite private delivery service, and you can't even get the address right?" Rufus queried.

"Apartment 306," the courier repeated. "These packages are for the new tenant. I have a key."

"Like hell you do," Will said, standing up straight, his hand straying to his empty hip out of habit. "There is no tenant in 306."

The courier set the stack of packages on the counter and pulled an ornate key from his shirt pocket. "I can assure you, there is. Now let me up like the good little toy cops you are, and we can carry on with our day."

Rufus grabbed for the key, but the courier sidestepped with effortless precision, already three paces back, the packages clasped neatly in one arm while the key dangled mockingly from his finger.

Will's face flushed, stung by the "toy cops" jab and the realization of what the key was—an original York Tower apartment key. "Fine. I'll take you up. But I'm telling you, that apartment's empty."

"Suit yourself," the courier shrugged, his expression unchanged. "You have your orders, and I have mine."

The elevator ride was tense and silent, with Will watching the courier from the corner of his eye. The man barely seemed to breathe, his wax-like face making it impossible to pin down his age. He could be anywhere from 30 to 50. Probably an elite athlete type who trained to lower their heart rate to near hibernation, Will thought bitterly. His cop instincts screamed that something was off about this whole situation, but he couldn't put his finger on what.

Outside apartment 306, Will gestured. "There you are."

The courier stepped forward, sliding the key into the lock and slipping through the open door with his packages before turning to face Will, his stance blocking any clear view inside. "Thank you for your assistance."

Frustrated, Will turned to leave, certain his eyes were playing tricks on him. Had he glimpsed someone else inside? The place was supposed to be empty. As he stepped toward the elevator, he felt a sharp sting and slapped at his neck. He checked his palm, expecting to find a squashed bug or spider, but found only a smear of blood.

Back in the lobby, Rufus looked up. "Everything okay?"

Will rubbed his neck. "Yeah, apart from being stuck in a rickety cage with a guy who wouldn't stop staring. I hate those elevators.

"They're older than God himself. And we need to call the exterminators. Something just bit me.'

"Let me see." Will felt Rufus' thick fingers probe his neck. "It's still bleeding."

"Probably a mosquito bite." Will rubbed at the bite again, though something deep in his gut told him mosquitoes didn't leave wounds that felt quite like this.

"What if it's a spider bite? Those can kill you."

Will rolled his eyes. "If you're worried I'm gonna turn into Spider-Man, I hate to disappoint you. I don t do Lycra."

Preoccupied with rifling through the first aid kit in the dark kitchen nook off to the side of reception, the men launched into a heated debate about the merits of the various Spider-Man actors.

Neither Will nor Rufus noticed the courier slipping silently out of the building, a small smile playing at the corners of his sharp mouth.

And from somewhere high above York Tower, a raven's harsh caw cut through the unseasonable rain, a single dark shape wheeling against the gray sky before vanishing into the growing storm.

2

TEE TIME TALES

The early morning sun cast long shadows across the fairway of Dyker Beach Golf Course as Will and Rufus stepped up to the first tee. Will squinted, fishing his sunglasses from his golf bag. The sun seemed unusually harsh today, each ray felt like a needle against his retinas.

"Your honor," Will said, gesturing to the tee with mock reverence. As he stepped up to the ball, he noticed the usual morning chorus of birds had weirdly fallen silent.

Rufus grinned as he set up his ball. "Watch and learn, rookie. Watch and learn."

As Rufus' drive sliced predictably to the right, Will chuckled, although the laugh made his head throb. "Nice one, partner. I think you knocked out a seagull." But there were no seagulls in sight — in fact, the sky above them was empty of birds.

Their banter continued as they sauntered down the fairway, together with their regular playing partners, Mike and Dave, also ex-cops. Will adjusted his sunglasses against the sunlight, wishing he'd thought to wear a cap.

"Did you guys hear the latest about those drones?" Mike asked, lining up his approach shot.

"They're looking for some escaped lab monkeys, 'cause they're worried people are so broke they're gonna eat them if they find them," Dave said.

Rufus snorted. "Yeah, right. The only thing I'm eating is this hot dog at the turn. And maybe Floss's alimony payments."

The foursome shared a laugh, the conversation flowing easily between old friends. As Will addressed his ball on the third tee, he rubbed at his neck. The bite should have healed by now, but it still felt tender, pulsing with each heartbeat. He'd avoided looking at it in the mirror this morning — something about what he'd seen in the mirror had seemed... off.

By the sixth hole, Will had developed a pounding headache. Even with the sunglasses, the light drilled into his skull.

"You okay there?" Rufus asked, eyeing him with concern. "You're looking peaked."

"Just tired," Will muttered, though 'tired' didn't begin to describe the strange sensitivity that made every sunbeam burn his eyes.

As they approached the ninth hole, Dave brought up their latest celebrity resident. "I can't believe you're working in the same building as Skylar Reeves?"

"That cape movie made stupid money,' Rufus said, before adding, "it's no wonder he's as reclusive as hell."

Will lined up his putt, a simple four-footer for par. As he bent to read the break, a sharp throb from the bite mark threw off his concentration. He jerked up, sending the ball skittering past the hole.

"Since when do you get the yips?" Mike teased.

"Must be coming down with something,' Will said. Or it's an allergic reaction, he thought to himself.

After finishing their round, they made their way to the PBA Hall on 86th Street for their customary post-game beers. In the dimmer light of the hall, Will's headache eased.

As Dave launched into another story about their old nemesis, Clifton Russell, Will rubbed at the bite, which felt warm under his fingers. Not a good sign.

"Speaking of things that should be locked up," Dave said

with a chuckle, "remember Clifton Russell? That slimy bootlicker with the evil career-ruining side?"

Groans echoed around the table. "Don't remind me," Will grimaced.

"The worst boss ever. Always throwing others under the bus to make himself look competent" he added.

As they settled into their regular corner booth, Mike leaned forward. "Hey, do you remember that series of apartment break-ins back in the day? Where they got past all the security systems?"

"Oh yeah, that was wild," Dave nodded. "Hundreds of reports from locked apartments, and not a single perp caught. As if they were ghosts."

"They never hit York Tower, though," Rufus said. "They never dared, not with such a crack security team on site."

They all laughed.

"You know what I don't get?" Will asked, his voice more serious than the moment called for. "These rich folks in the tower, they've got everything — money, fancy apartments, the best medical care. But half of them seem lonelier than my dad was in his state facility."

The table went quiet. Mike and Dave exchanged glances. Rufus stared into his beer.

"Your dad was in assisted living?" Dave asked gently.

"For the last three years of his life. Alzheimer's." Will's grip tightened on his glass. "Paid through the nose for 'premium care,' but he died alone on a Tuesday afternoon while I was stuck in traffic. The staff didn't notice for four hours."

"Damn, Will. I never knew," Mike said, almost reaching for Will's hand, before pulling back.

"That's why I actually give a damn about the old folks at York Tower," Will continued. "Someone should. Dad used to say 'Don't let them warehouse me like yesterday's newspaper.' Well, I failed him. But I won't fail the residents on my watch."

Mike raised his beer. "To your dad. And to looking out for people who can't look out for themselves."

They drank in respectful silence.

"Speaking of York Tower," Mike added, lowering his voice, "any word on what's going on up on the 3rd floor? My cousin works maintenance there, and said that they keep hearing weird noises up there."

Will's hand strayed to the throbbing bite mark. The courier's face flashed in his mind, and he remembered how still the man had stood unnaturally still, like a predator waiting to strike. The memory made his skin crawl.

"There's nothing going on, and they certainly haven't said anything to us," Will said quickly. Too quickly.

"Tommy swears he heard odd sounds last time he was there," Mike added.

Will took a long pull from his beer, buying time to steady his voice. "Probably just wind coming up the elevator shaft. Those old buildings make all kinds of noises. You get used to it after a while, although in the beginning Rufus used to shit his pants every time."

"Hey, watch who you're calling a baby!" Rufus protested. "And I only squealed like a pig the one time. Honestly thought there was a banshee living inside the elevator shaft."

The conversation shifted to lighter topics, but Will couldn't shake a growing sense of unease. Every time the door of the bar opened, letting in a shaft of late afternoon sunlight, he flinched.

Mike clapped Will on the back. "Same time next week?"

Will nodded, forcing a smile. "Wouldn't miss it for the world."

Walking to his car, Will caught his reflection in the club window and froze. For a moment it seemed like his image had blurred, as if he wasn't solid enough to cast a proper reflection. He blinked, and everything snapped back to normal.

Somewhere, in the back of his mind, a voice whispered a warning he couldn't quite make out.

3

ODORIFEROUS

Slumped over the security desk, Will halfheartedly flipped through a dog-eared magazine. He'd positioned himself carefully in the corner of the counter to avoid the line of sunlight cutting across the marble floor. Even the fluorescent lighting seemed too bright for his eyes, made worse since it had also started buzzing aggressively above him, like a swarm of angry wasps trapped behind plastic sheeting.

The lobby doors swung open, and Will recoiled as a fresh blade of light sliced through the space. A diminutive figure bundled in an oversized coat bustled in.

"Morning," Will grunted, barely looking up. It had been a rough night of very little sleep twinned with a killer headache. The bite on his neck had kept him awake, pulsing in rhythm with his heartbeat like some kind of biological metronome. Hopefully this wasn't the start of a brain tumor. He didn't have the funds to fix that.

"Good morning!" The voice was unexpectedly booming for such a small man. "We haven't been introduced yet. I'm Matthew Peart."

Will raised an eyebrow, finally lifting his gaze. The man before him barely reached the top of the desk as he extended a hand adorned with an ostentatious class ring.

Before Will could respond, Rufus lumbered in from his break, a half-eaten sandwich in hand.

"Mind if we swap spots?" Will asked quietly. "The sun's killing my eyes today."

Rufus gave him an odd look, but shuffled over. "Migraine?"

"Something like that," Will muttered, slouching into the shadowy corner of their workspace. Peart appeared to be an entitled wealthy resident, one who would undoubtedly come with complaints, he predicted silently.

"I'm Rufus, and this is Will," Rufus said, shaking the proffered hand. "And you're the new owner of apartment 326."

Matthew puffed up his chest. "Ah, what a welcome when the staff knows who you are. But sadly, I have concerns about the building's maintenance."

A complaint. Exactly as Will had predicted, and he had to suppress a groan. "Oh?"

"The smell!" Matthew's nose wrinkled dramatically. "It's like something died and is rotting in a wall cavity."

Will sniffed the air, detecting nothing but the usual blend of cleaning products and Rufus' lingering deodorant, which was stronger than usual. His senses had been sharper lately — picking up scents he'd never noticed before — but this supposed stench eluded him entirely. "I'm not picking up anything unusual, Mr. Peart."

"The smell is outside my apartment, and it's impossible to miss. It's strongest near the elevators. I've been taking the stairs just to avoid it. Someone else must have noticed. It's putrid. Decaying flesh mixed with... something else. Something sweet?"

Will's stomach lurched. Sweet decay. The words triggered something — that day with the courier. Hadn't there been a strange smell up on the third floor? He hadn't noticed it at first, but thinking back now... He swallowed hard, his hand unconsciously moving to his neck.

Rufus exchanged a puzzled look with Will. "Sorry, Mr. Peart, but I haven't smelled anything out of the ordinary."

Will dropped his hand quickly, realizing he'd been touching the bite mark again. He forced himself to focus on the conversation, even as that fragment of memory kept trying to surface. The courier's cold smile. The glimpse of something — someone — inside apartment 306. The metallic tang in the air that he'd dismissed as his imagination.

Matthew's face flushed. "The odor is very real. You need to get someone in to investigate the ventilation system."

"Look, we'll make a note of your complaint and pass it on," Will said, trying to keep his voice steady. "But I gotta tell you, you're the first person to mention any weird smells."

"There is something dead in the air ducts, or the elevator shafts, and given how much I'm paying to live here, I want it fixed," Peart hissed, complete with an audible stomping of his heeled boot.

As Peart stalked off toward the stairwell, Rufus leaned toward Will. "What's his deal?"

Will shrugged, but his mind was racing. Sweet decay. Decaying flesh. The locked apartment that wasn't supposed to have a tenant. "Don't know, but he's going to be a pain in the ass."

"Do you think it's possible that something died in the walls?" Rufus asked.

"Nah," Will replied, scratching absently at his neck. The wound felt warm under his fingers, warmer than it should be. "It's probably his ruined nasal passages. He's in real estate apparently, and you know what they're like... too many parties with an abundance of white powder." He tapped the side of his nose, but the joke felt hollow.

The building around them seemed to settle with a sigh, and Will caught himself listening for sounds that shouldn't be there. Footsteps where no one walked. Whispers where no one spoke. The elderly residents of York Tower deserved someone who would notice when something was wrong, someone who would investigate instead of dismissing complaints as drug-induced paranoia.

His father had died alone because no one had cared enough to check on him properly. Will wouldn't let that happen here. Not on his watch.

4

THE THIRD-FLOOR VIEW

Sarah Pike sat in the darkness of her third-floor apartment, listening to York Tower settle around her. Sleep had become elusive lately, her nights spent waiting for the inevitable. When Ethan's whimper finally pierced the pre-dawn silence, she was already moving, muscle memory guiding her through the shadowed hallway.

"No... please... don't..." Her son's voice, small and frightened, made her heart clench.

The air outside his door felt wrong — colder than it should be, despite the building's expensive heating system. Something shifted in her peripheral vision, a darkness deeper than the shadows that lined the hall. Sarah ignored it. Lack of sleep was making her imagine things.

Inside, Ethan's night light cast distorted shapes across the walls, transforming his model airplanes into twisted creatures. He lay tangled in his sheets, face contorted, fighting invisible hands.

"Sweetie?" She touched his forehead, finding his skin clammy but not quite feverish. "Ethan, wake up."

His eyes flew open, wild and unfocused. "Mom? Is he gone?"

"Who, baby?"

"The man." Ethan's voice trembled. "He was watching me again. From the corner."

Sarah's eyes darted to the shadowy corner by his closet. Empty, of course. Just like it had been every other night this week.

Unable to face another conversation about Ethan's mysterious visitor, she settled him back to sleep and retreated to the kitchen. The coffeemaker's gentle gurgle filled the silence as she watched the sunrise paint the Manhattan skyline. From here, everything looked pristine, unbroken. But like so much else in her life lately, she knew it was just an illusion.

The building woke up around her. Water rushing through pipes, and the hum of the elevator cables joined the muffled sounds of her neighbors starting their day. With the coffee growing cold in her hands, Sarah watched the city emerge from darkness. Her reflection stared back at her — at 43, she still looked every bit the high-powered attorney she'd been just a year ago, but now yoga pants and a sweater replaced her perfectly pressed suit, comfortable slippers instead of power heels.

Maybe it was just her own growing fear that by leaving her career to care for Ethan, she was slowly disappearing herself. That she was becoming invisible, just another stay-at-home mom whose concerns would be dismissed as maternal hysteria.

"Mom!" Zoe's voice shattered the morning quiet. "I can't find my history textbook and I'm going to be late!"

Sarah set down her untouched coffee. "Check under your bed. That's where it was last time."

She watched her daughter emerge triumphant from her bedroom, textbook in hand. At 12, Zoe was all long limbs and attitude, a perfect mini-me of Sarah at that age.

Before she could ask about Ethan, her son shuffled into the kitchen, still in his pajamas. "Mom, I don't feel good."

Sarah pressed a hand to his forehead. No fever, but the kid looked exhausted. Dark circles shadowed his eyes, and his skin had taken on an unhealthy pallor that reminded her uncomfortably of the elderly residents she sometimes passed in the lobby. "What hurts, buddy?"

"Everything's too bright," Ethan mumbled, squinting even in the apartment's dim morning light. "And I had that weird dream again."

Sarah's stomach tightened. Between the light sensitivity and lethargy, her mind immediately went to meningitis. "The dream about the man beside your bed?"

Ethan nodded, and Sarah's hand trembled as she smoothed his hair. She glanced at her watch. Letting him stay home meant rescheduling her interview at Burrells, the law firm she'd set her sights on for her reentry into the legal world. Not the first impression she'd hoped to make, but meningitis... she shuddered at the thought.

"Okay, buddy. Back to bed."

As Zoe headed out with a hurried "Bye, Mom!", Sarah's phone buzzed. A message from her husband Mark flashed on the screen: "They want another meeting this afternoon, which means another night in Chicago. Sorry, babe."

Sarah's jaw clenched. Another night alone in their bed. Another dinner for three, not four. Another night of the kids asking when dad was coming home. Another night of being the *only* parent dealing with whatever was happening to Ethan.

A knock at the door startled her. Before opening it, Sarah caught a whiff of something sweet and metallic, like old pennies left in the sun. The scent vanished so quickly she thought she'd imagined it.

She opened the door to find Mr. Peart, the new tenant on their floor, hopping from one booted foot to another.

"Good morning Mrs. Pike, sorry to intrude, but I knew you'd be awake, what with the kids and all. I was hoping to talk to you about the odor out here. It's becoming unbearable. Surely you've noticed?"

Sarah forced a polite smile. "I'm sorry, Mr. Peart. I haven't noticed any unusual smell. Have you spoken to maintenance?"

As Peart launched into a tirade about incompetent staff and health hazards, Sarah checked behind her. Curled up on the couch, Ethan had pulled a blanket over his head.

"I'll mention it to the front desk on my way out," she said, cutting Peart off mid-rant, desperate to close the door on the strong light and on the obnoxious man in the corridor. Something about his complaint made her uneasy, though she couldn't put her finger on why. "But I must go, as I need to call our pediatrician."

As she closed the door, Sarah leaned against it, and the frown lines between her eyes, the ones her husband had commented on three times last week, deepened. Burrells wouldn't wait — they'd made that clear. But as Ethan curled deeper under the blanket, she realized some choices made themselves. She picked up the phone and dialed the pediatrician's office.

"Dr. Ramirez's office, how can I help you?" a cheery voice answered.

"Hi, it's Sarah Pike. Do you have any appointment times available this morning? My son, Ethan, is sick."

Twenty minutes later, Sarah was guiding a sluggish Ethan into the elevator. As they descended, she noticed Will at the security desk, looking unusually disheveled with his uniform hanging loose on his frame.

"Everything okay, Mrs. Pike?" he asked, his eyes lingering on Ethan with what looked like genuine concern.

"Just a check-up," Sarah replied, forcing a smile. "Nothing to worry about. Everything fine with you?"

"Absolutely," he replied, but not with enough effort for her to believe him.

There was something in Will's expression that made her pause — a recognition, maybe. As if he understood exactly what she was going through with Ethan. The exhaustion, the sensitivity to light, the way her son seemed to be fading before her eyes.

The taxi ride to the doctor's office was quiet, Ethan leaning heavily against her side. Sarah tried not to imagine the worst-case scenarios, but she had an aunt who'd lost limbs to meningitis, so it was always at the forefront of her mind.

Dr. Ramirez's examination room was bright and

cheerful, making Ethan flinch and cover his eyes. The doctor listened to his chest, checked his throat, and asked a series of questions.

"How long has he felt unwell?" Dr. Ramirez asked.

"A couple of days, maybe. He was quieter than usual over the weekend," Sarah replied, realizing she wasn't entirely sure. "Then he started complaining about the light hurting his eyes and has been having nightmares."

Dr. Ramirez's expression grew more serious. "Any neck stiffness? Headaches?"

Sarah's heart raced. So they were checking for meningitis.

"Neck's fine," Ethan said. "I'm tired, and the light hurts my eyes."

Dr. Ramirez nodded thoughtfully. "I'll run some blood tests to be on the safe side. We'll check his iron levels, among other things." Seeing Sarah's panic, she added, "Don't worry too much. This sounds like one of those childhood viruses we can never quite pinpoint. They usually run their course within a week or two. The blood tests are just a precaution."

As the nurse prepared Ethan for the blood draw, Sarah held his hand, whispering words of encouragement. He was so pale against the white paper protecting the examination table.

"You're being so brave," she told him, squeezing his hand as the needle went in. Ethan's pallor faded even more as his blood flowed with a hypnotic slowness, as if time itself had thickened.

"Almost done," the nurse said, her cheerful tone faltering as Ethan's blood flowed into the vial. Sarah caught the way the nurse's eyes widened at the way the blood seemed to move — too thick, too dark, as if it were reluctant to leave Ethan's body.

Sarah tried to ignore the nurse's quick glance toward Dr. Ramirez as something unspoken passed between them. The dread in her stomach bloomed...

Later, as they waited for a taxi outside the clinic, another text from Mark arrived: "How are things at home? Miss you guys."

Sarah stared at the message, her anger surging. He wouldn't need to text if he was actually at home. She wanted to tell him about Ethan, about how worried she was and how much they... no, how much she needed him. Instead she typed: "All good here." Let him interpret that any way he wanted.

"Mom," Ethan whispered as they rode back to York Tower, "do you think the man will come back tonight?"

Sarah pulled him closer, fighting back tears. "There's no man, sweetheart. It's just dreams."

With Ethan dozing against her shoulder, Sarah gazed out the window, the city blurring past. And she allowed herself to remember her life before — one where she was still practicing law, where Mark was home for dinner every night, where Ethan was healthy and thriving, and where she couldn't keep up with Zoe's sports. But as the taxi pulled up to York Tower, reality returned.

Today was just another day in York Tower, pretending that her life was perfect. That their lives were perfect.

But deep down, remembering Will's concerned expression as they'd left that morning, Sarah suspected that she wasn't the only one pretending that life was perfect.

5

———

RAVENS AND WHISPERS

W ill watched the hearse pull away from York Tower, its tinted windows reflecting the gloomy sky. Inside was the body of Eleanor Lowenstein from 4B. She'd been found that morning, seated in her favorite chair by the window.

"That's three in a month," Rufus said, his chair creaking under his weight. "First Dunblane, then Bruce, now Lowenstein."

"Not normal," Will replied, scratching at his neck. The bite mark had been bothering him more lately, a constant reminder of the courier's visit. "Folks are dropping like flies."

"Maybe it's that smell Peart keeps going on about." Rufus pulled out his phone. "Hey, that pizza place on 86th is doing two-for-one tonight. Double pepperoni with extra cheese?"

The thought of greasy cheese and pepperoni made Will's stomach lurch. Even Rufus' coffee smelled wrong these days, acrid and too intense for his increasingly sensitive nose. "I'll pass. Not hungry."

"More for me then," Rufus shrugged, already typing in his order. "Gotta get my order in early, before they run out. I've been caught by that before and it was not pretty. Imagine a pizza place running out of dough?"

"I don't know how you can think about pizza when a dead body has just left the building?"

"Grief affects us all differently. Me? I eat my way through grief," Rufus said.

"You couldn't *stand* Mrs. Lowenstein. What'd you call her? I think it was a *desiccated, pinch-faced garden gnome.* Correct?"

"Her face did resemble a cat's butt. You've got to admit that? She had a smoker's mouth slapped onto a skinny garden gnome and the attitude of an Arizonian cactus. Her dying still makes me hungry."

Their banter was cut short by a loud thud against the lobby window.

"What the hell?" Rufus clutched his chest.

Will stepped to the window. Beyond the rain-streaked glass, a dark shape lay motionless on the sidewalk, wings splayed wide. "It's a raven," he said softly.

The lobby temperature dropped. Will turned to find the courier standing there in his brown uniform, his pale skin almost luminescent.

"I'll take care of this," the courier said, his voice as cold as the surrounding air.

"Where did you come from?" Will asked, but the courier was already moving past them.

They watched as he lifted the raven with eerie reverence. What had seemed like a lifeless husk shuddered in his grasp. The raven's eyes flicked open and locked onto Will.

"I have a way with animals," the courier's lips curved into a smile. "Now, please excuse me, I have a delivery for 306."

As the courier headed for the elevator, a large package under one arm, and the raven cradled in his hands, Will felt the bird's eyes boring into him. There was intelligence there, and something that might have been hunger.

His attention was diverted by the sight of Matthew Peart scurrying from the stairwell door, his nose wrinkled in disgust, a clipboard clutched tightly in his hand.

"Still hunting that smell, Mr. Peart?" Rufus called.

"Three other tenants have noticed it now," Peart

snapped. "All on the third floor. Something is rotting in York Tower, and none of you seem to care."

"We'll look into it," Will said, but Peart was already storming out.

When Rufus left for his break, the silence pressed in around Will. The lobby was never this quiet. Eight floors of apartments, dozens of residents, there should be noise — footsteps, conversations, the hum of life.

Then he heard them. Whispers. Not from anywhere specific — they seemed to come from the walls themselves, seeping into his skull. Will shook his head, but the voices only grew clearer.

He's changing.

Soon.

The hunger grows.

A scream pierced his thoughts. Will jerked upright, knocking over his coffee. The liquid spread across the desk like dark blood, and for a moment, he couldn't tell the difference. The rich, coppery scent that rose from the spill made his mouth water in a way that horrified him.

"What's that?" Rufus asked, pointing at the coffee, and seemingly unbothered by the scream.

Had he not even heard it?

"It's coffee," Will said quickly, grabbing a handful of paper towels. "Just coffee."

The scream had faded, but the whispers remained, rustling like dead leaves across concrete. The bite on his neck throbbed in time with his pulse. Will pressed his palms against his temples, trying to block out the sound. He swallowed hard, his throat dry.

"Perhaps you're being haunted by the ghost of Mrs. Lowenstein? Serves you right for being so rude about her!" Rufus joked.

The elderly residents of York Tower deserved better than low brow insults, Will thought. Mrs. Lowenstein had been a former Juilliard instructor, still giving piano lessons to the neighborhood children well into her eighties. Now she was gone, and Will couldn't shake the feeling that it wasn't from natural causes.

Although his father had died forgotten in a state-run facility, and the residents of York Tower had all the money in the world, Will still wouldn't let them meet the same fate — abandoned and dismissed, their concerns unheard until it was too late.

But as the whispers grew louder and the hunger in his stomach twisted like a living thing, Will wondered if *he* was part of the problem.

6

NIGHTFALL

The Marsdens' evening routine unfolded like a well-rehearsed play. Jacob cleared his plate as usual, while Leigh merely pushed her salmon around with her fork. He'd noticed she'd been doing that a lot lately. A frisson of worry passed through him as he watched her scrape the barely touched food into the trash. Was she coming down with something? But the thought dissipated as they settled into their usual positions on the couch with Netflix already queued up. After a brief debate, they settled on a documentary about sports doping, with Leigh in charge of the remote.

As the credits rolled, Jacob stretched and stood. "I'm just going to check the stars quickly. The forecast said it would be clear tonight."

Leigh's lips tightened in barely concealed irritation. "I'll get ready for bed," she said, her tone clipped. "Don't take too long."

Jacob watched her stalk off toward their bedroom, a familiar mix of guilt and resentment stirring in his chest. He turned toward his telescope, caressing the Unistellar eVscope eQuinox, a three-legged monster, and his pride and joy.

He opened the window, and the cool night air caressed his face as he peered through the eyepiece. His hands trembled as he adjusted the focus, something that had never happened before. He was tired. Nothing more.

This was his sanctuary, his connection to the vastness beyond Apartment 503. From the fifth floor of York Tower, the lights of the city spread out below him like its own galaxy of stars.

A sudden sting to his neck broke his concentration. He slapped at it, the sensation fading as quickly as it had come. Returning to his telescope, he caught a glimpse of Leigh's reflection in the window. He sighed, turning around, but she had already vanished.

"I'm coming," he muttered, frustration coloring his tone. Thirty-five years of marriage, and still he felt like a child being summoned inside. He loved his wife, but his real passion lay in the stars, in nights spent at Long Island's Custer Institute imagining everything beyond what the naked eye could see. Lately, he'd been too exhausted to make the trip out there. He'd missed the last three Saturday viewings — something he hadn't done in fifteen years of membership. Even setting up his own telescope was an effort tonight.

As Jacob shuffled toward the bathroom, a raven alighted on the sill of the open window. The large bird settled comfortably, preening its glossy feathers, its dark eyes observing the night as clearly as the telescope. Jacob stopped, startled by its presence. In thirty years, he'd never seen a raven up here — pigeons occasionally, sure, but never a raven. This one was huge, its feathers impossibly black. The size mesmerized him, its presence somehow wrong at this height. Shouldn't ravens be down in Central Park, harassing tourists? Or maybe over at Marble Cemetery with the rest of their gothic kin? He shuddered at that last thought and waved his hands at the bird. "Go on, get out of here!"

The raven tilted its head and regarded him with an intelligence that made him deeply uneasy before it took off into the darkness.

The bathroom was dark, but he didn't bother with the

light. Three decades in York Tower had etched every inch of their home into his memory.

He brushed his teeth mechanically, his mind still on the celestial bodies he'd left behind, and the raven's unsettling presence. The bird's eyes had seemed almost human in their awareness, as if it had been studying him rather than simply roosting.

As with every other night of their marriage, Leigh had left his pajamas warming on the heated towel rail. These tiny acts of service kept him in the marriage, whether he realized it or not.

Climbing into bed, Jacob was struck by the chill emanating from Leigh's side. "You're ice cold," he remarked, reaching for her.

"If you didn't leave the windows open, I wouldn't be freezing," she retorted, turning away and undoing her thoughtful deed with her thoughtless words.

Jacob sighed, settling into his pillow. Early in their marriage, she'd have come back with a saucy reply, but those days were long gone. Sleep came slowly, but when it did, he sailed through galaxies of stars — black holes of nothingness, and everything.

Hours later, in the hushed darkness of their bedroom, Leigh's eyes snapped open. She felt stifled, overwhelmed by heat, despite knowing that her husband had once again left the window open in the lounge. She pushed the duvet from her body, kicking it toward Jacob's side of the bed. Even the cool cotton sheets felt oppressive, clinging to her like a suffocating second skin. She peeled them away, exposing her body to the night air, but even then, she plucked at the silk of her nightgown.

With a sigh, she rolled toward her sleeping husband and observed the rise and fall of his chest. For a moment she smiled, and leaned toward him, as if she were about to bestow a kiss. But then her head dipped lower, toward his exposed neck, and without a moment's hesitation, she sank her teeth into his flesh.

She drank deeper and deeper until she finally withdrew,

a trickle of blood at the corner of her mouth. She rolled onto her side, leaving Jacob Marsden, her husband of thirty-nine years, an empty husk.

And perched on the open window's ledge, the raven cawed once — a sound of satisfaction that echoed through the pre-dawn silence like the toll of a funeral bell.

Later that morning, the neighbors would find Jacob's body, but Leigh would be gone, vanished like morning mist. The raven, too, would disappear, leaving only the memory of its presence and the echo of its cry.

The stars Jacob had loved so much continued their ancient dance, indifferent to the small tragedy that had played out below. But in the growing light of dawn, even they seemed dimmer somehow, as if the darkness had claimed a little bit more of the world.

THE DEPARTURE GATE

In Apartment 412, June Johnson's elderly hands fussed over the display of pink gardenias in her dining room. Their fragrance was a gentle counterpoint to the emotional weight of her daughter's imminent departure. From the guest bedroom came the rhythmic sounds of Sally packing—hangers clinking, drawers sliding, and the rustle of clothing. June loved her daughter fiercely, she had always loved her, but Sally's presence was like a sudden, brilliant light that bleached out the soft edges of June's carefully cultivated solitude.

Each movement, each thud of Sally's suitcase, reminded June of their vast differences. Where Sally moved through life with the momentum of a hurricane, June preferred the quiet spaces between moments. Their week together had been a dance of love and tension—Sally's well-intentioned recommendations, her barely concealed worry, pressing against June's independence like waves against a cliff.

The afternoon sun cast long shadows across York Tower's lobby as Sally wheeled her suitcase out of the elevator and toward the exit.

June followed Sally closely, their heated conversation drawing curious glances from Will and Rufus.

"Mom, please," Sally pleaded, her voice strained. "Just come visit Brookdale Village. You'll see how nice it is."

June's hand brushed her neck, a fleeting gesture. 'The

Blackwoods have been so kind to me here," she said, almost as an afterthought. "They look after everyone in the building. If I've told you once, I've told you a hundred times, Sally. I'm not leaving my home." There was something more than stubbornness in her voice.

"It's not safe for you to be alone in the city," Sally insisted. "Brookdale is top of the range. It's like a five-star hotel, more a luxury resort than a senior living facility."

"Safe?" June laughed, a sound that didn't quite reach her eyes. "This building, this apartment. It's the only place that's ever felt truly safe to me." Her voice echoed in the lobby. "And a fancy prison is still a prison. You're trying to institutionalize me!"

Will and Rufus exchanged a look, pretending to be engrossed in their paperwork as the women approached.

Sally's shoulders sagged. "Mom, I can't be here all the time, and Boise is so far away."

"I've lived in New York my entire life," June retorted. "I'm not leaving because you're feeling guilty about moving across the country."

"Are you going on vacation, Mrs. Johnson?" Will asked, stepping forward. The women didn't know it, but their conversation had triggered memories of Will's own father— the arguments about care facilities, the guilt, the inevitability of it all.

June forced a smile. "My daughter is leaving. I'm staying. And Sally needs to understand that won't be changing."

Sally turned back toward her mother. "Promise me you'll at least consider the idea?"

June paused before answering, her fingers stroking her throat. "I will, but don't get your hopes up. This is my home."

They embraced, and Sally climbed into a waiting cab.

June remained motionless as the cab pulled away from the curb. She hitched her purse higher on her shoulder as a brown uniformed courier approached the entrance. June held the door for him before stepping out onto the sidewalk, her gaze fixed on the departing taxi. She shivered as the man slipped past, before straightening her shoulders and striding into the bustling crowd.

Will's neck throbbed faintly as the courier passed by.

The uniformed man moved with such unnatural stillness as he made for the elevator bank. Will watched him punch the button for the third floor, knowing without checking that he was headed to the third floor, and apartment 306.

Only after the elevator doors closed did Will and Rufus share another glance. "There's something about that guy," Will muttered, rubbing at his neck. "Shows up like a ghost, only delivers to 306, barely talks. What do you think he's delivering?"

"My gut says drugs?" Rufus suggested, lowering his voice.

"Maybe..." Will said, though something deep in his bones whispered it was far worse than drugs.

"Where would you rather see your days out?" Will asked, changing the topic, his eyes following June's retreating figure through the glass doors. "In the greatest city on earth, or in Boise, like Mrs. Johnson's daughter?"

"Is that even a question?" Rufus cleared his throat dramatically. "Well, in Boise, you've got... potatoes. Lots of potatoes and clean air," Rufus said. "No smog, no subway fumes, and no homeless winos drunk in the middle of the potato fields."

Will scoffed. "Who needs clean air when you've got the intoxicating aroma of street vendor hot dogs?"

"Boise's got... nature. Trees and stuff," Rufus countered.

"We've got Central Park," Will said, "with the added treat of facing a mugger every other day. Keeps you on your toes."

Rufus stroked his double chin. "Boise's quieter. Peaceful."

"Peaceful?" Will laughed. "You mean boring. Here, it's a symphony of car horns and angry couriers, with more hearses than usual in the traffic..."

They laughed.

Rufus wiped a tear from his eye. "Imagine trying to

convince someone to leave this for Boise. It's like asking a lion to trade steak for tofu."

Will's laughter faded. "Yeah. New York's got its problems, but..."

"But it's home," Rufus finished.

Will nodded, watching through the window as June disappeared into the crowd. There was something in her posture—a new tension in her shoulders and a brittleness to her stride—that hadn't been there when Sally arrived. Whatever had transpired between mother and daughter this week, it had left its mark.

And somewhere in the building above them, Will could sense the courier's movements, and the whispers that followed in his wake.

The elderly residents deserved protection from whatever was stalking these halls. People like June Johnson, who had chosen to stay in the city they loved rather than disappear into the safety of assisted living. But as Will watched her vanish into the Manhattan crowd, he wondered if staying in York Tower was really the safer choice after all.

A MOTHER'S INSTINCT

Detective Iona Melville was knee-deep in case files when her son Finn burst into the kitchen, his backpack slung over one shoulder.

"Mom, can I go visit Ethan after school tomorrow?" Finn asked, eyes bright with excitement.

Iona looked up from her laptop, noting the unusual enthusiasm in her normally reserved son. "Ethan? You haven't mentioned him before."

Finn shrugged, dropping his bag on a chair. "He's in my class and he's been out sick for ages, and Mr. Gilligan asked if we could take turns visiting him because he's lonely."

Iona's investigative instincts stirred. Something felt off about a teacher organizing home visits for sick students. "How long has he been sick? And what's wrong with him?"

"I dunno," Finn replied, rummaging in the fridge. "A couple of weeks? Mr. G didn't say what was wrong, just that he's recovering and could use some company."

Iona felt a twinge of unease. Two weeks was a long time for a child to be out of school. "And you've never mentioned this Ethan before because...?"

Finn emerged with a juice box. "We're not best friends, but he's nice. And it's not fair that he has to miss so much school."

Iona watched Finn, noting his genuine concern. The kid had a good heart, always had. But something about this situation made her cop instincts twitch. "I'm not sure. I'd like to know more about Ethan and his family before agreeing."

Finn's face fell. "But Mom, everyone else is going! I'll be the only one who doesn't visit."

Iona sighed at the familiar social pressure argument. Every parent knew that particular guilt trip. "Tell you what, let me email Mr. G and get some more details. What's Ethan's last name?"

"Pike, Ethan Pike. He lives at York Tower," Finn said with a kind of reverence in his voice.

Iona tried to hide her surprise. York Tower was serious money—the kind of address that appeared in society pages and real estate fantasies. Nothing good would come from Finn seeing how the other half lived, developing expectations she could never meet on a detective's salary. "Okay, I'm not saying no, but I'm not making any concrete promises, understood?"

Later that night, after Finn had gone to bed, Iona sat at the kitchen table reading the email from Ethan's teacher.

Ethan Pike lived on the third floor of York Tower, a luxury apartment building she'd driven past countless times but never imagined entering. His mother, Amanda Pike, was a stay-at-home mom, and Ethan's father was frequently away for work. The doctors had cleared Ethan for visits from other students, but the email didn't elaborate about the boy's illness. On the surface, nothing seemed amiss, so Iona replied, confirming that Finn would take his place on the visiting roster. Given that Ethan's mom was on the PTA committee, and Iona had zero time to spare for volunteer work, she needed to stay on the right side of the school's power structure.

The next day, Iona found herself in the lobby of York Tower waiting for Amanda Pike. The scruffy security guard barely paid her any attention after ringing up to announce her arrival, seemingly more interested in slouching behind the reception desk than in doing his job. She waited with Finn in the opulent lobby, feeling underdressed despite her best efforts.

When a woman—Amanda Pike she assumed, stepped out of the elevator, Iona was struck by how put-together she looked, especially compared to her own work clothes.

Designer jeans that probably cost more than Iona's monthly grocery budget, silk shirt, and boots that screamed "I don't check price tags."

"Mrs. Pike? I'm Iona Melville, Finn's mom," Iona introduced herself.

Amanda's smile was warm but tired. "Please, call me Amanda. Thanks for coming by. Ethan's so excited."

As they rode the ancient elevator to the third floor, Iona noticed Amanda's restless movements—adjusting her sleeves, touching her hair, a pattern of nervous energy that her detective training automatically catalogued.

The third-floor hallway stretched before them, plush carpet muffling their footsteps. Despite the luxury, something about the corridor felt wrong. The overhead lights seemed dimmer here, creating pools of shadow between each fixture, and the temperature felt several degrees cooler than the lobby. Amanda's pace quickened as they passed the other apartment doors, though Iona doubted she was even aware of doing it.

The Pike apartment was immaculate, with the tempting scent of fresh cookies in the air. There was a boy on the couch, must be Ethan, pale and drawn, but his face had lit up at the sight of Finn.

Finn pulled out a small stack of papers from his backpack. "I brought your homework assignments," he said, handing them to Ethan. "And some comics."

"Thanks! Did you bring the new Spider-Man?"

"Of course," Finn grinned. "Wanna read it together?"

As the boys huddled over the comic, their excited chatter filled the room and Amanda pulled Iona aside. "I can't tell you how much this means," she said. "Ethan's been so bored. The doctors... they're still running tests. And with Mark away on business again, it's been..." she trailed off, her composure slipping for just a moment before she regained her polished demeanor.

"Your husband travels a lot?" Iona asked, keeping her tone casual.

Amanda's mouth tightened. "Yes. He's in Chicago this week. Again." The last word held a weight that Iona didn't miss.

"That must be difficult, especially with Ethan being ill," Iona observed.

"I manage," Amanda replied, her tone clipped. "I have to. Mark has to travel for work, new clients, and all that... Now, enough of that, it's wonderful to see Ethan so excited. He's been absolutely bored stuck inside. What is it you do, Iona? I don't think I've seen you at any of the PTA meetings."

Iona shifted slightly. "I'm a detective with the NYPD."

"Oh, how fascinating!" Amanda leaned in, her restless movements continuing—sleeve, hair, neck—repeated like a nervous tic. "Have you worked on any interesting cases?"

"Nothing newsworthy for a while now," Iona deflected, not wanting to discuss her work. She changed the subject. "Those cookies smell delicious. Did you bake them?"

"Baking is one of the few things I can do to keep busy while Ethan's been ill. Would you like to take some home?"

After politely declining and saying her goodbyes, Iona left Finn with a promise to pick him up after dinner. As they walked to the door, Iona spotted a dark smudge on the collar of Amanda's otherwise pristine white silk blouse.

"There's something on your collar," Iona pointed out.

Amanda's hand flew to her neck. "It'll be from a mosquito bite. I was at the track with Zoe yesterday, Ethan's sister. It's next to the river and the mosquitoes are terrible."

"Those river mosquitoes can be persistent," Iona said neutrally, knowing mosquito season was months away in November.

"Indeed," Amanda agreed, her smile a touch too bright. "I'll have to soak this shirt. I usually take insect repellent, but at this time of year, I didn't think we'd need it."

"Climate change," Iona said diplomatically as the elevator dinged and the doors opened. "See you later, and thanks for inviting Finn to stay for dinner. I've packed his swimsuit, just in case Ethan is up for a dip in the pool. You never know with boys!"

"Oh, that would have been great, but we don't use the pool. Ethan doesn't like the water, so he's never had lessons."

Every child should know how to swim, Iona thought, but kept her opinion to herself. The ornate elevator doors closed on the image of Amanda, one hand at her neck, staring into nothing.

In the lobby, the security guard remained fixated on his phone, oblivious to a young woman struggling through the door with an enormous floral arrangement in her arms.

"Let me help you with that," Iona said, hurrying to hold the door.

"Thanks," the woman huffed, maneuvering the flowers inside. "These are heavier than they look. Usually I get help," she gestured toward the guard, "but he's distracted today."

Iona stepped aside to let a courier pass, watching the guard's continued absorption in his phone. Any halfway decent criminal could walk right in, she thought. Or out.

As she walked back to her car, Iona's mind catalogued her observations: mosquito bites in November, a child who'd never learned to swim despite living in a building with a pool, a mother's nervous tics, and a security guard more interested in his phone than his job. None of it added up to anything criminal, but her gut wouldn't be quieted.

Still, Finn was happy, and that mattered more than her professional paranoia. Sometimes a sick kid was just a sick kid, and a worried mother was just a worried mother.

But as she drove away from York Tower's imposing facade, Iona couldn't shake the feeling that she'd just walked through a very expensive, and shaky, house of cards.

9

———

A FATEFUL RETURN

As the year slipped another week closer to Christmas, the York Tower lobby started to resemble Grand Central Station at rush hour, with the doors propped open to allow a near-constant flow of bodies to surge through the normally secure entrance.

Mrs. Johnson shuffled in, her arms laden with Macy's shopping bags, just as the Callahans emerged from the elevator, awash in a cloud of chiffon and aftershave.

Jim Callahan appeared to scowl as he guided his wife through the throng, until Celeste Callahan's emerald gown snagged on the velcro straps of Zoe Pike's gym bag

Amanda Pike, wrestling her family through the lobby, and drowning under her own collection of shopping bags and coats and scarves and gloves, gasped.

"Oh, Celeste!" Amanda exclaimed, freeing the delicate fabric. "I'm so sorry, look, no damage done. Say sorry, Zoe."

Zoe muttered something which could have been an apology, or the lyrics to whatever she was listening to under her headphones.

"You look stunning by the way. What's the occasion?" Amanda asked quickly, her words running over the top of themselves.

"A competition at the Rainbow Room. The annual qualification event for the Manhattan Dance Championships," Celeste preened.

"This is our year," Jim said, using his broad shoulders to clear a path. "It's only taken us twenty years of lessons to get this far. Come on, or we'll be late for registration."

The security desk was a scene of controlled chaos. Will and Rufus's heads swiveled constantly, trying to keep track of the comings and goings. A DoorDash driver argued loudly with a resident about a mixed-up order, while an Amazon courier attempted to deliver an avalanche of packages to a dozen different residents.

Mrs. Abernathy sat in the lobby, perched in a green velvet chair against the burnished wall, watching everyone with the intensity of a hawk as she waited for her Uber.

Tom Forrester, fresh from his daily commute, tried squeezing past the Callahans, but pulled up short at seeing Celeste in her gown. He whistled appreciatively. "You'll be the belle of the ball, Celeste," he grinned, before being swallowed by the crowd.

And at the front desk, the new florist was trying to wrangle a giant arrangement into a vase which was proving to be too small for the job. Water splashed over the desk, distracting Will and Rufus even further.

Amidst the pandemonium, as Mrs. Johnson struggled with her shopping bags, navigating around arguing children and puddles of water and Celeste's floor-length gown and a full-blown shouting match between the DoorDash driver and a bike courier who'd wheeled his ride into the lobby, a figure materialized beside her.

The courier, in his ever-present brown uniform, smiled politely. "Allow me to assist you, ma'am."

Mrs. Johnson blinked in surprise. "Thank you. I hadn't realized I'd bought quite so much," she said, handing him several white and red Macy's bags, before pressing the button for the second floor.

In the chaos of the lobby, the courier's entrance and exit with Mrs. Johnson went completely unnoticed. As the elevator doors closed on them, the lobby's frenetic energy continued unabated.

Outside apartment 206, Mrs. Johnson unlocked the door

and fussed over the courier. "Please, come in and let me fix you a cup of coffee. It's the least I can do. Have you got time?"

The courier smiled, his pale features softening. "That would be lovely, thank you. I have all the time in the world."

As the coffee machine whirred into life, June found herself opening up to attentive courier. "You know, my daughter wants me to move to Boise. Boise! Can you imagine?"

"It's a very different place from New York," the courier agreed, accepting the steaming cup with a nod.

"Have you been there?"

"A long time ago, on a vacation. But all that sky wasn't for me."

Mrs. Johnson fell into her armchair, sighing. "I feel the same way. My daughter thinks I'm too old for the city. That it's time for me to... what was her phrase? 'Settle into my golden years.' As if I'm ready to turn to stone in a Boise garden!"

The courier leaned forward, his eyes intense. "Time is such an interesting concept. At what point do we decide that we're too old to do the things we love?"

"Exactly!" Mrs. Johnson laughed. "I've got too much living left to do. If only time wasn't so cruel."

"Ah, time," the courier mused, setting down his untouched drink. "It's a fickle thing, isn't it? Relentlessly moving forward. Wouldn't it be marvelous to stop the clock while we got on with doing everything we desired?"

"A beautiful idea, but impossible," June said, her eyes misting over.

The courier chuckled and rose from his seat. "In my experience, nothing is truly impossible."

As the sun dipped below the Manhattan skyline, casting long shadows across York Tower, the courier bid her farewell. "Thank you for the drink, Mrs. Johnson. I'll see you again... soon."

As night fell over York Tower, its residents settled into their evening routines. In apartment 206, Mrs. Johnson slept fitfully, the words of her daughter taking root in her subconscious.

Outside apartment 206, the elevator dinged, its doors sliding open with a whisper. But no one stepped out. The hallway remained empty, save for a sudden chill that dropped the temperature by ten degrees.

A pungent odor, like rotting fruit mixed with something metallic, crept under the door of 206, seeping into the apartment like an unwelcome guest. The lock clicked, although no key had turned it. The door swung open silently, and inside, the temperature plummeted further.

Mrs. Johnson shivered in bed, her breath fogging in the air above her. She slept on, unconsciously curling into herself to preserve her body heat. A shadow detached itself from the darkness of the hall, gliding toward the master suite.

The curtains rustled in a nonexistent breeze, recoiling from the approaching evil.

And then the courier materialized beside the bed, a slow grin on his pale face. His form was barely perceptible against a floral wallpaper which was adorned with dozens of framed photographs of smiling faces. A pictorial patchwork of memories.

He loomed over the sleeping woman, his silhouette a slash of darkness against the night. Bending low, his breath an icy whisper against her neck, "Sweet dreams," he murmured in a voice that sucked the remaining warmth from her skin. "Your new life begins now."

His fangs sank into her flesh with terrifying ease, like a knife through overripe fruit. Her eyes flew open as she let out a strangled gasp, a gasp cut off as he clamped a hand over her mouth, a hand as cold and unyielding as marble.

He drank deeply, careful not to take too much. This was no killing bite, but a transformative one. As he withdrew, he left behind two perfect puncture marks on her neck. Straightening, he wiped a droplet of blood from his lip.

June Johnson's anesthetized eyes followed him as he moved to the window.

Twitching the curtains open, a sliver of moonlight sought him like a lover. "Sleep now," he whispered, before leaving the room as silently as he'd arrived.

June Johnson took one long, deep breath, before closing her eyes and drifting off to sleep. Her second breath wouldn't come until after a full sweep of the hand of her bedside clock.

And high above the city, a murder of ravens took flight from above York Tower, their cries echoing through the night like harbingers of what was to come.

10

FLICKERING LIGHTS

Will tugged at his uniform shirt, frowning. "Does this look loose to you?"

Rufus glanced up from his crossword puzzle, his special retirement-gift pen tapping incessantly against the security desk. "Huh? Oh, yeah, maybe. You shedding pounds or something?"

"Not on purpose," Will muttered, pinching the excess fabric. He couldn't remember the last time he'd eaten a full meal, but he didn't feel hungry either. Just... empty.

The lobby doors slid open, admitting the now-familiar brown-shirted courier. As always, he carried a package for apartment 306.

"Good morning, gentlemen," the courier nodded, his voice as cold as the wind that followed him in. "Shall I just go up?"

Before either guard could respond, Amanda Pike bustled through the lobby doors, her children in tow. "Hold the elevator," she called to the courier, who obligingly pressed the 'hold' button.

As the elevator doors closed on the odd group, the lights in the lobby flickered. Will and Rufus exchanged uneasy glances.

"That's the third time today," Rufus said, his pen tapping growing more insistent.

Will nodded, about to reply, when Mrs. Pike burst out of

the elevator, her face pale, with her children clasped beneath her arms.

"Mrs. Pike?" Will asked. "Is everything all right?"

She'd bent to kiss the head of her son before answering. "The elevator... it, well, it seemed to go up, then it gave a nasty jolt, and descended again. I think we'll take the stairs..."

"Probably a good idea!" Will replied, although something in her harried expression suggested that the elevator wasn't her only problem today.

The day progressed with more unexplained power fluctuations. The elevator shuddered to a stop between floors, twice, trapping residents for several tense minutes each time. By the afternoon, maintenance had been called three times, but the technicians couldn't find anything wrong with the electrical system.

As evening approached, Amanda returned to the security desk, her heels clicking a staccato rhythm on the marble floor. Will noticed a faint tremor in her hands as she pushed a stray hair back into her bun.

"Gentlemen," she began, her usually confident voice slightly off, "I hate to be a bother, but have there been any reports of insects in the building? Mosquitoes or fleas, perhaps?"

Rufus' pen stopped mid-tap. "Insects? In December?"

Amanda nodded, her hand moving to her neck. "I know it sounds crazy, but Ethan's been ill, and now I'm finding these marks... on the children and myself." Her voice dropped. "The doctors haven't been able to explain his condition—a virus they say, but these bites..."

Will assured her they would look into it, but as she walked away, he and Rufus exchanged skeptical looks.

"Mosquitoes. Right," Rufus snorted, resuming his crossword. "In the middle of winter."

"Could be bedbugs," Will offered, scratching at his own neck.

"Shush, we don't want anyone hearing that. Imagine what that would do to property values around here?"

"We're not a hotel. They wouldn't shut us down. I'm just saying that bedbugs are more likely than mosquitoes in December, in Manhattan," Will said.

The phone rang.

Will answered, his brow slowly furrowing.

"That was Mrs. Johnson's daughter, Sally, calling from Boise," he said after hanging up. "Says she hasn't heard from her mother in days. She's asking us to do a wellness check."

Rufus looked up from his crossword. "Off you go then. You know how Mrs. Johnson loves her daily chats with you."

Will hesitated. "The thing is... I could have sworn I saw her yesterday. Didn't you?"

Rufus frowned, thinking. "Come to think of it, yeah. But... something was different. She didn't want to chat like usual."

"Exactly," Will nodded. "It's getting late though. Why don't we check on her tomorrow? She's probably fine, and us banging on the door at this hour would send her into cardiac arrest."

Rufus' pen-tapping paused. "Since when have you ever delayed a wellness check?"

"This isn't the streets. It's York Tower. Nothing happens here."

As if to contradict him, the lights flickered again, plunging the lobby into momentary darkness. When they came back on, a shadow flew across the lobby windows, too fast and too large to be anything natural.

Will and Rufus both stiffened, their eyes locked on the spot where the shadow had been. For a long moment, neither spoke. Will rubbed his neck, where the bite mark pulsed like a second heartbeat. Rufus' fingers tightened around his pen, his knuckles white.

Neither man wanted to be the first to acknowledge what they thought they'd seen. To speak it aloud would make it real, and shatter the comfortable illusion that their biggest problems were elevator malfunctions and the resident's complaints.

Finally, Rufus cleared his throat. "Probably just a pigeon."

"Yeah," Will agreed, relief evident in his voice. "Just a bird."

Rufus resumed his nervous pen-tapping, but the rhythm was faster now, more agitated.

Will glanced at his buddy, and for a moment considered mentioning the sounds he could hear (or were they sounds he was imagining?). TVs tuned to different channels throughout the building, the muffled arguments between spouses, and worse, the love-making between adults married to other people. But the memory of the shadow they'd both pretended not to see held him back. Some things were better left unspoken. At least until he could figure out what the hell was happening to him. The bite on his neck throbbed again, and Will pressed his fingers against it, feeling the unusual warmth beneath his skin. Whatever was wrong with him, it was getting worse.

The elevator dinged softly across the lobby, despite no one calling for it. Rufus dropped his pen. And Will's heart leapt into his mouth. And somewhere in the building above them, in the maze of corridors and expensive apartments, something dark crept through the shadows. Patient and hungry. Marking time...

11

UNEXPECTED ARRIVALS

Iona Melville sat at her desk, reading the file she'd just been handed. Three deaths in York Tower over the past month. The building's name brought back memories of her recent visit with Finn—the marble lobby, the distracted guard who'd barely acknowledged them, the strange vibe she'd gotten from the mom.

Marion Bruce, 71, heart failure.

Elgar Dunblane, 88, another case of heart failure.

And Eleanor Lowenstein, 82, the latest victim. Found in a chair by the window, with a half-drunk cup of tea cold beside her. The official cause of death was currently pending autopsy.

"There's probably nothing in it," said Lieutenant Ortega from the doorway, a steaming cup of coffee in his hand.

"Three deaths in one month? In the same building?" Iona said shaking her head. "That's not normal. I knew there was something off about that place when I was there."

Ortega raised an eyebrow. "Don't waste too much time chasing ghosts at York Tower, when there's probably nothing more there than walking sticks and a hundred sets of dentures. Rich old folks die just like the rest of us, but my hand's been forced by the powers that be. The Deputy Commissioner's mother lives there. So when the report came in, my hand was forced," he shrugged.

"So it was the funeral home who contacted us?" Iona asked, flipping through the file.

"Yeah, Eternal Rest Funerals. They handled all the deaths, and apparently noticed a pattern. I don't see it myself," Ortega replied. "So all we need is a quick visit to dot the i's and cross the t's, and I promise we'll all be able to sleep tight in our beds, and the Deputy Commissioner will be happy."

YORK TOWER's glass doors opened with a whoosh, admitting a burly FedEx courier struggling with a large, shrink-wrapped object.

"Whoa there, big guy," Rufus called out. "Need a hand?"

The courier grunted, his face red with exertion. "Delivery for Apartment 306."

"306?" Will asked.

"We'll take it from here," Rufus told the sweating man, heaving himself off his chair.

As the courier gratefully relinquished his burden, Will grabbed the clipboard. "It's some kind of birdcage," he said, squinting at the form.

"Since when does 306 have deliveries by anyone other than our mystery man in brown?" Rufus asked, eyeing the package.

Will shrugged. "Since never. But I say we deliver this one ourselves, and have a look inside. You know, professional curiosity."

"You can take the man out of the badge, but you can't take the cop out of the man," Rufus proclaimed. "Come on, then."

They maneuvered the bulky package into the elevator, with the two men squeezing into the remaining space before the ancient machinery shuddered upwards to the third floor.

Will slid the master key into the lock of apartment 306

and the door swung open. The room before them was immaculately furnished with high-end pieces that looked like they belonged in a magazine, or in a museum.

"Holy shit—" Will started.

"Shiitake mushrooms," Rufus finished.

They stepped inside, the plush carpet muffling their footsteps. Everything was picture perfect, complete with a gilt-framed oil painting of a young woman, obviously long dead now, given the style of her dress and hair. Apart from the portrait in the dining room, there wasn't a single other personal touch in sight. No photos, no trinkets, not even a stray coffee mug or any evidence that anyone lived there.

"It's like one of those staged apartments they use for real estate showings," Will said.

Rufus nodded, visibly shivering. "Not a meth lab then."

"Nope," Will replied.

After placing the birdcage in the center of the room, both men stood silently, neither wanting to be the first to voice their unease.

"Let's get out of here," Will said.

Rufus didn't argue.

Back in the lobby, they were still discussing how the apartment had become fully furnished without them noticing when the entry buzzer sounded. Will glanced at the security monitor.

"What do you think?" Will asked, gesturing to the screen.

A sharp-eyed woman in a crisp suit waited outside, bouncing slightly on her low-heeled shoes.

Rufus whistled low. "That's a cop if ever I've seen one."

Will pressed the intercom. "Can I help you, ma'am?"

"Detective Melville, NYPD. Here to ask about some residents," came the curt reply as the woman flashed her badge to the camera.

The two exchanged glances. "Must be serious if they've sent a detective," Rufus muttered as Will buzzed her in.

As she entered, her gaze swept the lobby before settling on them.

"Detective Iona Melville," she announced, laying her

badge on the counter. "I'm here about the recent deaths in your building."

Will and Rufus straightened, recognition dawning on their faces.

"Melville?" Rufus blurted. "As in the Riverside Strangler case?"

The detective's expression remained neutral, but there was a flicker of pride. "That was some time ago. I'm here to talk about Marion Bruce, Elgar Dunblane and Eleanor Lowenstein."

The Riverside Strangler case had been all over the news a few years back. Melville had cracked it when everyone else had hit a dead end, catapulting her career forward.

"What can we do for you?" Will asked, while trying to maintain his professionalism while simultaneously wondering why she was there to discuss three old residents.

"Lowenstein lived on the fourth floor, Dunblane on the second, and Bruce on the sixth, is that correct?" At their nod, she continued, "I'm following up their deaths. Checking for any connections. Did any of them travel recently? Or receive any unusual visitors?"

Will scratched his head. "We usually know everything about everyone here. We even know what Mrs. Rodriguez is buying her grandkid for lunch today. Mrs. Bruce spent most of her time either here or shopping at the Strand Bookstore. Miss Lowenstein didn't get out much, but she painted a lot. And Elgar Dunblane was eighty-eight. That's a good run."

Detective Melville's expression shifted. "Look, I'm aware of your backgrounds in law enforcement, and I was hoping that, as former officers, you might be more... forthcoming with information that could assist in this investigation."

Will and Rufus exchanged glances, their postures straightening.

"Of course, Detective," Will said earnestly. "We want to help however we can. The thing is, we really don't know much beyond what we've already told you."

Rufus nodded, his earlier star-struck demeanor giving way to a more professional tone. "We keep pretty close tabs on everyone here—comes with the territory. But those three residents? They were just living their lives. Quiet, routine stuff."

"Trust me, if we'd noticed anything—anything at all—we would have called it in ourselves. Old habits die hard," Will said.

"Speaking of which," Rufus added, unable to help himself, "this whole setup is giving major 'Only Murders in the Building' vibes. You know, that show with Selena Gomez, Steve Martin and the other funny guy, the short one?"

Melville's face remained impassive. "I'm not familiar with it."

"Oh, come on!" Rufus exclaimed. "It's about these true crime podcast enthusiasts who start investigating a murder in their building. It's hilarious. You'd love it."

"I fail to see the humor in murder," Melville said coldly. "Let's get back to my original question. What can you tell me about those residents? Did they share any regular visitors? Were there any changes in their routines?"

Will and Rufus sobered quickly. "Of course, Detective," Will said. "It's just our way of coping, I guess. York Tower is usually pretty quiet compared to the real world."

"Usually quiet, except for the recent string of deaths," Melville pointed out.

"I would hardly call it a string..." Rufus said, before wilting under Melville's stare.

"Three deaths in a month is a string,' Melville said firmly.

Will and Rufus had no comeback for that truth. Neither of them had worked at York Tower long enough to know whether three deaths in a building mostly filled with rich, old people was higher than average, or not.

"Well, gentlemen," Melville said, closing her notebook. "If you think of anything else, please give me a call." She handed them her card and left, her heels clicking on the marble floor.

As the doors closed behind her, Rufus turned to Will. "Can you believe we just met Iona Melville?"

Will nodded, rubbing at his neck where the bite mark throbbed with renewed intensity. "Yeah, did you see that look she gave us? Like we were nothing more than mall cops? Remember when even the rookies treated us like we actually knew something?"

"Yeah, but we were carrying badges then. Now look at us. We're one step up from mannequins."

"But we don't have to deal with punk kids shoplifting, and it pays the bills. Speaking of which," Will chuckled, trying to lighten the mood, "who would be the murderer if this really was 'Only Murders in the Building'?"

Rufus leaned back in his chair, a glint in his eye. "My money's on that widow in 703, Mrs. Abernathy. She's got that whole 'sweet old lady who's actually a secret assassin' vibe going on."

"Nah," Will countered, "it's definitely that fitness influencer in 705, Cruz Collins. He's always so peppy—he's hiding something for sure. All those Starbucks lattes and yoga mats, with his oh-so-perfect blonde hair and white teeth. And that mustache."

They laughed, the tension dissipating. As they settled back into their routine, neither mentioned apartment 306 again, although it wasn't far from their minds.

And up on the third floor, the birdcage sat in apartment 306's pristine living room waiting to be filled.

And hiding in the darkest corners of York Tower, in the corners no one ever sees, something else was waiting too.

12

WELFARE CHECKS

Will and Rufus stood at the reception desk, discussing the delayed welfare check on Mrs. Johnson, the one Mrs. Johnson's daughter had asked for the day before.

"I'll go," Will volunteered, a touch too quickly. "With the elevators acting up worse than usual, those stairs will be murder on your knees. Besides, I could use the exercise."

Rufus' pen tapped against the desk, a staccato rhythm that grated on Will's increasingly sensitive hearing. 'Or we could both go," Rufus offered.

Will shook his head. "Nah, one of us should stay here."

Rufus nodded slowly, his expression unreadable. "But remember, announce yourself, knock three times, wait thirty seconds—"

"I know the drill," Will snapped. "I haven't forgotten."

As Will approached the stairwell, the usual sounds of the building multiplied into an overwhelming symphony. Radio talk shows, hair dryers, blenders, and a replay of an episode of Sesame Street. Despite the cacophony in his head, that last one made him smile.

Outside Apartment 206, Will paused, steeling himself. He rapped sharply on the door. "Mrs. Johnson? It's Will from downstairs. We're checking in on you. Are you okay in there?"

Silence.

Will counted to thirty, each second stretching uncomfortably.

Still no response. With a deep breath, he inserted the master key and turned it slowly.

The door swung open with a soft creak to reveal a darkened apartment. The air inside was stale and cold, carrying a vaguely familiar scent that made the hairs on the back of Will's neck stand up.

"Mrs. Johnson?" he called out, flicking the light switch. Nothing happened. "Great," he muttered, reaching for his flashlight.

The beam cut through the gloom, revealing a living room that looked lived-in, yet oddly untouched. A cup of tea sat on the coffee table, a thin film forming on its surface. The TV remote lay on the arm of Mrs. Johnson's chair, angled as if recently used.

Will moved deeper into the apartment, his enhanced senses on high alert. Each room told the same story—recently occupied, but with an underlying wrongness he couldn't quite pin down.

Finally, he reached the bedroom. As he pushed the door open, his flashlight beam fell on a figure in a chair by the window.

"Mrs. Johnson?"

The elderly woman didn't move, and gave no sign of having heard his voice.

"Mrs. Johnson, it's Will. Are you all right?" The room was freezing, and Will saw his breath misting in the air with every word.

There was no response from the woman.

His heart pounding, Will stepped closer. The woman's skin looked translucent under the flashlight. She wasn't moving. And she wasn't breathing.

"Oh, God," Will whispered, stumbling backward. He had to call this in and get Rufus to contact the authorities. Another death in the building. This wouldn't be good.

As he turned to leave, a voice stopped him cold.

"I'm fine, Will," Mrs. Johnson said, her tone flat and emotionless. "Fine."

Will froze, his hand on the doorknob. Slowly, he turned back. Mrs. Johnson hadn't moved, hadn't turned to look at him. But he knew he'd heard her voice.

"Mrs. Johnson?" Will managed, his voice barely more than a whisper.

Paralyzed between duty and fear, for what felt like an eternity, Will's training finally kicked in. Regardless of whatever was happening here, he needed help.

Will backed out of the room, and then the apartment, fumbling as he locked the apartment door behind him. As he descended the stairs, his mind whirled. What had he just witnessed? Was Mrs. Johnson alive or dead or something in between? But most importantly, how would he explain this to Rufus?

As Will reached the lobby, he saw his partner look up expectantly. Rufus' pen was poised mid-tap, ready to resume its nervous rhythm.

Will opened his mouth, then closed it again. How could he explain what he'd just experienced?

In that moment, surrounded by the too-quiet lobby of York Tower, Will made a decision that would change everything.

"She's fine," he lied, forcing a smile. "Must've been napping when Sally called. I didn't want to disturb her too much, but she said she's just fine."

Rufus' eyebrows rose slightly, but he nodded, seemingly satisfied. As Rufus' pen resumed its rhythmic tapping, Will settled back into his chair, the chill from Room 206 still clinging to his bones.

Whatever was happening upstairs, Will wanted no part of it.

The building around them seemed to exhale, as if it had been holding its breath. And from somewhere far above, Will heard the faint sound of laughter. Cold, brittle laughter that didn't belong to any human throat.

But when he looked at Rufus, his partner showed no sign of having heard anything at all.

13

A DAY IN THE LIFE

York Tower's lobby bustled with its usual morning activity as Will and Rufus greeted the residents starting their day

"Good morning, team," Rufus called out to the Callahan's, a couple in their early fifties, both dressed as though they'd stepped straight from the pages of a late 1990s edition of Vogue magazine.

"Good morning," Mr. Callahan replied, his tie a dash too short to be fashionable, and his hair a smidge too long for his age. "Not a bad day for this time of year, is it?"

Mrs. Callahan beamed. "We've just booked our flights for the World Champs. Our 25th wedding anniversary gift to each other."

"That's more than you get for murder!" Rufus said, grinning.

"What he meant to say was, that sounds fantastic!" Will added, frowning at his partner. "Have you booked any specific events?"

"Oh, the athletics mostly," Mr. Callahan said. "Sarah was quite the hurdler at college."

Sarah Callahan swatted her husband's arm. "Ancient history now, but we're both excited to see the sprints, and yes, the hurdles too."

"Don't forget to give us the dates when everything's

confirmed so that we can make a note in the file that you'll be away," Will reminded them.

As the Callahans headed out, Rufus stared morosely at their retreating backs. "Twenty-five years, and Floss couldn't even stick around for five."

"She's no great loss. Think about how much money you're saving on hairspray now that she's gone," Will laughed. It had been a running joke at the precinct about how Rufus' wife Floss maintained her helmet-like hair, and bets had been placed over the sheer amount of aerosol needed to keep it that way.

After she'd walked out of their marriage, Rufus had told Will that their final fight had centered on the outrageous cost of her salon appointments. Their marriage was doomed from the start—a cop could never satisfy Floss Matheson's social-climbing ambitions. She'd swept into his life wearing knockoff designer shoes and gel-tipped nails, a stark contrast to his modest lifestyle, and income. Their incompatibility was evident from day one, although Rufus was the last to see it.

A man in skin-tight cycling gear emerged from the stairwell, his designer backpack slung over one shoulder.

"Good morning, Mr. Forrester," Will said. "You're still biking to work, even in winter?"

The man flashed a broad white-toothed smile. "Gotta keep the ticker going."

Rufus chuckled. "You make me feel lazy just looking at you."

"It's never too late to start, Rufus," Tom Forrester winked. "I could always use a cycling buddy. They're few and far between at the bank. My colleagues are more interested in cigars than they are cycling."

As they chatted, there was a buzz at the lobby doors. The now familiar brown-shirted courier.

"Ah, our mysterious delivery man," Rufus said, buzzing the courier in. "I swear, we see him more than some of the residents."

The courier carried three packages under his arm, his

face impassive. "Apartment 306," he said, addressing Will and Rufus, but staring at Forrester.

Tom Forrester said his goodbyes and disappeared through the door leading to the lower parking garage.

"Quite the dedicated cyclist, that one," the courier remarked from his position by the elevators, his tone oddly flat. "Although in this city, such hobbies can be... short-lived. The traffic is unforgiving."

Will's skin prickled. Before he could respond, the elevator doors opened, and the courier was whisked away.

Rufus shook his head. "Cheerful guy, isn't he? Must be a real hit at parties."

"Yeah, a regular comedian," Will said, his mind automatically cataloguing the courier's words about cycling being "short-lived." Something about the way he'd said it felt like a threat.

The rest of the morning passed uneventfully. Residents came and went, sharing snippets of their lives. Mrs. Rodriguez proudly showed off pictures of her new granddaughter, born on the other side of the world in New Zealand. Mr. Kim from the fifth floor grumbled about his teenage daughter's latest infatuation—the son of a famous football player who'd asked her to go for a late night drive, after asking her if she could sneak out. The trio agreed that it sounded like the boy was bad news, and commiserated with Mr. Kim over the state of today's youth.

Then the lobby doors swished open, admitting a waft of floral fragrance along with Maggie Kendall, the building's regular florist. Her arms were laden with this week's delivery, but that didn't stop her from flashing Rufus a dazzling smile.

"My favorite delivery of the week," she chirped, her cheeks flushing as she settled the vase on the counter. "I'm here to brighten up your day."

"Maggie, you're the highlight of our week, too," Rufus said.

She leaned in, her voice dropping to a conspiratorial

whisper. "One day, you could come visit me at work for a change. There's a great coffee shop next door."

Will rolled his eyes. This dance between Rufus and Maggie had been going on for months.

As Maggie sashayed away to dispose of the previous week's flowers, Rufus' wistful gaze followed her.

"You know," Will said, unable to resist needling his friend, "you could just ask her out."

"She's far too young for me. It's just harmless flirting," Rufus huffed.

"I don't think she thinks that."

Rufus' response was cut short by the arrival of another resident, but the tips of his ears remained red for the rest of his shift.

As the day wore on, Will found himself thinking about the courier's comment about cycling being dangerous. Tom Forrester had been riding his bike to work for years without incident. But something in the courier's tone suggested he knew something they didn't.

Will touched his neck, feeling the unusual warmth beneath his skin. He couldn't help thinking that Tom Forrester's cycling days might be numbered. Why he thought that, he couldn't have said. But the thought should have prompted him to warn the man. But instead, Will found himself oddly curious about what would happen next...

14

UNSPOKEN SUSPICIONS

The acrid smell of pesticide enveloped the lobby like a toxic cloud, so intense that Will's heightened senses recoiled.

"Well, that's that," Rufus said, waving off the departing exterminators. "They didn't find a single dead critter or bug in the whole place."

Will nodded absently, the smell still threatening to overpower him. His mind was still on his encounter with Mrs. Johnson and the lie he'd told Rufus. The memory of her cold, lifeless form suddenly speaking had been haunting his dreams, making sleep an impossibility. Then there was the whole odd exchange with the courier over Tom Forrester's cycling.

Matthew Peart emerged from the stairwell, the fire door clanging shut behind him.

"Still avoiding the elevator, Mr. Peart?" Rufus called out.

Peart's nose wrinkled, whether from the pesticide smell or because it was his default expression. It was hard to tell. "Those exterminators must have missed something. There's definitely a dead animal decaying somewhere in this building."

"In the elevator shaft?" Rufus asked.

"That's what I'd put my money on," Peart replied. "I hope you haven't paid them yet because they certainly haven't done their job properly."

Peart's complaints were interrupted by the doorbell. Outside stood the now familiar brown-shirted courier. "Another delivery for 306," the courier spoke into the intercom, his voice as cold as ever, his eyes staring at Peart.

As Will buzzed the courier in, Peart scurried away, giving the courier a wide berth on his way out. The phone rang, and Rufus answered. A small sigh escaped his lips as he listened.

"That was June Johnson's daughter again," he said after hanging up. "She says she's flying in from Boise if her mother doesn't call back soon."

Will's stomach churned. "Did you tell Sally that we checked on her mom?"

"Yeah, I told her everything was fine." Rufus' eyes narrowed slightly. "It was fine, wasn't it, Will?"

Will forced a nod, avoiding his friend's gaze. "Yeah, of course. She's probably just forgotten to charge her phone or something. Or maybe after the grief her daughter gave her about moving, she's actively avoiding her?"

Rufus' pen began its nervous tapping again. "Yeah, probably. We just don't want another death on our hands this month, or the cops will really start asking questions... I've been thinking about Apartment 306."

Will tensed. "What about it?"

"Don't you find it weird? All these deliveries, but we've seen no one go in or out except that guy."

"Yeah, it's strange," Will said, relieved that Rufus wasn't pressing him about June Johnson.

Rufus leaned in, lowering his voice. "I've got half a mind to open one of those packages and find out what he's delivering."

"We can't do that," Will snapped.

Rufus raised an eyebrow. "Why not? If something fishy is going on, it's our job to know about it. Like we said in the beginning, it could be drugs. The building's a perfect front. Fancy apartments in a good part of town. Twenty-four hour security. I just don't know how they're doing the exchange when we haven't seen anyone else going into the apartment."

Will struggled to find a reason that wouldn't sound suspicious. "We can't just open someone's mail, it's... it's illegal."

"Since when did you become such a Boy Scout?" Rufus asked.

Before Will could answer, Amanda Pike entered the lobby, her children conspicuously absent.

"Mrs. Pike," Rufus called out. "I haven't seen the kids head off to school this week. Are they sick?'

Amanda Pike paused, her eyes darting around the lobby. "Oh, it's just that we, we've... decided to homeschool for a while. It's safer that way."

"Safer?" Will echoed.

"More convenient," she corrected. "Please excuse me, I'm in a hurry."

As she rushed off, Rufus turned back to Will. "Now that was weird. Since when is homeschooling safer than—"

He broke off as Will stiffened.

"What is it?"

Will blinked, coming back to himself. He'd heard... something. Whispers, maybe. Or screams. He couldn't be sure. The voices seemed to drift down from the upper floors, speaking words he couldn't quite make out.

"Nothing," he lied again. "Just thought I heard something."

Rufus' pen stilled. "What's going on, buddy? And don't tell me it's nothing. We've been partners too long for that bullshit."

How could he explain what was happening when he didn't understand it himself? "I'm just tired," Will said finally. "I've been having trouble sleeping, and I've lost my appetite. Trying not to worry about it, but my insurance won't cover... you know."

Rufus was clearly unsatisfied with Will's answer, but to his credit, he didn't push any further. "You know you can talk to me about anything. You should at least go to the doctor. It might be your iron levels or something simple like that."

"Yeah," Will agreed, guilt gnawing at him. "I know."

They'd been friends for a long time. They'd joined the force together and had retired together. Then they'd taken this job together at the urging of a former boss who'd held the position before them. Will wanted to share his concerns with his friend. But not yet. He wanted to do his own investigations, to assuage his, what would he call them? His own suspicions? His own fears? And after that, maybe he'd tell Rufus. Although at this point, he doubted Rufus would ever believe him.

Will waited until he was certain Rufus was safely ensconced in the bathroom before making a move. Grabbing the master key, he headed for the elevator, his heart pounding. The front desk would be fine for the few minutes he planned to be away.

He passed Mrs. Abernathy on her way out. As always, her steely gaze swept the lobby. For what, Will didn't know. He could only hope that she wouldn't say anything about him leaving the front desk.

The ride to the third floor took an eternity. As he approached apartment 306, he tried to slow his racing heartbeat.

With a deep breath, he inserted the key and turned it slowly. The door to apartment 306 swung open.

The room was immaculate, just as it had been when they'd delivered the birdcage. But something was different. Will's nose twitched at a familiar scent—musty and sweet, like decaying flowers.

He moved further into the apartment, noting once again the untouched furniture and the lack of personal items. Then he saw it—an opened package on the dining table. Will approached cautiously, his curiosity overcoming his fear. He peered into the box and gagged.

Inside were several small vials filled with a dark, viscous liquid. Will didn't need to open one to know what they contained. Instinctively, he knew. They contained blood.

Movement from the corner caught his eye. The ornate birdcage he and Rufus had delivered now housed several small, ash-gray birds. Their black eyes followed his every move as they hopped silently between the gilded perches. Will stepped closer. They looked ordinary at first glance—like common finches—except for their beaks. Each was tipped with an unnatural sharpness, and dark stains marred the edges. As he watched, one pecked viciously at another's wing. The wounded bird didn't even flinch. The metallic scent of fresh blood joined the musty sweetness in the air, making Will's newly heightened senses reel.

A noise from somewhere in the bowels of the building startled him and Will backed out of the apartment, locking the door behind him.

Instead of returning to the lobby, Will pressed the elevator button for the fourth floor. He needed some time to himself to decide what to tell Rufus. He could have been wrong. The vials could have contained nothing more than expensive ink, the sort you can order from exclusive suppliers who don't need to advertise. That's the sort of thing old money bought.

The elevator doors opened with a soft ding and the hallway stretched out before him. The air felt thick with disuse, which was odd, because unlike the third floor, the fourth floor was fully occupied.

He sniffed, searching for that musty, sweet scent he'd detected in Apartment 306. But it was noticeably absent from this floor.

From behind one door, he heard the muffled sound of a television. From another, the plaintive cries of a baby. Further down the hall, the melancholic strains of a violin drifted through the air. Normal sounds of life in an apartment building. And yet there was something artificial about the scene. It was too perfect, too staged. A television, a baby, and a violin. This was life imitating art, not real life.

Choosing the stairwell this time instead of the elevator, he climbed to the fifth floor, his breath catching at the unexpected exertion. As he emerged onto the landing, he caught a flicker of movement. Will spun around, but there was nothing there.

There was no Hollywood soundtrack on the fifth floor, save for a peal of laughter abruptly cut off, which made him jump out of his skin. The sense of wrongness grew until it gnawed at his bones. Will stood frozen in place. He'd been part of the thin blue line, he'd had a gun pointed at his head, and he'd been stabbed once. But he'd never felt like this before. Wrong. He felt wrong.

He continued going up.

On the sixth floor, he saw it again—a shadow lingering at the end of the hallway. Will blinked, and it disappeared. Now it felt as if the very walls themselves were watching him and he was almost ready to tear off his skin to escape their observation.

"Screw it," he muttered to himself, breaking the daze he'd been in. He stabbed at the elevator button and surged into the tiny space as soon as the doors opened, missing the shadow pooling on the polished floor outside the nearest apartment door.

When the doors opened onto the lobby, Will rushed out, straight into Rufus' angry stare.

"Where the hell have you been?"

Will opened his mouth, then closed it again. How could he possibly explain what he'd just experienced?

"I was checking out that noise I thought I heard," he managed.

"You left the desk unattended," Rufus said accusingly.

"Sorry."

"Did you find anything?"

Will hesitated, the weight of what he thought he'd seen pressing down on him. "No," he lied, hating himself for it. "Nothing out of the ordinary."

The vials of blood burned in his memory like a brand. And up above them, those strange birds with their razor-sharp beaks continued their grotesque feeding ritual, marking time until darkness fell.

15

ON TOP OF THE WORLD

The New York skyline glittered beyond the tinted windows of the York Tower penthouse, a view that had captivated Richard Blackwood for decades. But tonight, his attention was fixed on his wife, Elizabeth, who stood motionless on the terrace, her silk robe billowing in the evening breeze.

"My dear," Richard called softly, "you shouldn't be out there. The sun has barely set."

Elizabeth turned, an enigmatic smile playing on her lips. "The glass filters the worst of it, darling. Besides, our little friend is here."

As if on cue, a large raven landed on the railing. Elizabeth reached into a small bowl beside her, extracting a chunk of raw meat. The bird cawed loudly before snatching it from her hand.

"You spoil that creature," Richard said, joining her outside.

"He's got better manners than our kids," Elizabeth replied, feeding the raven another morsel. "Besides, he's our eyes and ears. And he brings me news about the city."

Richard's jaw tightened. "Does he tell you that someone is targeting our tenants? Because that's what I can feel. And it's not one of us. It's high time for James and Sarah to turn and join the rest of the family. There's safety in numbers, you know that."

"Now?" Elizabeth replied. "But what about Burton?"

Richard considered their other children from centuries past, now grown and scattered across the globe. They would come if he called, if he felt he needed them. But he didn't think they'd reached that stage. Not yet. "After all this time, I'm sure he's given up trying to destroy us. Especially after what happened in Rhode Island. I'm positive he's gone. It's someone else. I just don't know who, and that is what worries me the most."

Elizabeth paced the terrace, agitation clear in every movement. "But you don't know for certain? We have to be careful. James and Sarah aren't ready yet. The world is such a different place from when we changed their brothers and sisters. They don't need to know the full truth. Not yet."

"They're Blackwoods," Richard said firmly. "This is in their blood, whether they understand it or not. Our legacy will continue, with or without their full comprehension. But there's someone else out there, and until I know who that is, I worry about James and Sarah, about their safety."

"Perhaps it is time we brought James more fully into our world," Elizabeth agreed. "But 21st-century New York City isn't a small town in 1790s Vermont. We can't just disappear if things go wrong this time."

Richard stepped closer to his wife, placing his hand on her arm. "Which is precisely why we need James. And Sarah."

"Or they could reject us entirely," Elizabeth countered. "Sarah's already suspicious. If we lose both our children..."

"Though the blood in their veins may change, the bond of love that binds us was forged long before their first breath," Richard quoted.

The city lights flickered below, casting strange shadows across the penthouse floor. The raven's wings rustled, a sound that spoke of countless secrets.

"If we don't act," Richard said, "all of us are at risk. I can feel a change in the air, and not a good one. We need to be prepared. This detective might just prove to be useful."

"Or she could expose us," Elizabeth said.

"In this world of endless distraction and disbelief? No one would believe her," Richard replied. "But her presence may be enough to put a stop to whoever is encroaching on our life."

The raven finished its meal and preened its glossy feathers, its black eyes reflecting the city lights like tiny mirrors. Below them, York Tower hummed with its usual evening rhythm.

Televisions flickering to life, families settling in for dinner, the elderly residents drawing their curtains against the night.

But something felt different tonight. Richard could sense it in the building's very bones. A restlessness. A hunger that had been awakened and was growing stronger.

"The security guard," Elizabeth said suddenly, as if reading his thoughts. "He's changing. Was it you?"

"Will Taylor," Richard nodded. "It wasn't me, but yes, someone has changed him. But the change is slower than normal, which is why it took me so long to notice. And that scares me."

"I know you think Burton has gone, but could it be his handiwork? Or one of his followers?"

"But why would he draw it out like this?" Richard frowned. "It's not Burton's style."

Elizabeth moved to stand beside him, her hand finding his. "Perhaps he's learned patience in his old age."

"Or perhaps," Richard said quietly, "it's something much bigger. Someone we have yet to encounter? A threat larger than we can face alone?"

The raven cawed once, sharp and clear in the night air, before spreading its wings and taking flight. They watched it disappear into the darkness.

"We should warn James and Sarah," Elizabeth said.

"Warn them of what? That monsters are real? That their parents are among them?" Richard's laugh was bitter. "They'd think we'd lost our minds."

"Then what do you suggest?"

Richard watched the city pulse with life. Somewhere in

the maze of streets and buildings, something was waiting. Planning. Preparing to strike at the heart of everything they'd built.

"We do what we've always done," he said finally. "We survive. And we protect what's ours."

The raven's cry echoed across Manhattan one last time as two ancient predators prepared for a war centuries in the making.

16

HUNGER PANGS

W ill trudged up the creaky stairs to his fifth-floor walk-up, the keys jingling in his hand. The hallway lights flickered, casting eerie shadows that reminded him too much of York Tower. He shook off the thought as he reached his door.

His two-room apartment welcomed him with familiar, if somewhat shabby, comfort. Will tossed his keys onto the small table by the door and headed straight for the bathroom. The face that greeted him in the mirror looked gaunt, with dark circles under his eyes and hair that was at least three weeks overdue for a cut. He tilted his head, examining the bite on his neck. The surrounding skin was still red, with thin, dark lines spreading outward like spiderwebs.

"Damn it," he muttered, prodding gently at the wound. It didn't hurt, which worried him more than if it had been painful. He'd put some ointment on it later, after his shower.

Will stripped off his now oversized uniform shirt. He'd had to punch a new hole in his belt twice this month already. The weight loss might have been welcome if it didn't feel so... wrong.

His stomach growled, reminding him that he couldn't remember the last time he'd eaten a proper meal. He hadn't been able to finish his usual lunchtime sandwiches once this week. Their moldy remains mocked him from the trash bin, which he'd forgotten to empty.

Will headed to the kitchen, determined to fix himself something substantial.

As he opened the refrigerator, a wave of nausea hit. The usual smells of leftover takeout and half-empty condiment bottles had turned putrid, overwhelming him. Will slammed the door shut, leaning against it as he tried to stop heaving at the repulsive odor.

The aroma of sizzling peppers mixed with garlic wafted through the thin walls of his neighbor's apartment. Normally, Mrs. Ramirez's cooking smelled delicious, often tempting Will to knock on her door with some flimsy excuse just to score a plate of her famous enchiladas. But now, the scent turned his stomach, and he rushed to the bathroom, retching unproductively into the toilet.

What the hell is wrong with me? Will splashed cold water on his face and stared at his reflection again, noting the pallor of his skin and the sharp angles of his cheekbones. Cancer. The word flashed through his mind. It would explain his shrinking appetite, the lack of hunger, and the general feeling of wrongness plaguing him. Cancer had carried away both of his parents, and it hadn't been pretty. As long as he didn't see a doctor, he could pretend he wasn't dying. There was no way he wanted to go through what his parents had. It was a completely futile exercise trying to keep the disease at bay. He'd rather just fade away. Isn't that what they'd called it back in the day? The wasting disease?

He wandered back to the kitchen, opening cupboards aimlessly. Nothing appealed. Not the canned soup, not the stale crackers, not even the emergency chocolate bar he kept hidden behind the coffee filters.

Will's gaze fell on the bowl of apples on the counter. Selecting a small paring knife from the knife block, he chose the least rubbery fruit, long past its best-by date. And on his first pass, the knife slipped, and sank into the fleshy webbing between his fingers.

"Son of a bitch!"

He dropped the apple, and the knife clattered to the floor. Will grabbed a handful of paper towels to staunch the blood flow. And then the scent hit him like a freight train. Rich, coppery, intoxicating. His mouth watered, and for the first time in days, he felt hungry.

Horrified, he ran his hand under a stream of running water, ignoring the pain. What was he thinking? This wasn't normal. None of this was normal.

Struggling to ignore the metallic taste filling his mouth, Will stumbled to the bathroom, searching for his first aid kit, where he clumsily wrapped his hand in gauze before securing it with tape. A smear of blood beckoned him from the lip of the sink. A smear no larger than his thumbnail. The smear was so red, so fresh, that he could almost taste it.

He wiped at the smear with his fingertip, examining it for a moment before licking it.

He licked it once.

But once was enough.

A lightning bolt of sensation erupted through his body, every nerve ending alive and screaming with a hunger so profound it obliterated thought, replacing confusion with a razor-sharp clarity that felt more like remembering than discovering.

Will staggered to his bedroom and collapsed onto the unmade double bed, his hand aching, and his hunger growing. As he drifted into an uneasy sleep, one terrifying thought echoed in his mind: The taste of his own blood had been the most satisfying thing he'd eaten in days, and deep down, he craved more.

But underneath that craving lay the growing certainty that his own blood was just an appetizer. What he really wanted was warm, fresh, and flowing through someone else's veins.

Someone like Mrs. Holley next door, whose heartbeat came through the thin walls, steady and strong and utterly tempting.

Will pressed his face into his pillow, trying to block out

the sound, but it followed him into his dreams—the rhythmic pulse of life that called to the growing darkness inside him.

17

THE LONELY HEIGHTS

Matthew Peart sat at his mahogany desk, the glow of his laptop casting deep shadows on the angular planes of his face. His online dating profile stared back at him, as empty as his social calendar. He toggled between two photos: one in a bespoke suit, which in his mind spoke to his serious side and promised a man with a steady income. The other was him on a tennis court, racquet in hand, and he thought it conveyed healthy vitality.

Neither image captured the truth: Matthew Peart, 52, painfully average in looks, shorter than most men, extraordinarily above average in net worth, and lonely as hell.

He closed the laptop. What was the point? He should simply write 'Loaded' in his bio and watch the messages flood in. But that wasn't what he wanted. Was it?

A waft of something foul pulled him from his reverie. "Damn it," he muttered, striding to the door to check the towel he'd stuffed at its base. The expensive gardenia-scented candle on his desk was losing the battle against the stench.

Matthew glared at the door as if it were personally responsible for the odor. He'd only been living in York Tower for two weeks, a gift to himself after closing the biggest deal of his career.

This was supposed to be his slice of real estate paradise. Instead, he felt like he was living above a poorly managed sewage treatment plant.

He returned to his desk, pulling up the building management's contact information for what felt like the hundredth time. This was unacceptable. He was Matthew Peart, for God's sake. He'd once negotiated a multi-billion-dollar real estate acquisition over eighteen holes of golf with a man who owned his own island. Surely he could get someone to find the source of a bad smell.

As he began composing yet another strongly worded email, his mind drifted to the other residents. He couldn't believe that they couldn't smell it too? Or was he being oversensitive, a habit his ex-wife had often accused him of?

Matthew shook his head, banishing thoughts of his failed marriage. His therapist had done her best to train him to look forward, not backward. His ex-wife was an ex for a reason, and that reason wasn't him. After the divorce, his income had plummeted, making his once-luxurious lifestyle feel like a distant memory. The Blackwoods had been his salvation. Their arrangement stretched back further than the last decade, into murkier territory that Peart preferred not to dwell on.

Working for them wasn't always straightforward. Their requests were cryptic, their expectations sometimes bizarre. But they paid well, and after his divorce, that was exactly what Matthew needed. This apartment in York Tower? A perfect example of their peculiar generosity. Secured at a price that would have been impossible otherwise, with a lease that seemed too good to be true.

Which made the current situation even more frustrating. How could he not resolve a simple odor problem when he'd been working with the Blackwoods for a decade? They were meticulous, almost obsessively so. Dealing with a foul odor should be child's play compared to some secrets he'd buried for his clients.

He refocused on the email, his fingers flying over the keys as he detailed his grievances. This apartment, this building, was meant to be perfect. Instead, it was becoming a malodorous prison.

He hit send with more force than necessary, then leaned back in his chair. Even from the third floor, the city looked a damn sight better from up here than it did up close. Much like his dating profile photos.

Matthew appreciated the illusion. Life was a game, and the richer you are, the more likely you are to win.

Matthew stood and walked to the bar cart in the corner. As he poured himself a generous measure of scotch, he caught his average reflection in the mirror he'd paid thousands for at Christie's.

The reflection hid an important truth: for 15 years, Peart had been a key player in a game far bigger than real estate. A game where the rules were murky and the stakes higher than anyone could imagine.

"To success," he toasted his reflection sardonically. "May it smell sweeter than this."

He drained the glass in one gulp, savoring the burn. Tomorrow he'd call the Blackwoods directly. Enough tiptoeing around building management. If anyone could solve this problem, it was them.

They'd made much bigger problems disappear before. What was one bad smell compared to the secrets he'd helped them bury?

The smell wafted under his door again carrying with it something that made his skin crawl. Something that reminded him of the mortuary where his father had been laid out, all those years ago. Sweet decay mixed with something metallic.

Matthew poured another scotch, a double this time. Some problems were better faced with liquid courage. And if the Blackwoods couldn't fix this, well... he knew enough about their business to make other arrangements.

The thought should have scared him. Instead, it made him smile.

Outside, a raven alighted on the fire escape, its eyes gleaming in the apartment's warm light. It cocked its head, studying him with an intelligence that made Matthew step back from the glass. The bird watched him for a long moment, then spread its wings and disappeared into the night.

Matthew finished his drink and went to bed, unaware that his complaints had been heard by more than just building management. And by someone other than the Blackwoods...

18

WILTED PETALS

Outside York Tower, a cold, blustery fall morning delivered a city painted in gray. Razor-sharp wind blew through the streets, punishing commuters for daring to venture outdoors. Rain soaked the pavement, dampening the colorful petals of the huge floral arrangements the florist struggled to protect as she unloaded her van. Each gust threatened to destroy the blooms as she wrestled with the bouquets. The wind had whipped her hair out of her normal messy bun, and to the casual observer, it was difficult to see where her vibrant red hair ended, and the flowers began.

"Good morning Rufus, are you ready to be dazzled by today's blooms?" Maggie, the florist, chirped into the intercom, her green eyes twinkling.

Rufus chuckled, buzzing her in. "Always, Maggie. Your deliveries are the highlight of my Thursdays."

She threw a flirtatious wave towards Rufus on her way to the elevator. Her first stop was the penthouse with their standing weekly order. As the ancient elevator ascended, she hummed, stopping as the doors opened to reveal Richard Blackwood silhouetted against the tinted windows.

"Good morning, Mr. Blackwood," Maggie said.

"Good morning, Maggie," he nodded, his eyes following her as she began replacing last week's arrangement.

She worked quickly, conscious of his gaze on her. There

was always an intensity about him which made her skin prickle. As she turned to leave, he spoke again.

"How long have you been delivering here?" he asked.

Maggie paused. "Two years this month."

"Sounds about right," he murmured, his accent carrying a trace of something old, something foreign to New York. "Time certainly flies. I've enjoyed your dedication to your role, and I've heard that you've excelled at expanding your customer base. An impressive feat in this city. It hasn't gone unnoticed."

Maggie smiled, his praise sending an unexpected warmth through her chest. Richard Blackwood had rarely spoken more than a few words to her in all the time she'd been delivering flowers to York Tower.

She thanked him, his praise allaying her earlier feelings of unease, and smiled to herself as she carried on with the rest of her deliveries.

Her other rounds passed in a blur. The Callahans on the sixth floor were arguing good-naturedly over where to place their orchids. Tom Forrester on the fifth, barely looked up from his laptop as she swapped out his arrangement. Unusually, there'd been no answer at Mrs. Johnson's apartment on the second floor, so she would have to leave her arrangement at the front desk.

As she returned to the elevator, she found it already occupied by the courier she'd seen on countless other occasions. His brown uniform crisp and his smile impossibly charming.

"Good morning," he said in a velvet whisper that curled around her. "Those flowers look heavy. May I hold them for you?"

Maggie nodded and he relieved her of the large bouquet.

As the elevator started, they were jerked upward to the third floor instead of down to the lobby. The courier glanced at the button panel. "I see the elevators are still playing up," he murmured. "This may be fortuitous? Perhaps if you have a moment, you could share your professional opinion with my employer on which are the best cut flowers to have on display in his apartment?"

With Mr. Blackwood's praise still ringing in her ears, Maggie nodded and followed him out onto the third floor. The courier gestured toward apartment 306, adding, "He will undoubtedly want to arrange for weekly deliveries, like the other tenants. These really are quite exquisite."

When the courier opened the door to the apartment, Maggie's first impression was that it was immaculate, and beautifully furnished, like a high-end showroom. After that, her attention was drawn to an ornate birdcage where several ash-gray birds shifted silently on their perches, their eyes following her.

Maggie moved toward the cage, her florist's curiosity drawn to these unusual specimens. "What beautiful finches," she said, leaning closer. "I've never seen this variety before."

"Geospiza septentrionalis," the courier said, his voice still silky soft. "More commonly known as vampire finches. Native to the Galápagos."

As if on cue, one bird pecked viciously at its cage-mate's wing. A drop of blood welled up, and the attacking finch drank eagerly. The wounded bird didn't flinch, as if this bloodletting was routine. Maggie stepped back, unsettled by their behavior, before her eye was caught by an odd display on the opposite wall.

"Beautiful, aren't they?" the courier gestured to the display of glass vials. "Like your flowers, but far more precious."

Despite her growing unease, Maggie remained professional. "What are they?" she asked, filling the silence.

"Life itself," the courier replied, moving behind her with an unnatural grace, his closeness unnerving her even further. "Would you like me to show you how they work?"

Faster than humanly possible, the courier's teeth sank into her neck before she could answer. The needle-like points both paralysing and anaesthetising her simultaneously. She couldn't have fought back even if she'd wanted to.

As Maggie's life drained away, her last thought was of Rufus and of his shy smiles and awkward compliments, of how she should have asked him out herself. All the while, the birds watched with black, knowing eyes, nature's tiny mirrors, as her life drained away.

After sating his own thirst, the courier carefully collected Maggie's blood in one of the ornate vials, adding it to the collection on the wall. Each vial was representative of a life stolen. A future ended.

"Such a shame," murmured another voice, watching from the shadows as Maggie's body crumpled to the floor. "But we require fresh stock, and young blood is always the sweetest."

Like all their victims, Maggie's body would soon decay with inhuman speed, leaving little evidence of her existence, save for a sprinkling of dust on the expensive Turkish carpets.

"My pleasure, as always," the courier replied, before wiping his mouth and slipping from the apartment, his perfect smile back in place.

Descending to the lobby, the courier walked calmly past the security desk as if nothing about the day was anything other than ordinary. Of course for the courier, today was much like every other day.

And in the third-floor garbage chute of York Tower, the petals of Mrs. Johnson's undelivered floral arrangement turned black and fuzzy with decay, the sickly scent of rotting stems joining the growing miasma of death in the building.

THREE WEEKS LATER, as the uniformed security guard opened the lobby doors for her, Charlotte pushed her flower cart inside.

"You must be the new florist," Will said, his tone neutral. "Charlotte, right?"

She nodded, offering a small smile. "That's right. Maggie's replacement. And from what I've heard, I've got big shoes to fill."

"I'm sure you'll be fine," Will replied, scratching at his neck. "I'm Will, and my usual partner in crime is off on his break, but his name is Rufus. He was rather fond of Maggie, so you've got some work to do there," Will smiled.

Charlotte's own smile faltered a little, but she nodded and headed for the elevators, passing a well-groomed Asian man with a suit bag draped over his arm. As she waited with her cart outside the elevators, she overheard the conversation between Will and the other man.

"Good morning, Mr. Kim."

"That's not Maggie," Mr. Kim said quietly, but clear enough for Charlotte to hear.

Will shook his head. "No, it's not, and it sounds like she won't be returning."

Mr. Kim sighed. "My daughter keeps asking when she's coming back. Maggie was helping her with a school project on botany."

"I know," Will replied, his tone somber. "Mrs. Abernathy came down yesterday in a real state, worried that Maggie was booked to do the flowers for her granddaughter's wedding next month."

"And the florists haven't said anything?" Mr. Kim pushed.

"Her boss said it's like she vanished into thin air. They waited as long as they could, but they had to replace her," Will added.

Mr. Kim lowered his voice further, and Charlotte strained to hear. "You don't think she's dead?"

"In my experience, people disappear all the time, for a variety of reasons. It's probably either boyfriend related, or money issues. I imagine New York is an expensive city for a florist. It was bad enough as a cop to stay afloat."

Their voices trailed off as Charlotte entered the elevator,

but as she made her deliveries, the whispers followed her. Where was Maggie? Why had she left so suddenly? Had she moved to a different company?

In the penthouse, Charlotte bristled under Richard Blackwood's eye and his unreadable expression. "Is Maggie no longer doing the arrangements?" he asked, his voice void of any discernible emotion.

Charlotte's hands stilled. "She doesn't work for Buds & Bows anymore. I'm her replacement."

"Replacement?" A single word, weighted with something Charlotte couldn't quite define.

She met his gaze, forcing her voice to remain steady. "She stopped coming to work. I was brought in to continue her routes."

The silence between them stretched, uncomfortable and charged.

"She will be missed," he said, a statement that felt like a warning.

Charlotte let out her breath. Coming face-to-face with one of the Blackwoods had been her biggest fear, and she'd survived.

Later, as she was loading the wilted dying arrangements into her van, a shadow fell across her.

"Karl," she replied, without turning around. "I wondered if you'd show up."

"Any problems?"

Charlotte's eyes did a quick sweep of the road before answering. "Blackwood didn't suspect a thing."

Karl stepped closer. "Just remember why we're here. Don't get too complacent, because I won't always be here to help."

As Karl walked away, Charlotte turned back to the van. Among the wilted flowers, barely visible, was a flash of vibrant red—a strand of long, red, hair.

Charlotte plucked it out, letting it fall to the ground. The wind caught it and carried it away—much like the woman it had once belonged to, now lost to the shadows cast by York Tower.

19

———

NIGHT SHIFT

The lobby was eerily quiet as the clock ticked toward 6am. Karl Middleton stifled a yawn, his eyes scanning the security monitors one last time before his shift ended. The elevator dinged and out stepped Will and Rufus, ready to take over.

"Morning, boys," Karl greeted, his voice carrying a hint of an accent that was hard to place.

"How was last night?" Rufus groaned, settling into his chair.

Karl shrugged. "Quiet as a graveyard. Just the way I like it."

Will chuckled. "You're an odd one, Karl. Most guys your age would be out partying, not working nights."

"I'm saving up for college," Karl replied with a grin.

"Oh, yeah?" Rufus perked up. "Where you thinking of going?"

"Somewhere back home in Vermont. Maybe Bennington College."

Will raised an eyebrow. "You don't sound like you're from there."

Karl's smile tightened. "Manchester, born and raised. It's just a dot on the map, but it's got some interesting history."

"Like what?" Rufus asked, always eager for a good story.

"Well, for one, it was one of the first capitals of Vermont before it became a state. And it's where President Lincoln's son Robert had his summer home. I mean, it's not the White House, but it's still impressive for a town of only a few thousand people." Karl said.

"Although Manchester's got stories most people don't want to hear. Some history is better left buried," Karl added after a short pause.

Rufus nodded, not quite catching the weight behind Karl's words. "Must be nice to have a summer home. I've got a summer home and a winter home. The only difference is whether I turn on the AC or not. So, what brought you to the Big Apple?"

Karl's eyes darted to the monitors before answering, and for a moment his accent seemed to slip. "Just wanted a change of scenery, I guess. Manchester can be a bit... constraining sometimes. Too many old families with too many old secrets. New York's got opportunities you can't find anywhere else."

"Can't argue with that," Rufus chuckled. "Though I bet the crime rate's different?"

Karl's expression darkened for a moment. "You'd be surprised. Every place has its problems. Sometimes the worst monsters are the ones who've learned to blend in with polite society."

An uncomfortable silence fell over the lobby. Will cleared his throat. "Well, thanks for looking after the place last night, Karl. Go get some rest."

Karl gathered his things, and as he headed for the exit, he paused. "Hey, you ever notice anything strange? Here?"

"Strange how?" Will asked, his hand twitching toward his neck.

Karl shook his head, as if deciding against sharing something. "Never mind. It's probably just my overactive imagination," Karl said, but his tone suggested otherwise. "See you tonight."

As the door closed behind Karl, Rufus turned to Will with a sigh. "Not big on sharing, is he? And just when his story was getting interesting? Manchester I couldn't care less about. But our building? I'd like to know what he was going on about. Sometimes it's like getting blood out of stone talking to the younger generation."

Will was staring at the back of their new security guard. There had been something in Karl's voice when he mentioned old families and buried secrets which didn't sit right. And that accent. It tugged at his memory, although he couldn't place why.

"Can we not talk about blood? I haven't eaten, and I was looking forward to the bacon roll I grabbed on my way in."

Rufus laughed. "Yeah, I've seen you turn green around the gills at bloody crime scenes. Go eat your bacon roll, I'll hold down the fort."

The morning passed uneventfully, with residents coming and going, until later that afternoon, when a harried-looking DoorDash courier, balancing several bags, stabbed at the buzzer.

"Delivery for Pike, apartment 304," he announced.

Rufus buzzed him in and then called up to 304. "Mrs. Pike? Your DoorDash is here." He caught himself before adding the word "again," though the thought tempted him.

"I'll be right down," came the terse reply.

As the DoorDash driver set the bags on the counter, Rufus leaned forward, curiosity piqued. "What'd she order this time? You're here so often, we should get you your own key."

The driver rifled through the bag for the receipt. "One rare steak sandwich, two cheeseburgers, and two strawberry sundaes."

As the bag opened, a sickly sweet smell filled the lobby and Rufus noticed Will's face turn pale, almost gray.

"You okay?" Rufus asked, genuine concern in his voice.

Before Will could answer, Amanda Pike burst out of the elevator, her face a mask of barely contained frustration.

"You took your time," she snapped.

As she grabbed the bags, the bottom of one gave way, spilling a mess of ice cream and strawberry syrup across the polished floor.

Rufus watched as Amanda's frustration boiled over.

"Oh, for crying out loud!" she exclaimed. "Is it too much to ask for a simple delivery without a disaster?"

The driver stammered out an apology, but Amanda cut him off. "Save it. I've got two hungry kids upstairs and no dessert. It's like living in a third world country here sometimes."

She stormed back to the elevator with the remaining bag, never once turning around.

Rufus and the poor courier exchanged bewildered looks. "No tip for you, I'm guessing," Rufus said, grabbing paper towels from under the counter. "She's not usually like that."

The driver shrugged. "It happens. Are you okay to clear this up? I've got other deliveries, and I need the money."

"Get out of here," Rufus replied, thinking about his own financial struggles—even with his police pension and wage from York Tower, some weeks were tight.

As he cleaned the sticky mess, Rufus kept glancing at Will. His partner looked worse by the minute, sweating, his complexion still that unhealthy gray.

"You look like you're about to lose your lunch," Rufus said. "And if you are, can you do it in the john? There aren't enough paper towels here for me to clean that up as well."

"That smell... the artificial strawberry... it's making me sick. I'm gonna step outside for some air," Will stammered.

As Will hurried out, Rufus finished cleaning, puzzling over Amanda's uncharacteristic outburst. "Not quite the gourmet meals she usually orders," he muttered to himself, shaking his head. "Who the hell orders a rare steak sandwich from DoorDash?"

20

THE VIEW FROM ABOVE

In the dimly lit penthouse of York Tower, Richard Blackwood's silhouette appeared stark against the bronze-tinted windows that stretched from floor to ceiling. The New York skyline lay before him, a glittering map of electric stars dulled by the specially treated glass.

These windows, installed when they'd modernized York Tower in the 1960s, had been considered an extravagance by his competitors. Bronze-tinted glass wouldn't become commonplace in high-rises until the '70s and '80s. But he'd insisted, citing the need for privacy for his tenants.

Privacy was certainly part of it, but not in the way most assumed.

He raised a hand, watching as the skin on his palm rippled and shifted, almost of its own accord. With a grimace, he stepped back from the window, retreating further into the shadows of the room. Even filtered sunlight was becoming problematic these days—a sign that his last feeding had been too long ago.

The tinted glass wasn't just for show. It filtered out the harmful rays of sunlight that could betray their true nature. The Blackwoods had built an empire on secrets, and this building was a sanctuary hidden in plain sight.

Richard moved to his desk, his fingers trailing over a stack of reports. Complaints about strange noises, unexplained maintenance issues, the latest financials... all the mundane details of running a luxury apartment building. But beneath it all lay a darker truth that stretched back over two centuries.

His eyes fell on a framed photo of his son, James. The boy had no idea of the legacy he would inherit, the true nature of the family business. Richard's jaw clenched. How much longer could they keep up this charade? The modern world was becoming increasingly difficult to navigate—security cameras everywhere, social media making anonymity nearly impossible, DNA databases that could trace bloodlines back generations.

Not like the simple days in Manchester, Vermont, when a man could disappear into the wilderness and start fresh. When Rachel had been alive and the future had seemed full of possibilities instead of centuries of running from Burton's twisted revenge.

A soft chime from his computer drew his attention. An alert from building security—that detective had been around again. Melville. She didn't know what she was getting into. None of them did.

He turned back to the window, his reflection ghostly in the glass. York Tower had stood for decades, a beacon of luxury and prestige, built on blood and shadows. But it had served its purpose well—a perfect hunting ground disguised as respectability.

As the sun dipped, painting the sky in hues of orange and red, Richard felt the familiar stirring in his veins. Night was coming, and with it, the hunger. Though tonight he'd have to be more careful than usual. Burton was out there somewhere, and the last thing Richard needed was to give his old enemy more ammunition.

He smiled grimly, remembering Elizabeth's observation from the night before: "You know, darling, for creatures of the night, we certainly do spend a lot of time worrying about real estate taxes."

Even after three centuries together, his wife still made him laugh.

A harsh caw broke the silence of the penthouse.

Richard's head snapped toward the sound. On the railing of the outdoor terrace, a large raven had perched, its feathers glossy black in the fading light. Its unblinking eyes stared at Richard with an intelligence that made his ancient blood run cold.

Richard moved toward the terrace doors, sliding them open—taking a nimble step back as the evening light hit him. The raven didn't flinch. Instead, it cawed again, the sound echoing across Manhattan like a death knell.

"What news do you bring, my dark friend?" Richard murmured, more to himself than to the bird. But deep down, he already knew. Burton's messengers had found them. After all these years of hiding in plain sight, the hunt was about to begin again.

The raven tilted its head, as if considering his words. Then, with a final piercing cry, it spread its wings and took flight, disappearing into the gathering darkness.

Richard closed the doors, the evening's chill lingering on his skin. As he turned from the window, his reflection caught his eye—for just a moment, he looked exactly like the young man who had loved Rachel Burton in a small Vermont town over two centuries ago. Before the turning. Before the endless running. Before everything had gone so terribly wrong.

And as the sun set and the citizens of New York City prepared themselves for bed, the lord of York Tower prepared to feed. But first, he had a phone call to make. Elizabeth needed to know that their past had finally caught up with them.

The raven's cry echoed once more across the city, and Richard shuddered. Some sounds, once heard, could never be forgotten. Just like some debts could never be repaid.

As the raven soared away from York Tower, its wings cutting through the air with predatory grace, the bird's keen eyes took in the sprawling cityscape below. A kaleidoscope of lights and shadows, millions of lives pulsing through the urban arteries like blood through veins.

It swooped low over Will's apartment building in

Queens. where Will tossed restlessly in his sleep, plagued by dreams of copper pennies and warm flesh.

The raven's shadow briefly eclipsed his bedroom window, and Will's dreams shifted, becoming darker, more urgent.

Next, the raven glided past Rufus' home in Brooklyn, where the warm glow of a television flickered through drawn curtains. The bird's shadow briefly blocked the streetlamp, causing Rufus to look up from his late-night snack—a leftover meatball sub that was probably past its prime, but hey, waste not, want not.

Banking sharply, the raven headed toward Iona Melville's residence, where it perched momentarily on a fire escape. Through the window, it observed Iona hunched over case files at her kitchen table, unaware that she was investigating forces beyond her comprehension. Her coffee had gone cold hours ago, but she barely noticed, lost in the puzzle of York Tower's mounting death toll.

The bird then took off toward the heart of the city, flying over the empty apartment of the missing florist, Maggie. A faint scent of decay drifted upward from the building, wrapped in a shroud of abandonment that only the raven's supernatural senses could detect.

The raven's presence sent ripples through Central Park. Other birds dove for cover, bats changed direction, and the insects fell silent—all of nature recognizing a predator far older and more dangerous than anything that belonged in the modern world. Even the rats seemed to burrow deeper into their holes.

It observed a couple laughing on a moonlit bench, oblivious to the dangers that stalked the shadows. A homeless man huddled under a bridge, his dreams haunted by creatures he couldn't name. Teenagers drinking by the reservoir, their laughter echoing off the water while something ancient watched from the darkness above.

The bird saw it all—the joy and the sorrow, the light and the dark that coexisted in the city. It was a witness to the complex tapestry of human life, and to the supernatural currents that ran beneath the surface, unseen by most.

As dawn approached, the raven circled back toward York Tower. It landed once more on the terrace railing, locking eyes with Richard Blackwood through the tinted glass. Predator recognizing predator. Master acknowledging servant.

The message had been delivered. The hunt would begin soon.

The raven took flight once more, disappearing into the pre-dawn darkness. But its presence lingered like a dark promise of the night to come.

And somewhere in the city, Isaac Burton smiled.

21

A DAUGHTER'S DILEMMA

On the following Tuesday, which for most of New York was just an ordinary day of an ordinary week, the shrill ring of the lobby phone cut through the quiet morning air. Rufus answered, his eyes rolling skyward as his expression grew more exasperated with each passing second. "Yes, yes, I understand... No ma'am, we haven't noticed anything unusual... Of course, we'll check on her right away."

Will raised an eyebrow as Rufus hung up. "Mrs. Johnson's daughter again?"

Rufus nodded, his pen tapping an agitated rhythm on the desk. "Sally's really worked up. Insists on speaking to her mother directly."

"Guess we better do another wellness check," Will sighed, his stomach rumbling ominously.

Rufus cocked an eyebrow toward Will's shrinking frame. "I was running late and skipped breakfast," Will said, trying to ignore the ravenous hunger which was now his constant companion. In truth, he hadn't kept down the toast he'd eaten for breakfast, with the black coffee not far behind.

"We'll go up together," Rufus said, levering himself off his ergonomic chair.

Will swallowed his objections and followed Rufus to the elevator. For the first time, the irritation from the bite on his neck seemed to radiate down his shoulder. The transformation was spreading.

As they approached Mrs. Johnson's apartment on the second floor, an unsettling quiet enveloped them. The everyday sounds of life—televisions, conversations, the hum of appliances—which usually filled the hallways were absent, replaced instead by an oppressive silence that felt unnatural.

"Where is everyone?" Rufus asked, his voice sounding too loud in the stillness.

Will shrugged, though his enhanced senses had picked up something else—a faint odor that made his mouth water despite himself. He tried to push the thought away. It was probably just his imagination, another symptom of whatever was wrong with him.

Rufus knocked on the door. "Mrs. Johnson? It's Rufus and Will from downstairs. Just checking in."

After a long pause, they heard movement inside and the door opened a crack, revealing Mrs. Johnson's pale face, partially obscured by an elegant silk scarf wound tightly around her neck. "Hello, boys," she said, her voice flat and emotionless. "Is there a problem?"

"Your daughter has been trying to reach you," Will explained, fighting the urge to lean in and inhale deeply. That metallic scent was stronger now, unmistakable and oddly comforting.

Mrs. Johnson's expression didn't change. "I'm fine. I've been busy."

Rufus frowned. "Mind if we come in and check, just to put her mind at ease?"

"That won't be necessary," Mrs. Johnson replied, blocking the doorway. Behind her, Will caught a glimpse of a darkened apartment. "Are you having trouble with your electricity?" he asked.

"I'm conserving power," she answered without missing a beat. "Everything's fine."

Will's gaze was drawn to her scarf. Was that a dark stain near the edge? The scent grew stronger, and he felt his canine teeth ache in a way that should have terrified him but instead felt oddly natural. Before he could look closer, Mrs. Johnson stepped back.

"Mrs. Johnson," Rufus pressed, "your daughter's worried sick. Couldn't you just give her a quick call? She's thinking about flying out here."

"She's the one that moved away once she had no further need of me," Mrs. Johnson repeated in that same emotionless tone that had haunted Will since his last visit. The door closed with a solid click, leaving Will and Rufus standing in the silent hallway.

As they walked back to the elevator, Will picked up a faint sound from several floors above—the rustle of paper, followed by a soft, contented hum. He dismissed it, focusing instead on the more troubling concerns at hand.

"That was weird," Rufus said as they entered the elevator. "I thought money was no issue for her. That was always the impression I had. Why would she need to be saving money by turning off her lights?"

Will nodded, his mind racing. The smell of blood—because he was sure now that's what it was—lingered in his nostrils, making him simultaneously nauseated and ravenous. It reminded him of something from long ago, stories his grandmother used to tell about the old country. Stories about creatures that lived in the shadows and fed on the living.

"Maybe she gave away all her money to one of those Nigerian princes?" Rufus joked as the elevator doors closed. "Did you smell something off in her apartment? Or was I imagining things? Maybe that little Napoleon Peart was right after all?"

Will froze. What did Rufus smell? The blood? Something else? "I... uh... maybe? What kind of smell?"

Rufus shrugged. "Can't quite put my finger on it. Kind of musty, maybe? Like old books mixed with something sweet. It's probably a dead mouse in the walls somewhere. Or a rat."

Will relaxed slightly. "Yeah, maybe. When are they due for pest control?"

Before Rufus could answer, the elevator doors opened, and they spotted Peart pacing at the counter, his face a mask of agitation and what looked suspiciously like vindication.

"Ah," he said, his voice higher than usual. "I'm glad you're here. There's been a... development with the smell."

Rufus sighed. "Mr. Peart, we've been over this—"

"No, no, you don't understand," Peart interrupted, practically bouncing on his toes. "It's not just me anymore. Mrs. Pike smells it too, and Mrs. Rodriguez from 301. We all agree—it's getting worse."

Will and Rufus exchanged glances. "Worse how?" Will asked, his own supernatural hunger gnawing at his insides like a living thing.

"It's... changed," Matthew said, lowering his voice dramatically. "At first, it just smelled like something had crawled into the walls and died. But now..." He paused for effect. "Now it smells metallic. Like blood. And I know blood —I watch enough true crime shows. I think someone may be killing animals and dumping them in the elevator shaft. Or the garbage chute."

Will felt his heart skip a beat. He opened his mouth to speak, but Rufus beat him to it.

"Mr. Peart, I'm sure there's a perfectly reasonable explanation. Perhaps a pipe has burst somewhere in the building. We were just discussing getting maintenance in to check the pest situation—"

Peart shook his head vehemently. "This isn't a burst pipe, and it's definitely not mice. This is something else entirely."

Rufus' expression hardened, his voice taking on the authoritative tone he'd used countless times during his years on the force. "Mr. Peart, we appreciate your concern, but I think you're jumping to conclusions. As a former police officer, I've encountered my fair share of crime scenes. I know what blood smells like, and I can assure you, there's no such odor in this building."

Peart looked like he wanted to argue, but something in Rufus' stern gaze made him hesitate. Still, he couldn't resist getting in the last word: "Well, I suppose we'll see who's right when they find whatever's causing it."

Rufus continued, "Now, we'll certainly look into the issue, but I'd advise against spreading rumors. It could cause unnecessary panic among the residents, most of whom are a lot older than you and don't need the stress."

Peart pressed his lips together in a thin line, clearly restraining himself. With a curt nod that somehow managed to convey both submission and defiance, he turned on his heel and marched toward the stairs, pointedly avoiding the elevator.

As his footsteps faded, Rufus turned to Will. "What a pain in the ass. Do you think he was the kid who reminded the teacher about homework assignments?"

Will, his mind focused on the lingering scent in his nostrils and the growing ache in his teeth, forced a shrug. "You know how some people love being the center of attention."

As Rufus turned away to answer another call, Will checked the security monitors. That same faint, coppery scent that had been haunting him seemed stronger a moment ago, but had faded away like morning mist.

The lobby lights flickered, plunging them and the security monitors into momentary darkness. As they came back on, Will heard a sound—a cry, abruptly cut off, coming from somewhere above them.

"Did you hear that?" Will asked.

Rufus looked at him, puzzled. "Hear what?"

Will hesitated. "I thought I heard... It's probably nothing."

But up on the sixth floor, Marion Bruce, a retired librarian who had moved into York Tower just three months ago, lay motionless on her kitchen floor. Her life had been taken swiftly, silently, by an assailant who had left no trace —save for two small puncture marks on her neck, hidden beneath her silver hair. A half-finished crossword puzzle sat on the table, the pen still uncapped. Marion Bruce had been looking forward to a quiet evening with chamomile tea and a fresh book of word games—she had been looking forward to cracking its spine. Now, she would never finish either.

The killer moved through the building like smoke, leaving death in his wake. Isaac Burton had waited centuries for this moment, and he intended to savor every drop of his revenge.

The Blackwoods had taken something precious from him in that small Vermont town so long ago. Now it was time to return the favor.

22

PERSISTENT INQUIRIES

The lobby bell chimed, and standing outside was Detective Melville. Her black suit looked almost funereal against the gray November weather. Rufus buzzed the doors open, and she stepped into the lobby. Her heels clicked sharply on the floor.

Will suppressed a groan. As Melville approached, a new scent hit him. A blend of coconut and something citrusy. Her shampoo, he realized with a start. He'd never been able to smell it from this distance before.

"Our favorite detective is back," Rufus muttered. "I wonder who's kicked the bucket now?"

"I really wouldn't joke about it," Will replied under his breath.

"Gentlemen," Melville interrupted, approaching the security desk. "I'm here about Mrs. Johnson."

The lights in the lobby flickered. Will's stomach dropped. "Mrs. Johnson? Is there a problem?"

Melville's eyes narrowed. "Her daughter called. Says she hasn't heard from her mother in days. Despite your assurances that everything was fine."

"She called the police?" Will asked.

Will tried to focus on the conversation, but the mix of scents assaulting his nose made it difficult.

Rufus cleared his throat. Will caught a whiff of the lotion Rufus had been using on his dry hands. And coffee.

The distinct scent of filter coffee. "We did check on her, Detective. Just yesterday, in fact."

"And?" Melville pressed.

Will stepped in, trying to keep his voice steady. "She seemed... fine. A bit more reclusive than normal. But that's not unusual for some of our older residents. They tend to become more insular."

"I see," Melville said. Her tone made it clear she didn't believe them. "Well, I'd rather check for myself."

"They sent a detective down to check on an old lady?" Rufus asked, eyebrows raised. "At one of the best addresses in town?"

"It's a favor for a friend. I used to know Sally Johnson years ago. She called me," Iona said. A small blush graced her cheeks. The slight increase in her body temperature sent another dizzying wave of coconut shampoo toward Will.

"Sally?" Rufus asked.

"Mrs. Johnson's daughter," Iona said. "Just buzz me up, please."

"I'll take you up," Will said. "Better that someone who knows her is there. Safety first and all that."

"I'm a detective," Melville said.

"Yeah, but she doesn't know that," Will replied.

As they rode the elevator to the second floor, Will wondered what they might find. Would Mrs. Johnson still be in that chair? Pale and unmoving? Or worse, would she be dead? The confined space of the elevator intensified Melville's scent. It mixed with lingering traces of Rufus' lotion and the metallic smell of the elevator itself. Will felt his hunger rising and swallowed hard.

The elevator stopped. As they stepped out, Will gagged on the now-familiar coppery scent filling the hallway. He glanced at Melville. She showed no sign of noticing anything amiss. He knocked on the door of 206.

"Mrs. Johnson? It's Will from downstairs. There's a police officer here to see you."

Silence stretched for what felt like an eternity. Then, just as Melville was reaching for her radio, the door opened a crack. Mrs. Johnson's pale face appeared. Once again partially obscured by an elegant silk scarf.

"Yes?" she said. Her voice was as flat and emotionless as before.

Detective Melville stepped forward. "Mrs. Johnson, I'm Detective Iona Melville. Sally is very concerned about you. May we come in?"

Mrs. Johnson's eyes flicked between them. They lingered for a moment on Will. He could have sworn he saw a flicker of... something in her gaze. Recognition, perhaps. Or hunger. The apartment's scent made his skin crawl in the most pleasant way possible.

"That won't be necessary," Mrs. Johnson said. "I'm fine. My daughter clearly can't accept that I've moved on from her life."

Melville frowned. "Ma'am, I insist—"

"I said that won't be necessary," Mrs. Johnson repeated. Her voice was sharp. The door slammed shut, leaving them standing in silence.

Melville turned to Will, her expression incredulous.

How could he explain what was happening? He didn't understand it himself. He could barely think straight. The mix of scents threatened to overwhelm him. Melville's shampoo, the odor from Mrs. Johnson's apartment, and that ever-present coppery smell.

As he tried stammering out some explanation for Mrs. Johnson's rudeness, he heard a sound. It came from inside the apartment. It was faint, but unmistakable.

A low, hungry growl.

The sound stirred something deep in Will's memory. Stories his grandmother had whispered about the old country. About creatures that stalked the night and fed on the living. About families cursed to wander forever. About blood debts that could never be repaid.

He'd dismissed those stories as folklore. Children's tales meant to keep them indoors after dark. But now, standing in this hallway with the scent of blood thick in the air, Will wondered if his grandmother had been trying to warn him about something real.

Something that had followed them across an ocean and through the centuries. Something that had finally found what it was looking for in a luxury apartment building in Manhattan.

The growl came again. This time, Melville heard it too.

Her hand moved instinctively to her weapon. "What was that?"

Will met her eyes. For the first time since this nightmare began, he told the truth. "I think we're in trouble."

23

WITHERING SUSPICIONS

Melville's heels echoed through the lobby as she departed. Will and Rufus were left in uncomfortable silence. The detective had maintained an embarrassed quiet in the elevator back down. She barely acknowledged them before leaving. She even ignored the florist on her way out.

"Time to brighten up this place," Charlotte chirped. Her arms were laden with an enormous bouquet. She seemed oblivious to the tension behind the security desk.

Rufus eyed the flowers warily. His nose already twitched. "Charlotte, please tell me that those aren't—"

"Lilies? It's that time of year," Charlotte replied. "So stunning."

"My hay fever doesn't think so. Maggie knew that. Do you think next time you could swap them out for carnations or..." Rufus faltered. His mind fumbled for the names of any other flowers.

"Petunias or something," Charlotte offered.

"Petunias, yeah, them," Rufus sniffed dramatically.

As the florist returned to her van, Rufus turned to Will. His expression instantly sobered.

"So... what happened up at Mrs. Johnson's? Something happened. You look like you just swallowed a glass of broken glass."

Will hesitated before answering. "Something odd is

definitely going on. She was... different. She had all her lights off. And it was freezing in there. Like she had the AC cranked to arctic levels."

"Should we have mentioned the power saving thing to Melville? Maybe she's been scammed out of her millions?"

Before Will could respond, the elevator dinged. A figure emerged. Head down, collar turned up. Mr. Finch from the sixth floor. He strode across the lobby without so much as a glance in their direction. He disappeared out through the front doors.

"Well, good morning to you, too," Rufus muttered.

Will frowned. "That's not like him. Usually can't shut him up about his stamp collection."

"Speaking of the sixth floor," Rufus said, lowering his voice. "Have you seen Mrs. Bruce lately? I have no idea when I last saw her checking her mail."

A chill ran down Will's spine. He realized he couldn't remember either. "No, when was the last time you saw her?"

Rufus frowned. "At least a week? Maybe more. I just assumed you'd dealt with her. Or Karl had."

"Should we check on her?" Will suggested. He tried to keep his voice casual despite the growing unease in his gut.

"Might not be a bad idea. Better safe than sorry."

Just then, the lobby doors swung open. A gust of cold air and Matthew Peart entered. His face was set in its usual expression of mild indignation.

"Don't tell me it's lily season already," Peart said, sniffing the air. "Dreadful flowers."

Rufus groaned. "I've got enough trouble with my sinuses. Without you reminding me they hate lilies."

"My mother calls them the death flowers,' Peart said. "She'd never have them in the house. And I've followed her advice. Now, have you made any progress on the other odor?"

Will and Rufus exchanged glances. "These things take time."

"I didn't pay a small fortune for this apartment to live in

a building that smells like a slaughterhouse," Peart said. "I will speak with the Blackwoods directly."

"We're looking into it, Mr. Peart," Will assured him. "Honestly."

As Peart stalked off toward the staircase, Rufus spoke to Will. "You know, much as I hate to admit it, Peart has a point. That smell he keeps going on about... I'm thinking I can smell it too. Just the occasional whiff."

Will's pulse quickened. Should he tell Rufus about his bizarre experience with Mrs. Johnson? And about the vials of blood in Room 306? Not yet. He'd sound like a lunatic if there was a simple explanation. Maybe it was brain cancer affecting his judgment?

"Yeah," he said finally. "Maybe we should check in on Mrs. Bruce? You know, just in case?"

Will and Rufus stepped out of the elevator on the sixth floor. The air was noticeably colder than in the lobby.

"Is it just me, or is it freezing up here?" Rufus asked. He rubbed his arms. "That damn air conditioning needs a service, too."

Will nodded. He tried to cover his nose surreptitiously.

As they approached Mrs. Bruce's door, Rufus gagged. "Jesus Christ! What is that smell?"

Will's stomach churned, but not from revulsion. An intense hunger twisted his insides. He lurched into the wall, trying to steady himself.

"You okay, buddy?" Rufus asked, concern written all over his face.

Will nodded weakly. "Yeah, just... the smell."

"Once you've smelled it, you never forget it. Never thought I'd smell it working here, though," Rufus said. "This isn't going to be good. Are you ready?"

Will nodded again. His gaunt face was as pale as the marble tiles on the floor.

Rufus pulled out the master key. His hand shook as he inserted it into the lock. The door swung open. It released a wave of thick, putrid air.

Both men gagged, but for entirely different reasons.

Will's hunger became almost unbearable as they entered the apartment.

The living room was immaculate. Tidied within an inch of its life. Delicate Lladró figurines watched from glass-fronted cabinets. Their porcelain faces were frozen in eternal serenity and scrutiny.

Will fancied that the painted eyes of a giant laughing clown were following them. They crossed the threshold and moved further into Mrs. Bruce's apartment.

They found her sprawled on the floor of the kitchen. Her papery neck was torn wide open. The wound was jagged and savage. One slipper sat lodged under the refrigerator. The other still clung to her foot.

Will's nostrils flared against his will. The smell that had been driving him crazy suddenly crystallized. It became something terrifyingly specific: blood. Old blood, yes, but blood nonetheless. His stomach cramped with a craving so intense it made him dizzy. He could feel his teeth aching. Actually aching, as if they were trying to push through his gums. This wasn't the nausea he'd felt at crime scenes during his years on the force. This was something else entirely.

"Christ," Rufus turned away. His face was pale. "What could have done that? A dog? A really small, vicious dog?"

Will shook his head. He fought the urge to move closer to the body. Every fiber of his being screamed at him to bend down, to... No. He wouldn't even let himself finish that thought. He dug his fingernails into his palms. He used the sharp pain to focus. "She didn't have a dog... or a cat."

Silence took over. Rufus was probably thinking about procedure. About evidence preservation. About all the things Will should have been thinking about too. Instead, Will catalogued the different scents in the room. The smell of blood, with the metallic undertone of fear. She'd been afraid at the end. He could smell it. And worse, something deep inside him responded with a hunger that had nothing to do with food.

"I'll call the police," Rufus said. His voice was barely above a whisper.

Will didn't trust himself to speak. He could barely swallow past the need clawing at his throat. As Rufus fumbled for his phone, Will's gaze fell on the kitchen table. He was desperate for any distraction from the body and what it was doing to him. An unfinished crossword puzzle lay open. Mrs. Bruce's reading glasses waited beside it. Such a normal thing, such a human thing. Will clung to that normalcy. Even as his body betrayed him with wants he couldn't explain.

His eyes focused on the clue for seven across. "Seven letters. Fictional undead character." The D had already been filled in. As Rufus' shaky voice reported their grim discovery to the police, Will mentally filled in the answer:

D.R.A.C.U.L.A.

The word burned in his mind like a brand. Stories his grandmother had told about the old country came flooding back. Tales of bloodsuckers who stalked the night. Of families cursed to hunt the living. Of creatures that looked human but fed on blood to survive.

He'd always thought they were just fairy tales. Bedtime stories to keep children indoors after dark. But standing here, with Mrs. Bruce's blood calling to him like a siren song, Will wondered if his grandmother had been trying to warn him about something real.

Something that had followed European bloodlines across the ocean. Something that had been waiting in the shadows of American cities. Something that had finally found what it was hunting for in the marble halls of York Tower.

Will touched his neck where the bite mark pulsed. He was becoming one of them. Whether he wanted to or not.

24

AFTERMATH

The quiet routine of York Tower shattered like fine china. Police sirens wailed in the distance, growing louder with each passing second. Within minutes, the street outside was awash with flashing lights. Each pulse of blue and red sent needles of pain through Will's increasingly sensitive eyes. The colors painted grotesque shadows across the lobby's marble floors.

At the security desk, Rufus' face was ashen. He buzzed a steady stream of grim-faced officers and crime scene investigators into York Tower. Will leaned against the wall. His arms wrapped around himself, fighting the urge to flee. The lobby had become a torture chamber of sensations. The sharp tang of nervous sweat. The metallic click of handcuffs against utility belts. The thundering orchestra of dozens of heartbeats.

Curious residents trickled in. Each new arrival added another layer to Will's sensory assault. Mrs. Pike clutched her children close. Her anxiety rolled off her in waves that made Will's nose twitch. Mrs. Henderson's overpowering perfume cut through the air like a knife. The Rodriguez twins' racing pulses sounded like drums in Will's ears. They peeked around their mother's legs.

Mr. Forrester, still in his cycling gear, peppered Rufus with questions. The security guard was too shocked to answer. His fear-soured sweat made Will's stomach turn.

As if on cue, the lobby doors swung open. Detective Melville entered. Her sharp eyes took in the scene. They lingered on Will's pale face before she strode purposefully toward the elevators. Will could hear her heartbeat. Controlled and professional, even amidst the surrounding mayhem.

"Taylor, St John," she barked. "I need to speak with both of you. Separately. Is there somewhere private we can talk?"

Will swallowed hard. "There's a conference room the tenants use for meetings. Just off the lobby."

Melville nodded. "That'll do."

Will led her down the short hallway. Past the mailboxes, to the conference room. His hand trembled as he flicked on the lights. He flinched as the fluorescent tubes stabbed at his sensitive eyes.

"Please, sit," Melville gestured to one of the chairs around the polished table. The door clicked shut behind them. This left Will alone with the detective and her steady pulse.

"Run me through it again," Melville said. Her pen was poised over her notebook. "From the beginning."

Will took a deep breath. He immediately regretted it as Melville's scent filled his nose. Shampoo, coffee, and underneath it all, the steady pump of blood through her carotid artery. He gripped the arms of his chair. He forced his voice to remain steady. "I... we noticed we hadn't seen Mrs. Bruce in a while. Given what happened with Mrs. Johnson, we thought we should check on her."

"Had the door been forced? Did you notice anything before you opened the door? The smell, perhaps? Anything?"

Will wondered how to explain. He'd smelled the blood long before they'd reached Mrs. Bruce's apartment. Even now, with six layers of concrete and steel between them, he could still smell it.

"It was faint at first," he lied. He hated himself for it. "We thought maybe something had died in the walls. But when Rufus pushed the door open..."

He trailed off. He was unable to continue. The memory of the overpowering scent was too much to bear. And the hunger it had awakened in him.

Melville leaned forward. She slid a photo across the table. The movement sent another waft of her scent toward him. Will held onto the chair as if it were a life raft.

"Mr. Taylor, are you feeling alright? You look pale."

Will forced a weak smile. "It's been a while since I last saw a dead body. And a long time since I've seen one that brutal. You know what it's like. It kicks you in the stomach. The knowledge that people can do that to one another. I've never been good around blood."

"And where have you been after your shifts this week?"

The question caught Will off guard. He thought about his old routine. Beers with Rufus at O'Malley's, watching the game, complaining about the Yankees. But now the mere thought of a bar made the nausea stronger. The smell of beer. The press of bodies. The unrelentingly stupid conversations from every corner. He couldn't handle it anymore.

"I... I've just been going home. Watching TV," he stammered.

Melville's eyebrow arched. "So, no one can confirm your alibi?"

Will shook his head. "Can't you just check the CCTV? It'll show me leaving the building after my shift."

"We have checked the CCTV," Melville said. "There are no images of anyone entering or leaving Mrs. Bruce's apartment. But as I'm sure you know from your time on the force, CCTV can be manipulated."

Will's jaw dropped. "Are you suggesting I... Look, Detective, I can barely program my TV to record the game properly. I wouldn't have the first clue how to manipulate the CCTV footage."

Melville leaned back in her chair. Her eyes never left Will's face. "Is that so?"

The disbelief in her tone was clear. How could he

defend himself against suspicions he couldn't fully articulate himself?

"That's all for now," Melville said. "You're free to go. But don't leave the city without permission, okay?"

"One last thing. I want you to know we're reopening an investigation into the other recent deaths in York Tower."

The blood drained from Will's face. "What deaths?"

Melville's eyes narrowed. "Mr. Dunblane, Mrs. Lowenstein, Mr. Chang, and now Mrs. Bruce."

"We thought they were natural causes. They were all old," Will stammered. "Apart from Mrs. Bruce, of course."

Will was eager to escape the suffocating room. As he turned to leave, he glimpsed himself in the conference room's window. For a heartbeat, his reflection seemed to waver. Like a radio signal losing strength. He hurried out before Melville noticed. But the image stayed with him. The ghost of his humanity, already beginning to fade.

As Will stumbled out of the conference room, his mind reeled. Melville suspected him. How long before she connected him to whatever supernatural force was stalking York Tower? He touched his neck where the bite mark pulsed. His grandmother's stories echoed in his memory. Tales of bloodlines cursed across generations. Of Old World monsters following families to the New World. Of debts that could never be repaid.

He'd dismissed those stories as folklore. But now, with Mrs. Bruce's blood still calling to him from six floors above, Will wondered if his grandmother had been trying to warn him. About something that had crossed an ocean to find what it was hunting for.

Something that had turned him into its instrument of revenge.

The lobby chaos continued around him. But Will stood frozen in a moment of terrible clarity. He wasn't just becoming a monster. He was becoming someone else's weapon. Someone with a grudge that stretched back centuries. Someone who had followed the Blackwood family from a small Vermont town to the marble halls of Manhattan.

Someone who was finally ready to collect an ancient debt.

25

BLACKOUT

After his unsettling interview with Detective Melville, Will had stumbled out of the conference room. His mind was reeling. Rufus had tried to catch his eye, but Will had avoided his partner's gaze. He muttered something about needing air.

The city streets embraced him like an old friend. Will gulped in mouthfuls of air, trying to clear his head. He knew this city, born and bred. He'd been here when the towers came down. He'd lost friends in the rubble and chaos. He had grieved with the city. And he'd forged his way forward in the aftermath. New York was as familiar to him as his own shadow. Or at least, it used to be.

Now he was adrift. The familiar scents of his city had transformed. Hot dogs from the corner vendor now made his gorge rise. Meanwhile, the tang of blood from the butcher's shop three blocks away called to him like a siren's song.

A hunger gnawed at him. All-consuming, reminiscent of a stressful day on the beat. After the adrenaline subsided, he'd always been ravenous. Surely this was no different? Or was it the transformation? No matter how much he ate, the weight was melting off him. His belt had more holes than leather. He'd added so many new ones to tighten it.

Desperate to sate his appetite, Will ducked into a nearby cafe. He ordered a steak, rare. But after just two bites, he gagged. He barely made it to the restroom before emptying the meager contents of his stomach. Pale and shaking, he paid without speaking and left. He ignored the concerned looks from the staff.

Will's phone buzzed. Rufus' name flashed on the screen.

"Where the hell are you?" Rufus' voice was strained. "Get your ass back. The elevators are stuck between the third and fourth floors. I've called the engineers. But the residents and the police are going ballistic. I'm pulling my hair out here alone. No more of this weak-ass girly 'getting in touch with your emotions' shit, Will. I need you here."

Will managed an agreement and hung up. His feet were already carrying him back toward York Tower. When Rufus had yelled at him, the hunger had subsided. He could almost breathe again. But now it raged within him. As if it wasn't only Rufus calling him back to York Tower.

Will had no memory of re-entering the building. Or making his way to the third floor. His last clear recollection was staring up at the imposing structure from the street. Fighting the simultaneous urges to run far away and to rush inside.

Then, nothing but darkness until...

Will's eyes snapped open, his heart racing. The first thing he noticed was the cold, hard surface pressed against his cheek. He blinked, trying to focus. This wasn't his bed. Or his apartment.

Slowly, he pushed himself up to a sitting position. His head throbbed. His mouth felt like it was stuffed with cotton. He was sitting on the floor of York Tower's third-floor corridor.

"What the hell?" he muttered. His throat was on fire.

The last thing he remembered was Rufus' phone call. And returning to York Tower. How had he ended up here?

Will staggered to his feet. He used the wall for support. That's when he noticed it. He was outside apartment 306.

Without thinking, he stumbled toward the polished brass numbers. Will caught a glimpse of his own reflection.

Beyond skinny, pale, disheveled. Dark circles under his eyes. Almost unrecognizable.

Will pounded on the door. His fists hammered against the sturdy wood. The sound echoed through the empty hallway.

"Open up!" he shouted. "I know you're in there! What's happening to me?"

The door remained stubbornly closed. It absorbed the impact of his blows without so much as a shudder. Will's brassy reflection stared back at him. Wild-eyed and frantic, cadaver-like. His police buddies would be hard pressed to recognize him in a lineup.

After what felt like an eternity, Will's strength gave way. He slumped against the door. The hallway remained silent. The occupants of 306 gave no sign they'd heard him.

No, not silent. With his heightened hearing, Will caught sounds from within. The soft rustle of feathers. The clicking of tiny claws on brass perches. And beneath it all, a sound that made his new predatory instincts surge. The rapid heartbeats of the vampire finches. Punctuated by their quiet, satisfied chirps as they fed on each other. Will leaned closer. He was drawn by sounds and smells that would have been imperceptible to him just weeks ago.

He jerked back. He was disgusted by his own reaction. There were no occupants in 306, he reminded himself. Apart from the courier delivering almost daily packages and those blood-drinking birds, no one came in or out of the apartment.

Casting a final glance at his reflection, Will turned and aimed for the stairwell. He didn't trust himself in the confined space of the elevator. As he descended, the image of Mrs. Bruce's torn throat flashed through his mind. Nausea rushed through his body. What if he had hurt someone during his blackout?

Surely it was the transformation messing with his brain? He could no more murder someone than he could program a space shuttle. It just wasn't possible.

Will fumbled for his phone. His fingers shook as he

typed out a message for Rufus. "Not feeling well. Going home. Taking a sick day tomorrow, too." He hit send before he could second-guess himself.

As Will stumbled away from York Tower, guilt flooded through him. Guilt for abandoning Rufus to handle the crisis alone.

But that guilt was overshadowed by an irrational, overwhelming fear. His partner might be in danger if he stayed. Not from the malfunctioning elevators. Not the suspicious police officer, or angry residents. But from Will himself.

The next morning, Will's gaunt figure pushed open the heavy doors of the New York Public Library. His once-hefty frame was a shadow of its former self. Feeling foolish but desperate, he stood in front of one of the library's free computer terminals. His police training screamed at him not to be stupid. But he needed answers. There was only one thing he needed to research today. Vampires. Just thinking that word made him want to laugh. But then the laughter died in his throat. He remembered the blood, and the smell, and the taste. However, as he stared at the blinking cursor in the search bar, he realized how absurd this was. Shaking his head, he left the library. He felt more lost than ever.

Will's feet carried him almost unconsciously toward a familiar building. The Office of Chief Medical Examiner. How many times had he walked these steps as a cop? Seeking answers about victims?

Something else drew him now. The thought of Mrs. Bruce's body lying on a cold metal slab made his mouth water. The hunger that had been his constant companion roared to life. He doubled over on the sidewalk, barely able to breathe.

"Sir? Are you feeling okay? Can I help?" A young woman touched his arm. Her face was creased with worry. A tourist, for sure. No local would bother.

Will recoiled from her touch. "I'm fine," he gasped.

As he staggered away, an overriding thought took root. He had to see Mrs. Bruce's body himself.

But even in the state he was in, he realized he couldn't just waltz into the coroner's office. Or the funeral home. The woman was dead. She wouldn't rise from the afterlife and tell him what had happened. But he still needed to see her. To... not taste. That was the wrong word. To smell her? No, he shook his head. She would smell, of that he was sure. And he hoped it would tell him who had killed her. Yes, after the funeral was fine. And safer.

Realizing what he was considering made him sick. Grave robbing. But not as sick as the hunger inside made him feel. It ate away at his stomach lining, growing stronger with each passing moment.

Will hailed a cab. He had to get home before he passed out again. As the city blurred past the window, he closed his eyes. He shut out the world and the monstrous thoughts in his head. Vampires weren't real. Not here in New York. Not anywhere. It was just the transformation. Sweet, inevitable transformation.

His grandmother's stories echoed in his memory. Tales of Old World monsters following bloodlines to the New World. Of ancient debts passed down through generations. Of creatures that wore human faces but served darker masters.

She'd whispered those stories to keep him safe. To warn him about forces that had followed their family across the ocean. Forces that had waited in the shadows of American cities for the right moment to strike.

Will touched his neck where the bite mark pulsed.

The cab pulled up to his building. Will paid and stumbled inside. He was no longer just Will Taylor, security guard. He was becoming something else. Something hungry.

26

WHISPERS AND SHADOWS

Rufus shivered. "Christ, it's freezing in here. The night shift must've messed with the thermostat again."

Will frowned, puzzled. The temperature felt perfect to him. "It doesn't feel that cold to me."

The elevator doors opened. Mrs. Johnson emerged. Despite the season, she wore only a light cardigan over her dress. She walked past them as if they weren't there. Her gaze was fixed straight ahead.

"At least we know Mrs. Johnson is still with us," Rufus said dryly. "Though I'm not sure I'd call that 'alive' in the traditional sense."

Will felt a chill that had nothing to do with the temperature. Something about Mrs. Johnson's vacant expression struck him as wrong. He couldn't put his finger on why. Oddly, as he watched Mrs. Johnson disappear into the stream of humanity, he felt safer. With her out of the building than he had with her in her armchair upstairs.

The lobby of York Tower had always been a hive of activity. But now the buzz had taken on a nervous energy. Will noticed it immediately when he returned from his sick leave. The way residents' eyes darted around. How conversations hushed as people passed the security desk.

Mrs. Abernathy, the jovial widow from the seventh floor, was the first to approach. She leaned in close. Her voice was barely above a whisper. "I hate to be a bother. But with all these... incidents lately, are there any extra security measures in place?"

Will assured her they were doing everything possible. They were ensuring residents' safety. But he could see the doubt in her eyes as she hurried away.

Throughout the morning, a steady stream of concerned tenants found reasons to linger near the desk. Mr. Goldstein from 505 asked about the frequency of security patrols. The Thompsons from 412 inquired about installing additional cameras in the hallways.

It was Cruz Collins, the fitness influencer from the seventh floor, who drove home the extent of the unease permeating the building.

"I'm going to spend a few weeks at a friend's place upstate," he announced. His attempt at casual nonchalance was betrayed by the nervous tapping of his on-trend sports shoes. "It's annoying, really. I prefer the city in winter. But given the circumstances..."

He trailed off. His eyes darted toward the elevators. "You'll monitor things, won't you? Make sure no one... unsavory... gains access to my apartment?"

Will nodded. He assured him of their vigilance. As Collins walked away, Rufus leaned in. "That's the third 'vacation' announcement I've heard today. People are spooked."

Before Will could respond, a familiar voice shot through the lobby at full volume. "You still haven't fixed that smell. Pray tell me, why am I paying through the nose for service fees and security and maintenance? When you can't even bloody well clear whatever dead animal is lurking in the elevator shaft? Or is it another dead body?"

"Mr. Peart, can you please keep your voice down? You're disturbing the other residents," Rufus tried placating.

Peart paused by the stairwell door. His face was twisted into an ugly snarl. "Do you know what's disturbing the other residents? The vile smell that you idiots cannot, or will not, acknowledge and deal with. Are you merely incompetent?

Or are you waiting for me to die as well? So then you don't have to deal with my very real complaints."

At that moment, a movement outside the bank of elevators caught Will's attention. A shadow sliding across the gleaming chrome. But when he turned to look directly, there was nothing there.

Will tried to focus on Peart's complaints.

As the two guards tried to placate Peart, the lobby doors swished open. Mrs. Rosenberg, a frail octogenarian from the fifth floor, struggled through. Her arms were full of packages.

Mrs. Rosenberg's eyes widened. She caught the tail end of Peart's rant. "Is it true? Are we in danger?"

"Mr. Peart, please," Rufus pleaded. "You're scaring the residents."

Will rushed to her side. He almost choked on the scent of talcum powder radiating from her bundled-up body. "Everything's fine, Mrs. Rosenberg. Mr. Peart is rightfully concerned about some maintenance issues. Building management has yet to rectify them."

"Maintenance issues?" Peart blustered. His face was the same red as the carnations in the floral arrangement.

"Mr. Peart..." Will growled. His tone was more cop-like than that of an acquiescent concierge.

"Would you mind helping me to my apartment, Will?" Mrs. Rosenberg asked. Her voice was as tiny as her frame. "I... I don't feel safe going up alone."

"Of course," Will agreed. He shot Rufus a look that said, 'I'll handle her if you handle Peart.'

Will rode up in the elevator with the quivering Mrs. Rosenberg. When the doors opened, the corridor leading to Mrs. Rosenberg's apartment seemed longer than usual. The shadows were deeper.

A pair of mock Louis XV chairs sat in the foyer of the fifth floor. All the floors in York Tower had occasional furniture adorning the public spaces. All in the same style. Will had never taken any notice of them before. But as they exited the elevators, he could have sworn he saw someone sitting in one of the chairs.

He blinked, and the figure disappeared.

But as Mrs. Rosenberg slowly shuffled toward her apartment, Will watched the indentation in the chair's cushion. It was slowly filling out. As if someone had just vacated the seat.

"No!" Will yelled, dropping the packages.

Mrs. Rosenberg jumped. She clutched her chest. "What's wrong?"

A rush of cold air brushed past him. It was followed by the loud slam of the fire exit door. The one leading to the stairwell. The stairwell Peart always used.

Will's heart hammered in his chest. Had he been seeing things? No. He knew what he'd seen and felt. And this time there was no rational explanation. Only the irrational. "I'm so sorry, Mrs. Rosenberg," he said. He tried to steady his voice. "I... I thought I saw a spider. A big one. But I was wrong. You're safe."

"For now," he added silently. "For now."

With Mrs. Rosenberg safely locked away in her apartment, Will stood in front of the elevators. His finger hovered over the button. To take the elevator back to the ground floor would be sensible. Safer.

But the image of that indentation slowly rising in the chair's cushion haunted him. It aligned too perfectly with what he'd read about vampires during his clandestine research at the library.

Will's gaze shifted to the stairwell door. Whatever he'd sensed had gone that way. Following it would be reckless. Possibly suicidal, if his suspicions were correct. But how else could he confirm what he was starting to believe?

And then there was Rufus. His oldest friend. How could Will even begin to explain what he was thinking? "Hey Rufus, I think we might have a vampire problem in the building." He could already imagine the incredulous look on Rufus' face. But not telling him could very well risk

Rufus' life. What if Rufus ended up like Mrs. Bruce? Or worse, like Mrs. Johnson?

His grandmother's stories about the old country echoed in his mind. Stories about families with bloodlines that drew monsters like magnets across oceans and centuries.

"Some debts follow families forever," she'd whispered. "Old World grudges don't die just because you cross new waters."

Will touched the pulsing bite mark on his neck.

She'd been trying to warn him.

He was becoming part of someone else's war.

A conflict that stretched back to a small Vermont town. Where love had turned to tragedy. And tragedy had spawned an endless cycle of revenge.

The stairwell door called to him. Behind it lay answers. And probably death.

But staying ignorant might doom everyone he cared about.

Will pressed the elevator button. He would go down. He would tell Rufus everything. And together, they would figure out how to fight an enemy that had been hunting for over two hundred years.

The elevator dinged. The doors slid open.

And Will stepped inside.

27

BLOOD AND STEM

The bell above the door jingled as Karl stepped into *Buds & Bows*—one of the more upmarket and discreet florists in Manhattan, and a far cry from his native Manchester. It was as if he'd just stepped foot onto the set of *Bridgerton*. Such was the decadent decor covering every inch of the premises. Lush beauty dripped from every surface.

Behind the counter stood a young woman—Charlotte—carefully arranging a bouquet of lilies and roses. Her brow furrowed in concentration as she adjusted a stem just so.

"Almost done," she said without looking up.

Karl leaned against the counter, his easy smile in place. "No rush. I've got all the time in the world."

"What are you doing here?"

Karl's smile widened. "I needed something to brighten my day."

"And so you decided to bother me at work?"

"I'd hardly call this a bother, plus the Blackwoods asked me to order a small bouquet for a memorial in the lobby. For one of our residents who has just passed."

"Very thoughtful of them," Charlotte replied, applying the finishing touches to the arrangement she was working on.

Karl's gaze wandered around the shop, taking in the

colorful blooms and lush greenery. His eyes lingered on a vibrant red rose, its petals as dark as fresh blood.

"That is a Black Baccara," Charlotte said.

"The rose?"

"Developed by a French breeder, in some lights it appears almost black. Will you be wanting some of those in your bouquet?"

Karl nodded, his mouth turning upward. "That would be perfect."

As Karl collected the small bouquet, his fingers brushed against Charlotte's. "Perfect, as always," he said, his eyes lingering on her face rather than the flowers. "I'm sure our late resident would have appreciated their beauty. Although sadly the symbolism will be lost on my employers..."

As he turned to leave, Karl paused at the door. "Still on for later?"

Charlotte nodded. "Wouldn't miss it."

Karl's answering grin was radiant as he stepped out onto Madison Avenue. The bell jingled behind him. For a moment, he seemed frozen in time, then, with a subtle shift in his expression, he turned and strode toward York Tower. The blood-red roses were clutched tightly in his hand, ignoring the bite of a thorn Charlotte had neglected to remove from the stems.

THE SUN WAS SETTING as Karl and Charlotte strolled through Washington Square Park.

"Remember the last time we were here?" Karl asked.

Charlotte laughed. "How could I forget? You were convinced that we were being followed, and you made me run. Ducking and weaving through the park, when actually it was an idiot playing Pokemon Go."

"He was following us."

"Well, if he was, he didn't get very far in the end, did he? Although I'm positive he was telling the truth when he said he was playing a game," she teased, bumping her shoulder against his.

They walked in silence, their steps in sync, a habit formed over years of similar walks.

"Oh, I found this," Charlotte said suddenly, reaching into her bag. "And I remembered how sad you were when you lost your copy in one of your moves." She pulled out a worn book, its pages yellowed from multiple readings, the gilt lettering almost illegible.

Karl's eyes lit up. "I can't believe you found a copy."

"Well, what are friends for?" she said with a wink. "Although I still don't understand your obsession with old vampire novels."

"What can I say? I find them... inspiring." Karl stroked the copy of *Carmilla* by Sheridan Le Fanu. "It's funny how much you remind me of the main character in the book. Carmilla was one of the first female vampires in literature. She charmed her victims to gain their trust. Hence the comparison."

"Is that so? Perhaps I should read it?"

"Perhaps you should. It's... educational."

They laughed, and to any casual observer, they would seem like nothing more than old friends enjoying each other's company. But there was an undercurrent to their interaction, a tension. Karl's eyes darted past Charlotte's shoulder, scanning the shadows, while hers flicked over his, searching for any danger lurking in the distance.

As night fell fully, Karl suggested they head back. "It's getting late," his tone casual, but his eyes intense. "We wouldn't want to run into any... unsavory characters."

Charlotte smiled. "Perhaps they wouldn't want to run into us!"

They turned back, arm in arm. The city lights flickered on around them, casting long shadows that reached out toward them like the grasping fingers of drowning sailors.

As they walked, Karl's mind drifted to the stories his grandfather had told him. Tales of Old World monsters that had followed bloodlines across the ocean. Stories of a family curse that had started in a small Vermont town, where love had turned to betrayal, and betrayal had spawned centuries of revenge.

His grandfather had whispered about Isaac Burton, a sea captain who had lost everything to the Blackwood family. And about Rachel. The woman caught between two men, whose death had ignited a war that spanned generations.

Karl touched the *Carmilla* book in his jacket pocket. Some monsters, his grandfather had warned, were real. And some of them had been hunting the same prey for over two hundred years.

He glanced at Charlotte, her blonde hair catching the streetlight. She didn't know the truth about his family's history. About why they'd really come to New York. About the debt that needed to be paid.

"Penny for your thoughts?" Charlotte asked, noticing his distraction.

"Just thinking about home," Karl replied. "About stories my grandfather used to tell. Old family legends."

"Good stories or scary stories?"

Karl's smile didn't reach his eyes. "Both."

As they reached the edge of the park, Karl made a decision. Tonight, he would tell Charlotte everything. About Manchester, Vermont. About the Blackwood family. About Isaac Burton's centuries-long hunt for revenge.

About why he'd really come to York Tower.

The city hummed around them, oblivious to the ancient war being fought in its shadows. A war that had begun with a forbidden love in a small New England town. A war that would soon reach its bloody conclusion in the marble halls of Manhattan.

Karl squeezed Charlotte's hand. "There's something I need to tell you," he said.

"About the stories your grandfather told you?"

"About why we're really here."

28

THEY ALL FALL DOWN

Rufus settled into his chair at the security desk, a steaming coffee in his hand. The lobby was quiet, with most of their residents tucked away in their apartments for the night.

"You're not gonna believe what I saw yesterday," Rufus said, leaning back in his seat, a yawn splitting his face.

Will raised his head from the logbook he was reviewing. The letters had been swimming in front of his eyes for the past ten minutes. "What did you say?"

"What I saw yesterday, our boy Karl," Rufus leaned in, lowering his voice conspiratorially. "I saw him in Washington Square Park, with a woman."

"A woman? I thought with those eyebrows that he was batting for the other team."

"Haven't you learned by now that you can't judge a book by its cover?" Rufus smirked. "The funniest thing is that we know her. It's that new florist, the one who replaced Maggie."

"You're kidding," Will said.

"Scout's honor," Rufus nodded. "They looked cozy. Walking arm-in-arm."

"Typical that a pretty boy with fancy eyebrows gets the girl, and you and I are left high and dry every night."

Will frowned. Something about this didn't sit right with him. "It didn't take him long to move in on her, did it?"

"Nope," Rufus agreed. "How many weeks has Maggie been gone? Two? Charlotte's not the same as Maggie, though."

"I miss her too," Will said carefully. "I always thought you two had something going on."

Rufus' pen stopped its nervous tapping. 'Nah, nothing like that. Just harmless flirting." He sighed, checking his phone briefly before continuing. "She was far too young for me. Sweet girl, but... well, I've got other things on my mind these days."

Will caught the slight smile that crossed Rufus' face as he glanced at his phone. The kind of smile his partner usually reserved for good news about his fantasy baseball team.

"Don't you worry," Rufus added, pocketing his phone. "I've got more than enough on my plate to keep me going." Another smile crossed his face before he continued. "Though I gotta say, there was something odd about them, Karl and Charlotte."

"What do you mean?"

Rufus shrugged. "The way they were looking at each other... it was intense. As if they'd known each other for ages. I never took him for a fast worker."

"Did you see where they went?"

"Nah, I didn't want to play stalker. But get this—as it got dark, they both seemed to get... I dunno, twitchy? Like they were scared of the shadows or something.'

Will raised an eyebrow and gazed into the void of the empty foyer. Neither man noticed the shadow that briefly darkened the lobby window, nor the pair of gleaming eyes staring at them from outside before vanishing into the night.

The lobby grandfather clock ticked steadily toward midnight, its sound unnaturally loud in the quiet space. Will was about to suggest they do another round when the lights flickered once, twice, and then went out, plunging them into total darkness.

"What the hell—" Rufus' voice cut through the blackness, followed by a loud thud and a cry of pain.

Will's heart leaped into his throat. "Rufus?" he called out, panic rising. His mind was full of the worst-case scenario. "Rufus!" Will shouted again, fumbling in the dark, his hands outstretched. He could hear scuffling and a muffled grunt that might have been Rufus. But it might also have been something else entirely.

"Will?" Rufus' voice sounded strained.

Will tried to move toward the sound, but in the darkness, he stumbled, crashing into a giant potted fern. The sound of shattering ceramic filled the air.

A mechanical whir joined the chaos. The elevator bank. And all three elevator doors opened in perfect unison, the sound more ominous than comforting. Will held his breath, expecting... what? A monster? A vampire?

Just as abruptly as they had gone out, the lights blazed back to life. Will blinked, momentarily blinded. As his vision cleared, he saw Rufus sprawled on the floor near the security desk, rubbing his knee.

"Rufus! Are you okay?" Will rushed to his friend's side.

"Yeah, yeah," Rufus grumbled. "Tripped over my damn feet when the lights went out, then got tangled in my jacket. What the hell was that?"

Will helped Rufus to his feet, then turned to look at the elevators. All three stood open, their empty cars waiting for passengers who would never come.

"I don't know," Will said slowly, still staring at the elevators. "But it was a bloody funny power outage if the elevators could still run."

"Maybe," Rufus said, uncharacteristically quiet. "Maybe we should call someone about this?" As he reached for the phone, a cutting breeze swept through the lobby, ruffling the scattered papers and the upturned fern. The two men exchanged uneasy glances.

"Where'd that come from?" Rufus asked.

"Downstairs?"

Both men turned to face the door leading to the parking

garage. As a fire barrier, the door was always shut. But now it stood ajar.

"Do you think someone left the security gate open? Maybe the power outage..." Rufus left the rest of the sentence unsaid.

"One of us should check it out," Will said, his voice steadier than he felt.

"We both should," Rufus said, retrieving their flashlights from the desk drawer and shrugging into his overcoat.

The walk down into the parking garage turned colder and colder, and Will regretted not grabbing his own coat.

They emerged from the stairwell into the pitch-black garage, their flashlights cutting through the concrete darkness like knives. Every parking space held a gleaming testament to America's motor vehicle industry, and not much else. The complete silence was broken only by their footsteps.

"Hello?" Rufus called out, his voice echoing off the concrete walls. "Is there anyone down here?"

In the far corner, something shifted in the shadows. Will's beam found a pair of eyes, reflecting the light back at them. In the cat's mouth, something small and gray dangled limply.

"What the hell—" Will started, but was cut off as the huge cat burst from the darkness. Hissing and spitting, still clutching its prey. As it darted between their legs, nearly tripping Rufus, Will caught sight of ash-gray feathers. One of the strange birds he'd seen in apartment 306. The bird's unnaturally sharp beak hung open and lifeless. The cat disappeared up the ramp and through the open security gate, taking its grim trophy with it.

"Jesus," Rufus muttered, his hand on his chest. "That thing could have killed me."

"You and me both." Will's enhanced senses picked up the metallic scent of the finch's blood. He wondered how the cat had snared the bird from a locked cage in a locked apartment. And what that might mean. "At least we got it out before it mauled a resident. Though it looks like it already found itself a meal."

"It's a goner if I ever see it again," Rufus replied, oblivious to the bird's origins. "Let's see if I can shut the gate now that thing is out, and the power surge, or whatever it was, is over."

With the security gate jangling shut above them, they moved further into the garage. Will's flashlight stumbled over an odd shape ahead of them.

"Is that Forrester's bike?"

Tom Forrester's high-end racing bike lay on its side, abandoned in the middle of the garage floor. Instead of being locked away in the bike cage, where it lived.

Rufus whistled. "Forrester treats that bike better than most people treat their kids. He'd never leave it like this."

Will approached the bike. "So where is he?"

Tom Forrester was a creature of habit, religious about his cycling routine and fanatical about his equipment. He'd told them that was why he'd bought an apartment with 24-hour security on site.

"Should we check his apartment?" Rufus suggested, but there was a tone of reluctance in his voice. "Or call him?"

Will caught sight of something on the ground near the bike. He bent for a closer look.

"Rufus," he said.

On the concrete floor, barely visible, was a small, dark stain. Will touched it gingerly, his fingers coming away red. The sort of red that you want to lick from your fingers. A red that smelled sweeter than cotton candy at the county fair. A sticky red delight.

Will rubbed his fingers together, his stomach rumbling with a hunger he didn't want to acknowledge.

"Is that..." Rufus couldn't finish the sentence.

"Yes." There really was nothing more he needed to say.

As they stood there in the garage's oppressive silence, Will's mind drifted to the stories his grandmother had told him. About Old World monsters that followed bloodlines across oceans. About curses that could wait centuries for the right moment to strike. About debts passed down through generations like poisoned heirlooms.

She'd warned him that some hungers could never be satisfied. That some creatures would hunt the same prey for hundreds of years, patient as death itself.

Will touched his neck.

Tom Forrester hadn't just been attacked by a random predator. He'd been claimed by something ancient. Something that had been waiting in the shadows of York Tower for exactly the right moment.

Something that was turning Will into its instrument of revenge.

The blood on his fingers called to him like a siren song. And for the first time since this nightmare began, Will didn't fight the hunger.

He licked his fingers clean.

29

THE BED IS MADE

Will and Rufus stood in silence, staring at the bloodstain near Forrester's abandoned bike. "Maybe he just fell off," Rufus suggested, his voice uncertain. "He could've cut himself and gone up to his apartment to get cleaned up."

"We would have seen him on his way to the elevators," Will said absently, fighting the sudden urge to lean down and... what? Taste it? The thought both disgusted and tempted him. He shook his head, trying to clear it.

"Let's secure it first," Rufus said, "before checking his apartment."

As Rufus wheeled the expensive bicycle to a secure corner, Will locked his gaze on the crimson stain. His fingers trembled as they brushed his lips, the compulsion overwhelming and inexplicable. His tongue darted out before he could stop himself. Just one lick.

The metallic tang of blood hit his senses, sharp and vivid, but it was quickly overtaken by something extraordinary. Flavors so intense it felt as though his entire body was on fire. No Michelin chef, no earthly creation, could ever hope to replicate it.

The shock jolted him back to reality. Will's stomach twisted with both revulsion and a sick, clawing desire for more. What was he doing? What had he done? But the damage was done.

The lingering taste was one he knew he wouldn't be able to forget.

"Will? Earth to Will!" Rufus' voice cut through his daze. "Did you hear what I said?"

Will blinked, realizing Rufus had been talking. 'Sorry, what?"

Rufus' eyebrows arched. "I said we should head up to Forrester's apartment now. Look, are you feeling okay? There's something going on with you. You're distracted, and you're losing weight. Like, and not in a good way. For Pete's sake, is it cancer? Is that it?"

"I'm fine," Will lied, avoiding Rufus' gaze and his own trembling hand as he pressed the elevator button.

Lavender scented air greeted them as they opened Tom Forrester's apartment door, likely from the fabric softener Tom always used on his perpetually clean laundry. The dim overhead light cast a yellowish glow across the space, pooling in corners and leaving shadows to deepen in the recesses of the room.

The small kitchen was immaculate, with its granite countertops gleaming even under the artificial light. A half-full bowl of fruit sat on the counter, the bananas just beginning to spot. The humming of the refrigerator was the only sound breaking the oppressive silence.

Tom's black leather couch was free of dust, its cushions perfectly aligned. A neat stack of magazines rested on the coffee table, beside a lone mug that had been washed and placed upside down on a coaster. His bookshelves, arranged by height and color, gave the room a sense of studied curation.

Will's eyes were drawn to the bedroom door, slightly ajar. He nudged it open, revealing an untouched bed, its duvet smoothed out like an unbroken sheet of snow. A pair of house slippers sat neatly beside it, waiting for their owner to step into them.

No blood. No mess. No sign of struggle.

"So, he never came upstairs to clean himself up..." Will whispered as he leaned against the wall, his increasingly weak body unable to support his weight for any prolonged period.

Rufus joined him by the wall, and Will stared at Rufus' neck where a vein pulsed steadily, hypnotically.

The sound of rushing blood was almost deafening. And Rufus' earlier question echoed in his mind: "Is it cancer?"

Will wished it was.

The silence in the apartment felt wrong. Too complete. Tom Forrester was a creature of habit, methodical in everything he did. His bike, his apartment, his routine - all meticulously maintained. But now there was an emptiness that went beyond mere absence.

"This doesn't make sense," Rufus said, his voice barely above a whisper. "If he's hurt, where is he? If he's fine, why leave his bike like that?"

Will's enhanced hearing picked up something else. A faint scratching from within the walls. Mice, probably. Or something worse. The building was old, full of hiding places for things that preferred the dark.

His grandmother's stories echoed in his memory. Tales of bloodlines marked by ancient curses. Of Old World monsters that followed families across oceans, patient as death itself. She'd whispered about debts that could only be paid in blood. About creatures that could wait centuries for the right moment to strike.

"Some hungers never die," she'd warned him. "They just wait for the right prey to come along."

Will touched his neck where the bite mark pulsed. Tom Forrester hadn't just disappeared. He'd been claimed. Taken by something that had been waiting in the shadows of York Tower for exactly the right moment.

Something that was turning Will into its instrument of revenge. One drop of blood at a time.

"We need to call the cops," Rufus said finally.

"No," Will said, surprised by the firmness in his own voice. "Not yet. Let's give it another day. Maybe he'll turn up."

Rufus stared at him. "A day? Will, there's blood on the

garage floor and his bike is abandoned. This isn't some minor scrape."

"Twenty-four hours," Will insisted, though he couldn't explain why. Something inside him recoiled at the thought of more police in the building. More questions. More scrutiny.

More opportunities for discovery.

As they rode the elevator back down, Will caught his reflection in the polished steel doors. For just a moment, his image wavered, like a radio signal losing strength. He was becoming something else.

And deep down, beneath the horror and revulsion, Will felt a terrible satisfaction.

30

THE BLACKWOOD LEGACY

Detective Melville stepped into the opulent offices of Blackwood Real Estate Development, her black shoes sinking into the plush carpeting. The receptionist, a young woman with a messy pixie cut, looked up from her computer.

"Detective Melville for Mr. Blackwood," Iona announced, flashing her badge.

The receptionist's manicured finger hovered over her earpiece. "Mr. Blackwood will see you now," she said after a moment, gesturing toward a set of imposing mahogany doors.

James Blackwood rose from behind an expansive desk as Melville entered. At 35, he had the polished look of old money, in his tailored suit, with carefully styled hair, and a mouth full of expensive teeth.

"Detective," he greeted, extending a hand. "How can I help?"

Melville shook his hand firmly. "Mr. Blackwood, I'm here to discuss the recent incidents at York Tower."

A frown crossed James' face before he smoothed it away. "Ah, an unfortunate business. Please, have a seat."

As they settled into the leather armchairs, Melville pulled out her notebook. "Mr. Blackwood, are you aware of the several deaths in York Tower over the past two months?"

James leaned back, steepling his fingers. "Detective, York

Tower caters to a mature clientele. While any death is tragic, it's not uncommon given the demographic of our residents."

"You don't seem concerned?"

"York Tower is one of our flagship properties," James replied smoothly. "Built by my grandfather Richard Blackwood Sr., its reputation invites residents who desire the prestige of the address, and the level of security that we're renowned for. Most of those residents are at the upper end of the age spectrum, so no, I'm not overly concerned. I'm more saddened that we have lost several close friends and family members in such a short space of time."

"Colleagues?"

"Jacob Marsden was the architect who designed York Tower, and a beloved family friend. And the tragic death of Marion Bruce has affected us all. It's been a very difficult time."

Melville hadn't known that and was momentarily thrown off her stride. "Your family has been in real estate for generations, Mr. Blackwood," Melville said, her tone conversational but sharp. "I'm curious about how the family business got its start."

James shifted in his chair. "Our family has been in real estate since before my grandfather's time," he said.

Melville leaned forward. "From what I understand, most real estate dynasties have their... interesting origin stories. How did your family build such a significant portfolio?"

A flicker of wariness bloomed before he answered. "Hard work. Connections. An eye for valuable properties," he said, his words carefully chosen.

"And those connections?" Melville pressed. "I imagine navigating Manhattan real estate wasn't easy back then."

James' smile became rigid. "Are you suggesting something?"

Melville shrugged. "Just trying to understand the history behind York Tower. A building with such a long-standing reputation must have quite a story." Melville wasn't sure herself why she'd asked that question, but there was some kind of deceit simmering under the surface, somewhere, and she didn't like it.

She scribbled in her notebook before moving onto her next question. "And the ongoing maintenance issues reported by your residents? Foul odors, power fluctuations, problems with the elevators? If the address is so desirable, I find it odd that there's been no urgency to address those concerns."

James waved a dismissive hand. "Every building has its quirks, Detective. I assure you, we're dealing with it. As I said earlier, it is an old building, and decent, affordable engineers are as rare as honest politicians in this town."

As she stood to leave, a framed photo on the wall caught her attention. It showed a younger James standing with an older couple - presumably his parents - and a young woman who bore a striking resemblance to him.

"Your family?" Melville asked casually.

James nodded. "My parents, Richard and Elizabeth, and my sister Sarah. Sadly, I never got to meet any of my grandparents, so it's just the four of us."

Melville studied the photo for a moment longer. Something nagged at her about the image, though she couldn't put her finger on what. The parents looked remarkably youthful for people who should be in their sixties or seventies, given James' age.

"Thank you for your time, Mr. Blackwood. I'm sure we'll be speaking again soon."

Experience told her that Blackwood hadn't been completely forthcoming with his answers, and that always meant someone was trying to hide something. But what, if anything, did he have to gain from the premature deaths of the residents in his apartment building? She hadn't a clue.

As the door closed behind Detective Melville, James Blackwood loosened his tie, feeling the weight of responsibility on his shoulders. He moved to the window, gazing out at the Manhattan skyline, his eyes finding York Tower in the distance.

"Alice," he called, his voice tighter than he'd like. "Bring me a pot of tea, please."

While waiting for the tea, James dialed his father's number.

"James?" Richard Blackwood answered. "This is unexpected."

"Dad," James began, then paused, collecting his thoughts. "I think we have a problem with York Tower."

There was a brief silence before Richard spoke again. "What kind of problem?"

James poured his tea as Alice quietly exited, the familiar ritual helping to calm his nerves. "A detective came to see me. She was asking questions about the recent deaths there. And then a weird question about how our family got started in real estate."

"And what did you tell her?"

"Nothing specific," James assured him. "But with the market downturn and our recent investments not performing as expected, we can't afford any bad publicity."

"No, we certainly can't," Richard agreed. "The York Tower renovations are already stretching us thin. Have there been more complaints from the residents?"

James rubbed his temples. "A few. Mostly about maintenance issues. Nothing we can't handle."

"Right then," Richard said, his tone becoming more businesslike. "We need to tread carefully here. Have Sarah look over our liability coverage. And James, see if you can expedite those repairs. The last thing we need is for the current residents to start looking elsewhere.'

"Understood," James replied, jotting down notes. "What about the detective? Should we have our lawyer involved?"

"Not overtly," Richard cautioned. "Let's not give them the impression that we have something to hide. Keep me informed of any developments, and I'll brief Peart. There's a reason he pays a peppercorn rent for one of the better apartments in York Tower. It's about time he did more to earn his keep than simple conveyancing."

As they wrapped up the call, James felt the tension leave

his body. His father's steady approach always had that effect. Not for the first time, he wished his sister had taken over the day-to-day running of the company. But their father wouldn't have it. Sarah would never have let their finances descend into the mess that they had, economic downturn or no economic downturn.

But there was something else nagging at James. Something about the detective's questions that felt more personal than professional. The way she'd asked about their family's origins, about how they'd built their fortune. It reminded him of stories his father had told him as a child. Stories about the old country, about why they'd come to America, about enemies that had followed them across the ocean.

Stories about a place called Manchester, Vermont, where their family had once lived. Where something terrible had happened that changed everything.

James poured another cup of tea, his hand trembling slightly. His father had always been vague about those early days. About why they'd left Vermont so suddenly. About the debts that had followed them to New York.

About the man named Isaac Burton who had sworn to destroy their family, one generation at a time.

James had thought those were just old family legends. Cautionary tales meant to keep the children in line. But now, with bodies piling up in York Tower and a detective asking uncomfortable questions, he wondered if those stories might be more than just folklore.

He reached for his phone to call his father back, then hesitated. Some secrets, once disturbed, had a way of becoming more dangerous. And some family histories were better left buried.

But as James stared out at York Tower in the distance, he couldn't shake the feeling that the past was finally catching up with them. That the debts his family had thought they'd escaped were finally coming due.

And that Detective Melville might be the least of their problems.

31

PAPER TRAILS

Matthew Peart's office was a carefully constructed facade of order. Color-coded files lined the walls, each precisely aligned. The half-completed New York Times crossword puzzle lay abandoned, its blank spaces mirroring the uncertainties surrounding the Blackwood Real Estate empire.

The market was brutal. Rumors swirled that competing real estate developers were circling like vultures, waiting for the Blackwood company to show any sign of weakness. The recent string of deaths at York Tower and the subsequent maintenance issues couldn't have come at a worse time.

His phone rang, the caller ID displaying "Richard Blackwood." He took a deep breath before answering.

"Matthew," Richard's voice was tense. "We've had a police visit. Asking questions about the deaths at York Tower. They're exploring whether these deaths could be connected to our business dealings. Wondering if a competitor might have orchestrated something, or if an unhappy resident could be seeking revenge."

While Peart couldn't pinpoint who might benefit from the deaths, he knew that this was exactly the opportunity their competitors would exploit.

The call ended, leaving Peart worried about his future. The Blackwood empire was vulnerable, and therefore, so was he. He wouldn't be brought down again.

But where to start? Should he wait until the police made contact? Or should he get ahead of them in order to stop any damaging media revelations? It really wasn't a question.

Peart stood, decision made. If there were answers about York Tower's past, they would be in the basement storage - inherited from his father, along with the Blackwood family's legal business. He'd never had reason to delve into those dusty boxes before, but now... As he descended the stairs to the basement, he felt a familiar thrill - the same one he got when starting a particularly challenging puzzle.

Descending into the basement storage was like entering another world. Dust-covered boxes contained decades of the Blackwoods' family legal history. Each file was a potential shield against their competitors' attacks.

Prepping the files would be tricky given the Blackwoods had retained the same naming convention through generations - Richard Blackwood. All the way until the birth of James Blackwood. The first Blackwood not to be called Richard, as far as Peart could tell. He briefly wondered if James minded?

Property deeds from 1876 bore striking resemblances to those from 1957. Corporate registrations created intricate webs of ownership, shell companies nested within shell companies. A legal labyrinth designed to protect the family's assets.

But as Peart dug deeper, he discovered something that made his blood run cold. Scattered throughout the files were references to a place called Manchester, Vermont. Property transfers dating back to the 1790s. Legal disputes involving a family named Burton. And court records of what appeared to be a murder trial.

The documents painted a picture that didn't make sense. How could the Blackwood family own property in Vermont in the 1790s when the current Richard claimed his grandfather had started the business? The math didn't add up.

Peart pulled out a yellowed deed dated 1793.

The property description was for land in Manchester,

Vermont, transferred from one Isaac Burton to Richard Blackwood. But there was something odd about the signature - it looked remarkably similar to the Richard Blackwood he knew today.

"That's impossible," Peart said, examining the document.

He found more records. Probate documents showing property transfers from Richard Blackwood (deceased 1823) to Richard Blackwood (heir, 1823). Then from Richard Blackwood (deceased 1867) to Richard Blackwood (heir, 1867). The pattern continued through the decades, always the same name, always the same careful transfer of assets.

But it was the criminal records that made Peart's hands shake. Court documents from 1793 describing the brutal murder of one Rachel Burton, wife of sea captain Isaac Burton. The primary suspect? Richard Blackwood, who had allegedly been involved in an affair with the victim.

The case had been dismissed due to lack of evidence, but the records suggested that Isaac Burton had sworn vengeance against the Blackwood family. The final document in the file was a ship's manifest showing Isaac Burton departing New York harbor in 1794, destination unknown.

Peart sat back in his chair. Either the Blackwood family had an obsession with recycling names, or something far stranger was going on. The documents suggested a family history that stretched back over two centuries, involving murder, revenge, and a blood feud that had somehow followed them from Vermont to Manhattan.

He thought about Richard Blackwood's ageless appearance, the way he moved with an old-world grace that seemed out of place in modern New York. The stories Peart had heard about the family's reclusive nature, their aversion to publicity, their preference for conducting business at night.

"I can protect them," Peart said, but his voice lacked conviction.

If what these documents suggested was true, then the

Blackwood family was harboring secrets far darker than questionable business practices.

For a moment, he imagined a different life - one where he'd followed his passion for archaeology, unearthing ancient secrets instead of burying modern ones. But his father's voice echoed in his memory: "It's the law or the street, boy. Make your choice."

What Peart didn't understand was that some secrets, once disturbed, have a way of fighting back. And some family feuds never die - they just wait for the right moment to collect what's owed.

As he carefully returned the documents to their boxes, Peart couldn't shake the feeling that he'd just opened a door that should have remained closed. The Blackwood family's past was catching up with them, and he was caught in the middle of a war that had been raging for over two hundred years.

Outside his basement window, a raven perched on the fire escape, its black eyes watching as Peart tried to make sense of the impossible. The bird cawed once, a sound like laughter, before disappearing into the night.

Some debts, it seemed, could never be forgiven. And some enemies never forgot.

32

ECHOES OF LOSS

Detective Iona Melville sat across from Linda Chang in the precinct's family room, soft light filtering through gauzy curtains. Linda's hands trembled slightly as she raised her cup, the tremors a testament to her ongoing battle with leukemia.

"Thanks for coming in, Mrs. Chang," Iona said, her tone gentle.

Linda nodded, her gaze distant. "Dr. Marshall said Robert died from a stroke. It was unexpected, but not surprising at his age."

"Walk me through the day Robert died."

Linda's eyes misted over. "I was at the hospital for my treatment. Robert was supposed to pick me up, but after waiting for two hours, I couldn't reach him, so I took a taxi home." She paused, her breath catching. "I found him on the floor of our living room. He looked peaceful, like he was just sleeping."

"Did you notice anything missing or out of place?"

"The windows were open, which was unusual. Robert preferred air conditioning. He was always worried about his ship models. A strong gust could damage them." A wry smile touched her lips. "My husband was a collector. Someone could have taken fifty of his model ships and it wouldn't have made a dent. There were hundreds, filling every available space. But no, there's nothing missing.'

Iona nodded, making a note. "Did he mention feeling unwell?"

"He complained of being tired, but I thought it was just age and retirement," Linda said, guilt threading her voice. "I was so focused on my treatment..."

"Had Robert mentioned any visitors, or unusual activities?"

"Nothing out of the ordinary," Linda replied.

"Tell me about the funeral arrangements."

Linda's expression softened. "Dr. Marshall handled everything. Robert wanted to be buried at sea, but that wasn't possible, so we cremated him. I'm planning to scatter his ashes next month."

Iona's pen paused. "Dr. Marshall arranged the cremation?"

"He said it would be easier. I was overwhelmed."

"What are your plans for the model ships?"

For the first time, Linda smiled. "I'm donating them to the children's hospital. Robert would have liked that."

As the interview wound down, Iona couldn't shake the feeling something was off. The open windows. The quick cremation. The helpful doctor. It all seemed too neat, too convenient.

"If you remember anything else, call me," Iona said, walking Linda to the door.

Linda paused. "Why are you really investigating? Robert's death was natural. Wasn't it?"

Iona met her gaze. "We're covering all our bases."

After Linda left, Iona pulled out her phone. "O'Brien, run the physicians for York Tower victims. Check for overlaps."

"Got it. Anything specific?"

"Just give me the names."

Minutes later, O'Brien called back. "Four out of five had the same doctor. Dr. Marshall."

"What about the cremations?"

"Signed off on Chang and Lowenstein's. Dunblane's nephew arranged his burial."

Iona's mind raced. "Contact the Marsden and Dunblane families. See if they'll authorize exhumation."

As she hung up, Iona thought about the pattern emerging.

One doctor overseeing multiple deaths. Quick cremations eliminating evidence. It reminded her of stories her grandmother had told about the old country. About village doctors who served darker masters. About families that preyed on the elderly and vulnerable.

Her grandmother had whispered about bloodlines that carried ancient curses. About creatures that looked human but fed on life itself. About debts that followed families across oceans and through generations.

"Some monsters wear familiar faces," her grandmother had warned. "They smile while they drain you dry."

Iona had dismissed those tales as folklore. Old World superstitions that had no place in modern America. But now, with bodies piling up and a doctor conveniently present for each death, she wondered if her grandmother had been trying to warn her about something real.

She pulled the files on York Tower, spreading them across her desk. Each victim elderly. Each death signed off by the same physician. The bodies disposed of before any questions were asked.

The perfect hunting ground for predators who preferred easy prey.

Iona reached for her phone to call the medical board, then hesitated. What would she say? That she suspected a doctor of being involved in mysterious deaths? That elderly people in an expensive apartment building might be targets of some ancient evil?

They'd laugh her off the force.

But her grandmother's voice echoed in her memory: "Trust your instincts, little one. When something feels wrong, it usually is."

Iona dialed the medical board. Sometimes instincts were all a detective had to go on. And sometimes, a grandmother's tale turned out to be more than just a story.

She thought about her son Finn, about the sleepovers at York Tower, about how close she'd come to letting him spend more time in that building. The thought made her blood run cold.

Some monsters, her grandmother had said, were very good at hiding in plain sight.

Iona was beginning to think her grandmother had been right all along.

33

BEHIND CLOSED DOORS

Melville stood outside apartment 503, her frustration mounting with each unanswered knock. She'd been trying to reach Leigh Marsden on the phone for days, but to no avail.

"Mrs. Marsden? It's Detective Iona Melville. I just need a few minutes of your time."

Finally, a muffled voice came from behind the door. "Please, Detective. Leave me to my grief."

Iona sighed. "Mrs. Marsden, I understand this is difficult, but it's important that we—"

"I said leave!" The sharpness was unmistakable.

Defeated, Iona turned away. Every other resident had been willing to talk, but Leigh Marsden was a wall of silence. Grief only protected you from the law for so long...

Back at the precinct, Iona pored over her notes. Jacob Marsden's death fit the pattern of the others, but without speaking to his widow, she was missing crucial pieces of the puzzle.

"Any luck with Mrs. Marsden?" Ortega asked, appearing at her desk.

Iona shook her head. "She won't even open the door. I'm considering getting a warrant, but—"

"But we don't have enough probable cause." Ortega finished. "Keep trying, Melville. She has to come up for air. Or groceries."

Later, Will and Rufus were wrapping up their shift when the elevator doors opened. Leigh Marsden strode out, dressed in a short-sleeved blouse and a lightweight wrap, despite the freezing weather.

"Mrs. Marsden?" Rufus called out, concern filling his voice. "Have you forgotten your coat? It's freezing out there."

Leigh barely glanced their way before disappearing out the front doors and into the hectic street.

"Should we go after her? She needs a coat," Rufus asked.

Will felt an inexplicable unease. "No," he said, more forcefully than he'd intended. "She's an adult and can take care of herself."

"She's just lost her husband. She might not be thinking clearly."

Will's hand moved unconsciously to the weeping sore on his neck. "Trust me, Rufus. It's better not to get involved."

Rufus stared at him. "What's gotten into you? You've been acting strange ever since..."

"Ever since what?" Will snapped.

Rufus held up his hands in surrender. "Forget I said anything."

As they finished their shift in silence, Will debated whether to inform Melville about Mrs. Marsden emerging from her apartment. But a voice in the back of his mind whispered that it was better left unsaid. Will couldn't explain his reluctance, even to himself. A fog had settled over his thoughts, obscuring his judgment like morning mist over water.

After Will clocked off from his shift, he glanced in the direction Leigh Marsden had gone, shivering in the wind whipping through the darkened street. The woman hadn't endeared herself to the staff at York Tower, but he should have felt some level of concern for her. And the fact that he didn't, terrified him.

As the evening wore on, Karl Middleton sat at the front desk, his eyes constantly scanning the lobby. The quiet was broken by the automatic doors sliding open.

Mrs. Marsden walked in, her face flushed from the cold.

At the same moment, Mrs. Pike emerged from the elevator, supporting her son Ethan, who looked pale and weak.

"Oh my," Mrs. Marsden exclaimed, her voice dripping with concern. "Is the little one not feeling well?"

Amanda's eyes welled. "We're heading back to the ER. He's so lethargic and dizzy. He can't even get off the couch."

"Poor dear," Mrs. Marsden cooed, reaching out to stroke Ethan's face. "Such a pretty boy. It's a shame to see him suffer."

As her hand neared Ethan's cheek, Karl's instincts flared. Something about the gesture felt predatory, wrong. "Mrs. Marsden!" he shouted, his voice bouncing off the marble.

Mrs. Marsden's hand froze, mere inches from Ethan's face. Her eyes flashed with something alien and hungry. Then, as quickly as it had appeared, the look vanished. She scowled at Karl before hurrying to the elevator without another word.

Amanda stood by the elevator door, bewildered. "What was that about?"

Karl leaped up from his seat, but in his haste, he caught his foot on the edge of the lobby rug. Stumbling forward, his outstretched hand collided with the massive crystal vase on the desk. The vase teetered for a split second before toppling over with a sickening crash. It shattered on impact, the sound echoing through the lobby like a thunderclap.

Water erupted from the broken vase, carrying with it a cascade of flowers. White lilies and crimson roses scattered across the polished marble floor, their petals smearing wet trails. The spread of rose petals looked disturbingly like droplets of blood.

Ignoring the mess, Karl made it over to the Pikes, his eyes scanning Ethan with growing alarm. The boy looked ill, but there was something else... something that made Karl sick to his stomach. "Let me call you a cab. You shouldn't be walking in this weather."

Behind them, unnoticed in the commotion, the fallen

lilies and roses began wilting at an alarming rate, browning and curling as if days had passed in mere seconds.

Once the Pikes were safely in a cab, Karl returned to the lobby. For a long time he stood and stared at the elevator Mrs. Marsden had disappeared into, his distorted reflection staring back. The sweet old widow act might fool others, but Karl knew better. He'd seen that look before, in the stories his grandfather had told him.

The big question was, how much time did they have before it was too late to do anything about it?

And Ethan Pike... Karl's brow furrowed. Something was very wrong with the boy. He suspected he knew what it was, and the knowledge filled him with dread. The boy was only nine. Such a short life to be caught in the crossfire of a centuries-old war.

Karl looked down at the wilted flowers. "When flowers die in the presence of evil, it's time to run," his grandfather had said.

Karl wouldn't run. He couldn't.

34

CONNECTING THE DOTS

Iona was reviewing her case notes at the kitchen table when Finn burst through the door, excitement radiating from his face like sunshine.

"Mom, can Ethan sleep over this weekend? Please?" he asked, bouncing on his toes.

Iona felt a twinge of discomfort. After her last visit to York Tower, she'd secretly hoped that Finn's friendship with Ethan Pike might peter out naturally. She didn't like the thought of running into any of the residents accidentally with her son in tow. But looking at Finn's face, her only child, her maternal wishes wavered.

"Ethan Pike? What's the occasion?" she said, her tone neutral.

Finn explained about Ethan's mom taking his sister to a track camp, an absent nanny, and Ethan's dad being away. "Please, Mom? Ethan's back at school now, just not full time. The doctors say it's probably an autoimmune thing, but he's definitely not contagious."

Iona weighed her options against the words 'probably an autoimmune thing' and the huge smile on her son's face. He was eleven, and this was the first time he'd ever asked to have someone over for a sleepover.

Professionally, she knew she should distance herself.

Personally, she couldn't bear to disappoint Finn. "Sure," she agreed reluctantly. "When would he be coming over?"

"Tomorrow after lunch. Do you really mean yes, Mom? Like yes, for real?"

"Yes!" she laughed, as her son threw his arms around her and burrowed his face into her neck, laughing.

"But you have to finish the rest of your homework tonight then, because you'll run out of time over the weekend otherwise. Okay?" she said, disentangling herself from his skinny arms.

"Okay, Mom. I love you. Thank you."

"I love you too, buddy."

Together the pair sat at the table, the blue glow of Iona's laptop screen illuminating her furrowed brow, and next to her, Finn, chewing on the end of his pencil as he tackled his math homework.

"Mom, what's seven times eight again?" Finn asked, breaking her concentration.

"Fifty-six, honey," Iona replied automatically, her eyes never leaving the screen. "Remember the trick I taught you?"

Finn nodded, returning to his worksheet as Iona refocused on her notes about the York Tower deaths.

So many deaths in one month. All seemingly natural causes, but the sheer number in such a short time frame set off alarm bells in Iona's mind. She pulled up the files.

1. Eleanor Lowenstein - Heart failure
2. Robert Chang - Stroke
3. Jacob Marsden - Apparent heart attack
4. Marion Bruce - Murder? Pending autopsy
5. Elgar Dunblane - Heart failure

The first two bodies had been cremated before any suspicions were raised. Jacob Marsden and Elgar Dunblane had been buried, so Iona was preparing the paperwork for a disinterment order. Marion Bruce's body was currently with the Medical Examiner, awaiting autopsy.

Iona rubbed her temples, feeling a headache coming on. Her Lieutenant, Dan Ortega, still thought they were chasing shadows. "Natural causes, Melville," he'd said. "Rich old folks die too, you know. Apart from Bruce."

But something didn't sit right. It was the funeral home, Eternal Rest Funerals, that had first raised concerns. They'd noticed the unusual cluster from York Tower.

"Mom, I'm done," Finn announced, sliding his completed homework across the table.

Iona glanced at the neat rows of multiplication problems. "Great job, sweetie. Why don't you go get ready for bed? I'll be up in a few minutes to tuck you in."

As Finn scampered away to his room, Iona returned to her notes. Studying the building plans for York Tower, she wondered what she was missing.

Her phone buzzed with a text from the Medical Examiner:

"Preliminary results on Bruce - no obvious cause of death. Tox screen pending. Anomalies in blood work."

Iona's pulse quickened. Anomalies could mean anything, but it was the first lead she'd had.

She quickly typed out an email to Lieutenant Ortega, updating him on the ME's findings and reiterating her request for the disinterment order for Jacob Marsden.

As she hit send, Iona heard Finn calling from upstairs. "Coming, honey!" she called back, closing her laptop.

She climbed the stairs, still thinking about her notes. The deaths at York Tower couldn't all be coincidental natural deaths. Life didn't work that way, not in her experience.

As she tucked Finn into bed, kissing his forehead, Iona knew that there was some key piece of information somewhere that she'd missed. She knew she'd seen it, she just didn't know what it was. But she would remember, she always did.

"Mommy?" Finn's sleepy voice pulled her from her thoughts.

"Yes, sweetheart?"

"Are you going to catch the bad guys in your files?"

Iona smoothed his hair. "I'm going to try, kiddo. Now go to sleep."

She turned off the light and closed Finn's door, her mind still on the fifth floor of York Tower and the growing pattern of deaths.

Lost in thought, she misjudged the top step, her toe catching the edge of the newel post. A sharp pain shot through her foot, and she bit her lip to stifle a cry. Hobbling down the stairs, she glanced back to see a smear of blood on the cream carpet.

"Damn it," she muttered under her breath. She knew from experience that blood stains were a nightmare to remove from carpet.

After wrapping a kitchen towel over her injured toe, she gathered cleaning supplies and returned to the stairs. As she worked on the stain, her mind wandered back to York Tower. More precisely, to the apartment of Marion Bruce. There had been a notable absence of blood or any bodily fluids at the crime scene.

Iona's hands stilled. How had she missed that? In a typical death scene, even from natural causes, there were usually bodily fluids. But Bruce's apartment had been immaculate, almost surgically clean.

She kicked herself mentally. She should have insisted on examining the apartments of the other four victims. A rookie mistake, one she wouldn't have made earlier in her career. Why hadn't she bothered about examining the other apartments? Was it because of the money involved? Had she fallen into the trap of assuming that because the building was high-end, and the people involved were wealthy, that there couldn't have been a crime?

As she finished cleaning the carpet, Iona planned out her next steps. First thing Monday morning, she'd request access to those apartments. If they hadn't been rented or sold, there might still be clues to find. And if they had been... well, she'd cross that bridge when she came to it.

With her toe throbbing but her mind sharp, she recalled one of law enforcement's most famous mantras - follow the money. But in this case, Iona wagered the same could be said about blood.

Her grandmother's stories slipped back. Tales from the old country about creatures that drained the life from their victims. About families cursed to hunt the living. About bloodlines that carried ancient debts across oceans and through generations.

"Some monsters leave no trace," her grandmother had whispered. "They take everything, even the blood. Leave nothing but empty shells."

Iona had always thought those were just scary stories meant to keep children indoors after dark. But now, with bodies piling up in an expensive apartment building and no blood at the crime scenes, she wondered if her grandmother had been trying to warn her about something real.

Something that had followed European bloodlines to America. Something that fed on the elderly and vulnerable. Something that was very good at making murder look like natural death.

Iona nervously tidied their modest apartment the next day. As she straightened the throw pillows on the couch, the doorbell rang.

She opened the door to find Amanda Pike, impeccable in a cashmere turtleneck, tailored black slacks, and elegant flats. Ethan stood beside her, overnight bag in hand, hopping from one foot to the other, while Zoe fidgeted impatiently behind them.

"Please come in," Iona said, acutely aware of her own casual attire - gray Old Navy joggers, a Gap crewneck sweatshirt, and slippers. Her hair was in a messy bun, her face freshly scrubbed.

"Thank you so much for this, Iona," Amanda said, ushering Ethan inside. "You're a lifesaver."

"Mom, we're going to be late!" Zoe whined. "Coach Demus is only there this afternoon, and I don't want to miss any of it!"

"I know, sweetie," Amanda replied, checking her watch.

To Iona, she added, "Lashinda Demus, legendary hurdles coach. A once-in-a-lifetime opportunity, I'm told."

Iona nodded. "Of course. I was going to offer you a coffee, but I think if I did that we'd have a murder on our hands," she joked, nodding toward Zoe who was already at the door, waiting to leave.

"A murder?" Amanda asked, puzzlement crossing her face before she realized the joke. "You're probably right. Bye Ethan, be good for Iona. Love you."

Ethan waved his mother goodbye, and as the boys disappeared to Finn's room, Amanda turned to leave. "I've packed his medications and a list of emergency contacts. I'm hoping to be back by eight o'clock tomorrow night, which is late I know—"

"We'll be fine," Iona assured her. "Safe driving, and good luck, Zoe."

If Zoe heard her, she didn't respond, and Amanda's attention was fully focused on the expensive Rolex on her wrist.

Closing the door, Iona listened to the boys' laughter in the other room. She couldn't shake her professional misgivings about becoming entangled with a resident from York Tower, no matter how benign they appeared.

But as she heard Finn's genuine happiness echoing through their modest apartment, she pushed those concerns aside. This weekend she was just a mom helping another mom.

Even if that other mom lived in a building where people kept dying under mysterious circumstances...

35

AS CLEAN AS A WHISTLE

Iona stood outside the front entrance of York Tower, a small team of officers at her back. As she waited for the doors to open, she rehearsed her opening line in her head. The early morning sun streamed through the floor-to-ceiling windows, casting long shadows across the marble floors. The ethereal glow brought to mind the afterlife - if such a thing existed - and Iona couldn't help but wonder if the recently deceased residents of York Tower were now basking in a similar, otherworldly light.

As they entered, two of the officers, Bish and O'Brien, broke into grins at the sight of Will and Rufus.

"Well, well, if it isn't the retirement squad," Bish chuckled.

O'Brien joined in, "Living the dream, eh, boys? No more chasing perps down dark alleys?"

Rufus' pen paused mid-tap. "You should try it sometime, O'Brien. Your knees will thank you."

Will managed a weak smile. "How's the beat treating you guys?"

"Same old, same old," Bish shrugged. "Though I hear you've got all the excitement up here."

Iona cleared her throat, bringing the banter to a halt. "Gentlemen, we have a job to do. Good morning," she nodded.

"I need access to the apartments of Mr. Chang, Mr. Dunblane, Mr. Marsden, Mrs. Lowenstein, and Mrs. Bruce."

Rufus' pen resumed its nervous rhythm on the polished countertop. "Ah, I think you'll find that most of those apartments have been cleaned. There's nothing left to see."

Iona's eyebrow arched. "Let me be the judge of that, Mr. St. John. Now, if one of you would be so kind as to escort us up?"

Will cleared his throat, his voice raspy. "And, uh, we'd need to see a warrant. Building policy, you understand."

"Of course." She reached into her jacket pocket and produced an official-looking document, sliding it across the counter. "Here's the search warrant, signed by Judge Holloway this morning."

Rufus picked up the warrant, his eyes scanning the page. He shared a look with Will, and Iona watched a silent conversation passing between the men. After a moment, Rufus nodded, his jowls trembling slightly.

"Seems to be in order," he said, handing the warrant back. "Will can escort you up."

Will stood, his movements unsteady, his uniform hanging loose on his frame like he was wearing someone else's clothes. Someone at least three sizes larger. "I'll take you up," Will offered, coughing slightly, as if trying to clear his throat.

For a moment, Iona wished she'd brought a face mask, but she'd fallen out of the habit post-pandemic.

As they rode the elevator, Iona pushed herself into the opposite corner as she studied Will, who was looking anywhere except at her. Dark circles shadowed his eyes, and his skin had an unhealthy pallor. "Are you sick, Mr. Taylor?" she asked.

Will's eyes met hers, and Iona could have sworn she saw a flicker of something in his gaze. Fear? Guilt?

"Long shifts. You know how it is."

"Can't be as bad as being a beat cop," she countered.

There was no reply before the elevator doors slid open.

They stepped out onto the second floor and approached Mr. Dunblane's former apartment.

Will fumbled with the master key. As the door swung open, Iona was hit by the sterile smell of industrial-strength cleaners.

"Jesus," she muttered. "Smells like an operating room."

"Commercial cleaners, it's a clause in the building management contract. After anyone moves out, or dies. They get brought in."

The apartment had indeed been emptied, stripped of all humanity, but Iona moved methodically through the rooms, searching for anything out of place.

In the bedroom, she paused by the window. "When was this apartment cleared out?"

Will shrugged. "A week after Mr. Dunblane passed, I think. His nephew came and took care of everything, and then we called the cleaners in."

Iona nodded, her gaze fixed on the windowsill. The cleaners clearly weren't as thorough as they claimed. A single, long dark hair lay there, barely visible against the white paint. She carefully bagged it before moving on to Robert Chang's apartment.

Detective Melville stood in the doorway of Chang's apartment, her eyes widening as she took in the scene before her.

"My God," she muttered, stepping into the room. 'It's like a miniature maritime museum."

Delicate sailing ships perched on bookcases, their rigging a complex web of tiny ropes. World War II battleships lined the windowsills, their guns forever aimed at unseen enemies. Even the coffee table hosted a fleet of merchant vessels, frozen in time on a sea of polished wood.

Melville moved deeper into the apartment, her trained eye cataloging details. A half-finished model sat on a workbench in the corner, tools laid out with surgical precision. A magnifying glass on an articulated arm loomed over the project.

The walls were lined with bookshelves, each groaning

under the weight of maritime reference books. *Naval Warfare Through the Ages* and *Shipbuilding Techniques: 15th to 19th Century*, were nestled beside *Ships and Seafaring in Ancient Times* by Lionel Casson, and the absolute classic, *The Rise of the Roman Empire* by Polybius.

A framed certificate on the wall caught her attention: 'Robert Chang, Secretary, Ship Model Society of New Jersey'. Beside it hung several ribbons and a photograph of Chang, beaming next to an elaborate model of a Spanish galleon.

Melville's radio crackled to life, startling her. "It's Bish. We've finished with the Marsden apartment. Where do you want us next?"

She keyed the mic, her eyes still roaming the room. "Up here in the Battle of Actium."

"The battle of what?"

"Chang's apartment. You'll understand when you get here."

Not a boat out of place. It was as she turned to leave that Melville's gaze fell on a small model of the Titanic, perched precariously close to the shelf's edge. She reached out to steady it, then paused, her hand hovering inches away.

"What happened to you, Mr. Chang?" she whispered.

With a final glance at the frozen fleet, Melville stepped out, closing the door on Robert Chang's silent armada.

Mrs. Lowenstein's apartment, number 405, was the next on their list. As they approached, Iona noticed Will's eyes darting around the hallway, avoiding hers.

"Mr. Taylor," Iona said, "is there something you want to tell me?"

Will's head snapped toward her, his eyes wide. For a moment, Iona thought he might confess to... something.

"No, nothing at all."

Inside Mrs. Lowenstein's apartment, Iona's frustration grew. It too had been scrubbed clean, with any potential evidence long gone. She was about to call it quits when something caught her eye.

On the living room floor, partially hidden under the

floor-length curtains, was a tiny glass stopper. Iona carefully extracted it, holding it up to the light. It was delicate and ornate, the kind you might find on an antique perfume bottle.

"Mr. Taylor, do you recognize this?" she asked.

"I don't even know what that is."

Iona pocketed the stopper.

She'd think about it, and Will's reaction, back at the office. Now wasn't the right time, and certainly not with an audience.

Outside Mrs. Bruce's apartment on the sixth floor, Iona caught Will rubbing at his neck again.

"Does your neck hurt, Mr. Taylor? From an accident?" she asked, her voice deceptively casual.

Will jerked his hand away from his neck. "I'm fine. Just... brings back memories, you know?"

"I've got the number of a good chiropractor if you need one," Iona said.

"What?"

"For your neck."

"My neck?" Will replied.

"You keep rubbing at it. Did you hurt it at work?"

"Golf," he replied, the word sharp, like a knife.

Iona let it go and stepped back as Will unlocked the door to apartment number 612.

Unlike the sterile emptiness of the other residences, Mrs. Bruce's home remained fully furnished. The Times crossword sat on the kitchen table, the pen lying uncapped beside it. A cold cup of tea, a fine film formed on its surface, stood nearby.

Melville noted the stacks of library books on the coffee table, the framed photo of a much younger Mrs. Bruce in front of the New York Public Library. As she approached the kitchen, Will hung back, his discomfort palpable.

"Mr. Taylor?" Iona called, "Could you come here a moment?"

Will shuffled forward. As he neared the kitchen, his face paled.

"Something wrong?" Iona asked, her eyes sharp.

"N-no," Will stammered. "Just... it's sad, you know? Seeing someone's life just... stopped."

"I'd have thought you'd be used to it, after all your years on the force. But I want you to look at this."

Iona held up a small, ornate glass stopper, similar to the one she'd found in Mrs. Lowenstein's apartment. "Does this look familiar to you, Mr. Taylor?"

Iona watched Will's hand shoot up to his neck, like a tic he couldn't control. "Should it?" he asked.

She turned the stopper over in her gloved hand. "It looks like the one we found in Lowenstein's place, don't you think?"

Will's Adam's apple bobbed as he swallowed hard. "Maybe they shopped at the same place? Rich people and their fancy perfumes, you know?"

Iona's eyes narrowed. "Maybe."

Once they returned to the lobby, Rufus looked up from his crossword. "Find anything?"

Iona's hand closed around the two stoppers in her pocket. "Maybe," she repeated. "I'll be in touch if I have any more questions."

As she walked outside into the New York morning with the rest of her team, Iona's phone buzzed. A text from the lab:

"Anomalies in Bruce's blood work confirmed. Acute anemia, unknown cause. Full report to follow."

Iona stared at the message. Anemia. Severe blood loss without external bleeding. It reminded her of stories her grandmother had told about creatures that drained their victims dry, leaving no trace except empty husks.

"Some monsters," her grandmother had whispered, "take everything. They leave the body but steal the life. No blood, no spirit, just empty shells that used to be people."

Iona had thought those were just old country superstitions. Tales meant to frighten children into staying close to home. But now, with bodies dropping and blood mysteriously missing, she wondered if her grandmother had been trying to warn her about something real.

Something that had followed bloodlines across the ocean. Something that had been waiting in the shadows of American cities for the right moment to strike.

Something that was very good at hiding in plain sight.

And up in apartment 306, a figure stood at the window, watching Detective Melville's retreating form with cold eyes. The figure's hand absently stroked one of the many vials on the nearby table, its glass stopper a perfect match to the two in the detective's pocket.

36

THIEVES IN THE NIGHT

Richard Blackwood stood by the windows of their Manhattan townhouse, his reflection a ghostly silhouette against the night. Elizabeth sat in a high-backed chair, her fingers tracing the edge of a centuries-old leather-bound journal.

"The detective," Richard said, his voice low, "is asking questions about York Tower's history. About our real estate portfolio."

Elizabeth looked up, her eyes reflecting centuries of carefully guarded secrets. "How much does she know?"

Richard turned, the moonlight catching the silver threading of his perfectly tailored jacket. "The internet changes everything. What we could bury for generations is now a simple search away."

She nodded, understanding the new vulnerability of their kind. "I remember when we acquired that land. The Lenape tribe didn't even understand the concept of land ownership as we did. It wasn't theft to us then - it was survival."

"Survival has always been our priority," Richard said, a hint of defensiveness creeping into his tone.

Elizabeth's laugh was soft, brittle. "And yet, survival looks different now. Now, there are digital trails, genealogical records, land surveys... DNA tests."

Richard moved to the ornate sideboard, pouring two

glasses of deep red liquid. Wine, to any casual observer. "Do you think someone knows? Truly knows?"

"About the land?" Elizabeth raised an eyebrow. "Or about us?"

The silence stretched between them, heavy with unspoken history.

"What concerns me," Elizabeth continued, "is why someone would start asking questions now. After all these decades of silence. Why would they choose to target us this way? It doesn't make sense."

Richard's hand unconsciously moved to an old scar near his neck - a remnant from a confrontation long ago. "You think this is about more than just the land?"

"I think," Elizabeth said carefully, "that someone is playing with us."

Richard set down his glass with deliberate precision. "Burton."

The name hung in the air between them like a curse. Elizabeth's fingers stilled on the journal's leather binding.

"After all these years?" she whispered.

"We both know he swore an oath over Rachel's grave," Richard said, his voice hollow. "In that godforsaken Vermont cemetery, while the town watched her body burn. He looked right at me through the smoke and flames and promised he'd destroy everything I held dear."

Elizabeth closed the journal, her knuckles white. "That was over two centuries ago, Richard. In Manchester. We were different people then."

"Were we?" Richard moved to the window again, staring out at the city lights. "I loved her, Elizabeth. Before I even knew what I was, before the hunger, before any of this. Rachel was... she was everything good I thought I could be."

"I know," Elizabeth said softly. "And Burton turned her into a weapon against you."

"He turned her into what we are," Richard corrected. "But she never forgave him for it. Even after the transformation, even when the hunger consumed her, she still loved me. And that's what drove him mad."

Elizabeth joined him at the window, her hand finding his. Three centuries of marriage had taught her when to speak and when to simply be present.

"He made her feed on that poor girl, Hilda," Richard continued. "Made her watch as I tried to save my second wife. Made her participate in the very cycle that destroyed us all. All to prove that love couldn't survive what we'd become."

"But it did survive," Elizabeth reminded him. "We found each other. We built this life."

"After Rachel died," Richard said bitterly. "After Burton's experiments finally killed the only woman I'd ever loved. After he realized he couldn't corrupt what was already lost."

The city sprawled before them, oblivious to the ancient grief being relived in their elegant townhouse. Somewhere out there, Burton was moving his pieces into place. The chess game that had begun in a small Vermont town was finally reaching its endgame.

"The deaths at York Tower," Elizabeth said. "The residents who've been disappearing. It's him, isn't it?"

Richard nodded. "He's not just killing them. He's turning them. Building an army of the recently dead, all carrying his hatred. All programmed to destroy what we've spent centuries building."

"Then we fight," Elizabeth said simply.

"With what?" Richard laughed bitterly. "He has the advantage of surprise. We don't even know how many of our tenants are already his creatures. How many of our security staff. How many of our business associates."

"We have James and Sarah."

"Do we?" Richard turned to face his wife. "James doesn't even know what we are. Sarah thinks we're just eccentric real estate moguls. How do we protect them from an enemy they can't see coming?"

Elizabeth was quiet for a long moment. When she spoke, her voice carried the weight of centuries. "The same way your father protected you in Manchester. The same way we've always protected our family."

"By running?"

"By doing whatever it takes to survive." She moved to the sideboard, refilling their glasses with hands that didn't shake despite the magnitude of what they were discussing. "Burton wants to finish what he started with Rachel. He wants to prove that love can't survive what we are. But he's wrong, Richard. We're living proof that he's wrong."

Richard accepted the glass, noting how Elizabeth's eyes had taken on the golden sheen they always got when she was preparing for battle. After three centuries, he knew that look well.

"What are you thinking?" he asked.

"I'm thinking," Elizabeth said, raising her glass in a toast, "that Isaac Burton is about to learn why the Blackwood family has survived this long. We don't run from fights - we end them."

Outside their window, a raven cawed once before disappearing into the night. But for the first time in decades, Richard Blackwood smiled.

The war that had begun with Rachel's death was finally going to end. One way or another.

"To family," Elizabeth said.

"To survival," Richard replied.

They drank, and in that moment, the scared young man who had fled Manchester in 1793 finally died. What remained was a creature old enough and strong enough to face his past.

Burton wanted a war? He could have one.

37

———

TRACE EVIDENCE

Iona Melville stood in the forensics lab, the fluorescent lights highlighting the bags under her eyes. Across from her, Dr. Samantha Webb, the department's lead forensic scientist, peered through a microscope.

"So, what can you tell me about those stoppers, Sam?" Iona asked, suppressing a yawn.

Dr. Webb looked up, pushing her glasses back up her nose. "Not much yet, I'm afraid. They're definitely old, probably antique. Hand-blown glass, which makes them pretty unique. We're running tests for trace evidence and DNA, but it'll take time."

Iona nodded, rolling the second stopper across the lab bench. "How long?"

"A couple of days, minimum. It isn't exactly top priority, Iona. We've got three homicides and a string of assaults backed up."

"I know, I know," Iona sighed. "It's just... something's not right about this case. If it even is a case."

Dr. Webb's eyebrows rose. "You think it isn't?"

Before Iona could answer, a text arrived from her son, Finn: "Mom, don't forget about the field trip form!"

Iona groaned inwardly. The school trip. She'd promised Finn she'd chaperone, but with the York Tower situation...

"Everything okay?" Dr. Webb asked.

"Yeah, mom stuff," Iona replied, pocketing her phone. "Let me know as soon as you have anything on that glass."

Iona knew she needed more. The stoppers were her only tangible lead, but without context, they were meaningless.

In the bullpen, she found Bish and O'Brien reviewing their notes from the search.

"Anything?" she asked hopefully.

Bish shook his head. "Nothing at all in the other apartments, Detective. They were cleaned out, just like the rent-a-cops said."

Iona ignored the dig about Will and Rufus. That would probably be them in another decade or two. "And what about Mrs. Bruce's place? Did you find anything like a perfume vial or anything that our mystery stoppers would fit?" Iona pressed.

"Nothing," O'Brien replied. "No fancy perfume bottles missing their stoppers anywhere."

Iona pinched the bridge of her nose. "Thanks, guys."

At her desk, she pulled up the case files. Of the York Tower deaths, two had been cremated, two buried, and one was still with the coroner. She needed to see those bodies.

She picked up her phone to dial the District Attorney's office. "This is Detective Melville. I need to request exhumation orders for Jacob Marsden and Elgar Dunblane."

Twenty minutes and one heated argument later, Iona hung up. The DA wasn't convinced there was enough evidence to justify exhumation without concrete proof of foul play.

Her phone buzzed again. Another text from Finn.

"Mom!!!!!! Did u sign the form yet? It's due tmr!"

Who taught these kids to write?

She'd been so wrapped up in things, she'd neglected Finn. Again.

She could take the time off for the field trip - her lieutenant had practically ordered her to use some of her accumulated leave. But could she justify stepping away from the investigation, even for a day?

As if on cue, Lieutenant Ortega appeared at her desk. "Melville, go home. You've been here for fourteen hours straight."

"But, sir—"

"No buts. Go home, hug your kid, get some sleep. The case will still be here tomorrow."

Will Taylor's face flashed in her mind, together with his nervous demeanor, and the way he'd reacted to the stopper in Mrs. Bruce's apartment. He knew something about the stoppers, she was sure of it. She slammed her hand against her desk. Exhaustion would not help solve the case, and sadly neither would a field trip to the Metropolitan Museum of Art, so help her God, but that's what she had to look forward to tomorrow.

The marble halls of the Metropolitan Museum of Art buzzed with children's excitement. Iona trailed behind Finn's class, her detective's mind only half-present.

"Remember, kids," Ms. Patel called out, her blue eyeshadow glinting under the museum lights, "keep your eyes peeled for the items on your scavenger hunt list!"

As the class moved through the galleries, Iona's eyes constantly swept the room, counting heads and scanning for potential risks. Her thoughts kept drifting back to the glass stoppers and Will Taylor's strange behavior.

"We're entering the *Ancient Ritual Objects* exhibition," Ms. Patel announced. The class filed into a dimly lit room filled with glass cases. Haunting music drifted from hidden speakers - a discordant melody that sent a slight chill down Iona's spine.

"Mom, come look!" Finn's voice cut through her reverie. "I found something like that little glass top you brought home!"

Her son beamed at her and she beamed back, until she leaned in and looked. A set of tiny, ornate vials - displayed with their stoppers - and a placard beside them.

Blood Reliquaries, c. 1450 CE
Origin: Snagov Monastery, Romania.

Her breath caught. The glass stoppers were identical to those from York Tower. Same intricate engravings and craftsmanship.

"Finn, why don't you check the next item on your list?" she said, her voice tight.

As her son scampered away, Iona discreetly photographed the display.

An elderly docent materialized beside her. "Fascinating pieces," he said. "Some scholars believe they're connected to Vlad the Impaler."

"Really?" Iona's detective instincts sparked.

"Supposedly linked to the monastery where he was buried," the docent continued. "Though his body was never found. Legend says these particular vials were used to preserve the blood of his enemies. Or his victims, depending on which story you believe."

Her phone buzzed with a message from Dr. Webb: "Preliminary results on stoppers. Traces of unidentified organic substance. Possibly blood. Call me ASAP."

Iona glanced from her phone to the ancient vials, her grandmother's stories flooding back. Tales of Old World monsters that followed bloodlines across oceans. Of creatures that preserved their victims' essence in ornate containers. Of ancient debts that could only be paid in blood.

"Some monsters," her grandmother had whispered, "keep trophies. They collect the life force of their prey in beautiful vessels, like precious wine."

Iona had thought those were just fairy tales. But standing here, looking at medieval blood reliquaries that matched evidence from a modern crime scene, she wondered if her grandmother had been trying to warn her about something very real.

Something that had brought Old World hunting practices to New World prey.

"Mom!" Finn called. "We're moving to the next room!"

"Coming, honey," she responded, her mind racing.

The docent smiled as she turned to leave.

"Remarkable how some traditions survive, isn't it? How the old ways find new homes in unexpected places," the docent said.

Iona felt a chill that had nothing to do with the museum's air conditioning. With a deep breath, she pocketed her phone and followed her son's class, carrying the weight of a centuries-old mystery with her.

The case could wait a couple more hours. Right now, she had a different hunt to finish.

But tonight, she would call Dr. Webb. And tomorrow, she would demand those exhumation orders.

Because some monsters, her grandmother had warned, were very good at hiding their true nature. But they always left traces of what they really were.

And Iona was starting to think she'd found those traces in a pair of medieval blood reliquaries, displayed in plain sight in one of the world's most famous museums.

38

UNEARTHED SECRETS

Iona stood in the City Morgue, her gaze fixed on the two sheet-covered bodies before her. The room's stark illumination leached color from everything, turning the stainless steel surfaces into mirrors that reflected her own tense expression. As always, the strong smell of disinfectant struggled to mask the underlying scent of death and made her stomach turn.

The exhumation orders had finally come through, but at a cost to Iona's conscience. She'd stretched the truth beyond her comfort zone, treading a fine line between thorough investigation and potential misconduct. She kept repeating to herself the mantra: the ends justify the means. Yet, she knew other officers who'd been fired for less.

In her meeting with the District Attorney, Iona had woven a tale of a warped blood cult preying on York Tower's elderly residents. She'd presented the mysterious glass stoppers as evidence of ritual objects, their connection to the deaths tenuous but intriguing. Marion Bruce's autopsy results, showing acute anemia, had been her strongest argument, lending credibility to her theory of foul play.

But it was the additional evidence that churned Iona's stomach with guilt. Hours spent combing the dark web had yielded dozens of disturbing posts about blood rituals and vampire worship.

None of it was connected to York Tower or to the Blackwood family, but it had tipped the scales in her favor.

Standing there, awaiting the pathologist's arrival, Iona recognized she'd veered from her usual by-the-book approach, pushing her to cross a line she'd once deemed inviolable.

Dr. Samantha Webb, the pathologist, entered the room, snapping on a pair of latex gloves. "Are you ready for this?"

Iona nodded, steeling herself. "As ready as I'll ever be."

Dr. Webb pulled back the sheets, revealing the bodies of Jacob Marsden and Elgar Dunblane. Iona's breath caught in her throat. Despite having been buried for weeks, the bodies looked... fresh.

"Is that... usual?" Iona asked, fearing the answer.

Dr. Webb frowned. "Well, there's minimal decomposition. The skin is still supple, no significant discoloration. And here," she pointed to Marsden's fingernails, "look at this growth."

Iona felt sick. "But... they've grown! That's not possible, is it?"

Dr. Webb smiled. "You know, it's funny. I just listened to a podcast about this very thing on my commute last week. *Lore*, it's called. In this episode, they talked about historical cases of suspected vampirism."

"Vampirism?" Iona echoed. The word sounded ridiculous, even as her mind raced to connect it with everything she'd seen.

"Oh, not actual vampires, obviously," Dr. Webb chuckled. "But in the 18th and 19th centuries, people would exhume bodies and find them in a similar state. They'd take it as evidence of vampirism."

"What do you mean?" Iona asked. The last word she wanted to write in her evidence notebook was *vampirism*.

Dr. Webb straightened, her voice taking on a lecturing tone. "In medical school, we learned about these cases as examples of how superstition can arise from misunderstood natural phenomena. In Serbia in the 1720s, there was a case where multiple bodies were exhumed and found to be 'fresh.' They described them as having new nail and hair growth, plump skin, and even blood in the mouth."

Iona's eyes widened. "Isn't that what we're seeing here?"

"Exactly. But now we know that these are natural processes of decomposition. Hair and nails appear to grow because of skin retraction. The 'plump' appearance is because of bloating from gases. The 'blood' in the mouth is just fluid from the lungs."

Iona tried to reconcile this scientific explanation with the supernatural claims she'd been hearing. Her grandmother's stories about Old World monsters suddenly seemed less like folklore and more like historical documentation.

Dr. Webb leaned in closer to Marsden's neck. "But this *is* interesting," she muttered, her Christmas earrings jingling inappropriately in the solemn moment.

"What?" Iona asked, stepping closer.

"There are two small puncture marks here on the neck," Dr. Webb said, pointing. She moved to Dunblane's body and examined it as well. "And here, too, in almost the same location."

Iona's hand tightened on her notebook. 'Caused post mortem?"

"The marks are clean, precise. Not like any animal bite I've seen." She paused, then added, "The placement, the depth, the lack of tearing... it's peculiar."

"Peculiar how?" Iona pressed.

"Well," Dr. Webb said, "as a first guess, I'd say these marks were made with some kind of tool or instrument. But for what purpose, I couldn't say."

"Dr. Webb," Iona asked slowly, "have you ever come across cases where the scientific explanation... just wasn't enough?"

The pathologist looked up, her eyes meeting Iona's. For a moment, a gleam of uncertainty crossed her face. "There are always anomalies in science, things we can't explain... yet."

As they prepared to leave the morgue, Iona couldn't

shake the feeling that she was dealing with something beyond normal police work. The medieval blood reliquaries at the Met, the puncture wounds, the unnatural preservation of the bodies - it all pointed to something her grandmother would have recognized immediately.

"Some debts," her grandmother had whispered, "follow bloodlines across centuries."

Iona had thought those were just stories to keep children from wandering too far from home. But now, with two impossibly preserved bodies bearing identical wounds, she wondered if her grandmother had been trying to warn her about creatures that had followed European bloodlines to America.

Creatures that had been waiting in the shadows of cities like New York for the right moment to settle ancient scores.

Outside the morgue, Iona pulled out her phone and called Dr. Webb's lab. "Sam, I need you to expedite those tests on the glass stoppers. And I need you to check something else - see if there are any historical records of similar puncture wounds. Specifically, look for cases from New England in the 1790s."

"New England? That's oddly specific."

"Just a hunch," Iona said. "Sometimes the old cases hold the key to new ones."

As she hung up, Iona thought about Will Taylor's nervous behavior, his reaction to the blood reliquaries, the way he kept touching his neck. She thought about the Blackwood family's impossible longevity and their real estate empire built on convenient deaths.

Most of all, she thought about her son Finn, who had spent time in that building with those people.

Some monsters, her grandmother had warned, were very good at hiding in plain sight. They built respectable lives, accumulated wealth and power, and everyone trusted them.

Iona was beginning to think her grandmother had been right about everything.

39

FAMILY TIES

Sarah Blackwood stood in her father's office, holding a stack of documents. Her hands were shaking.

Her father had asked her to handle what should have been a simple task - sorting through the paperwork for the new Healthy Homes Standards. The city was cracking down on residential buildings after that scandal in Queens, demanding updated ventilation reports and air quality assessments.

But as she'd dug through the property files, looking for the original HVAC specifications, something caught her eye. An unfamiliar name kept appearing in the small print, alongside that of Peart, their lawyer.

"This doesn't make sense," she said, spreading the papers across Richard's mahogany desk. "I was going through the property files for the HVAC certification, but look at this. Another company seems to own minority shares in all our properties. Why wouldn't you tell me?"

Richard barely glanced at them. "You're probably reading them wrong. If Matthew has signed off, then I'm sure everything is fine."

"That's just it, Dad. Burton Holdings goes back further than fifteen years. Always as a silent partner, and it predates Peart."

She pulled out several documents.

"Look. 1972, a 12% stake in our Vermont development.

1988, 15% of our Washington property. 2003, 18% of the Oregon Plaza. The percentage keeps creeping up, and it's always signed off by Peart, or our agent before him."

Richard froze. "Did you say Burton Holdings?"

"I did. It's like..." Sarah frowned at the documents. "It's like someone's been using our properties, our developments, but..." She looked up. "Dad?"

Richard had moved to the window. The city stretched out below them, a maze of lights and shadows. "Burton," he whispered. "What a fool I've been."

"Pardon?"

But he'd dismissed her with the flick of his wrist.

Sarah stood at the window of her bedroom, her reflection ghostly in the tinted glass. In her hand, she clutched a USB drive containing all the property documents she'd compiled. Her finger traced the Blackwood crest etched into the metal, a reminder of the legacy she both cherished and questioned.

A knock at the door broke her reverie. "Sarah? It's James."

She pocketed the drive. "Come in."

James entered, his tailored suit a stark contrast to Sarah's casual attire. "Father wants to see us. Both of us."

Sarah's jaw tightened. "I can't. I'm heading upstate with some friends later tonight. He could have spoken to me earlier, but he didn't seem interested."

James frowned. "Upstate? To Fir House?"

She shrugged. "No one else said they were using it this weekend."

"Father said he wanted to see us," James replied, his tone tense. "Besides, you should have checked with me first. I might have had plans up there."

Sarah didn't reply to his barb. Their relationship was friendly, but sibling rivalry was never far from the surface. They'd both learned how to inflict the sharpest wounds with just their words.

"Later, James," she said, opening the door and ushering him out, not even trying to smile.

The winding road to Fir House was pitch black by the time Sarah's car crunched up the gravel driveway. The grand silhouette of the Blackwood summer home loomed against the starry sky.

Sarah grabbed her overnight bag and made her way inside. The familiar scent of pine and old wood enveloped her as she entered. Hargreaves, ever-efficient, had left the lights on and a tray of refreshments in the kitchen.

She glanced at her phone out of habit, but as expected, there was no signal. Her friends should have arrived by now. A twinge of worry nagged at her.

Sarah's eyes fell on the key rack by the back door. The key to the pavilion hung there, its brass surface gleaming. Her father's sanctuary and the only spot on the property with reliable cell service.

Grabbing the key, Sarah stepped out into the night. A raven's call pierced the darkness, but she paid it no mind. This place, with its towering pines and secluded paths, had been her summer playground for as long as she could remember.

The pavilion stood a short distance from the main house, a sleek structure at odds with Fir House's rustic charm. As Sarah approached, key in hand, the crunch of tires on gravel broke the silence.

Relief washed over her. Her friends had arrived. She turned, ready to greet them, the USB drive heavy in her pocket.

But as the car's headlights swept across her, illuminating the pavilion behind her, Sarah realized with a start that this wasn't her friend's car. The vehicle was larger, more imposing.

Before she could react, the car door opened, and a familiar figure stepped out. Her father, closely followed by both her mother and brother.

Shit.

"Hello, Sarah," her father's voice cut through the night air. "We need to talk. There are some things you need to know."

Sarah took an instinctive step back. Something in her father's voice made the hair on her neck rise. The USB drive in her pocket felt like it was burning against her leg.

"What things?" Her fingers clutched the drive in her pocket like a talisman.

"The truth about our family. About what we are." Richard moved closer. "About what James must become."

"Dad?" James' voice held an edge of uncertainty she'd never heard before. "What are you talking about?"

"I'm sorry, son." Richard's face... changed. Sarah blinked hard, certain she was seeing things. Her father's features were sharpening, his skin taking on an unnatural pallor. When he opened his mouth to speak again, she saw his teeth elongating before her eyes.

"Jesus," Sarah whispered. This couldn't be happening. People's faces didn't do that. Teeth didn't just grow. "What's wrong with you?"

"Elizabeth," Richard called, his voice thick around those impossible teeth. "Hold Sarah back. She shouldn't interfere."

Their mother stepped forward, her grip on Sarah's arm like iron. "It must be done, darling. To protect all of us."

"Mom?" Sarah's voice cracked. "What's happening?"

James struggled against their father's grip, but Richard's strength was overwhelming. With terrible gentleness, he tilted his son's head, exposing his neck.

"I love you, James," Richard whispered. "This is the only way to keep you safe."

Sarah's scream died in her throat as her father's teeth sank into James' neck. For one terrible moment, she could only stare, her mind refusing to process what her eyes were seeing. Blood, dark and horrible, ran down James' expensive suit, staining the collar black in the dim light. Her brother's struggles grew weaker, his movements becoming sluggish, and something in Sarah snapped. She fumbled for her phone with trembling hands, but Elizabeth knocked it away with casual force.

"They wouldn't be able to help, darling," her mother

said, voice terrifyingly gentle. "No one can. This is family business."

The phone skittered across the ground as James' knees buckled, held up only by their father's inexorable grip.

"Stop it!" Sarah clawed at her mother's grip. "You're killing him!"

"No, darling," Elizabeth's voice was soft. "He's saving him."

Richard pulled back, his chin dark with blood. James sagged in his arms, barely conscious. With precise movements, Richard bit his own wrist and pressed it to James' mouth.

"Drink, son," he commanded. "Live."

Sarah watched in horror as James' throat worked, swallowing their father's blood. Her mind reeled, trying to make sense of what was happening. His body convulsed, back arching impossibly. A sound escaped him - not quite a scream, not quite human.

Sarah's legs gave out. She slid down to the ground. Her phone forgotten, its useless screen still showing no signal. Nothing in her world made sense.

James' convulsions stopped. When his eyes opened, they held a predator's gleam. His face, so familiar, now seemed carved from marble. When he smiled, his teeth were sharp.

"Welcome to the family," Richard whispered. "Truly, this time."

"Inside," Richard commanded, helping James to his feet. "The change is easier somewhere warm."

Sarah felt her mother's iron grip loosen slightly. "Come, darling. The night air isn't good for your brother right now."

Still numb with shock, Sarah let herself be guided into Fir House's grand living room. The familiar space felt alien now - the antique furniture, the old paintings adorning the walls, the drinks cabinet that had fascinated her as a child - all of it transformed by the horror she'd just witnessed.

Richard moved over to Elizabeth, placing his hand on his wife's waist. Sarah watched as her mother poured something dark into a crystal glass - not wine, she realized with growing horror. Her parents shared a look heavy with unspoken history.

"Do you remember Paris?" Elizabeth asked softly, her fingers tracing the rim of her glass. "1944. All those Nazi officers who mysteriously disappeared from their posts?"

Richard's smile held no warmth. "They tasted of fear and blind obedience. Like sheep who'd forgotten they were sheep." He looked out the window.

"We told ourselves we were doing our part for the war effort. That some monsters needed to be eliminated by bigger monsters," he continued.

"And now here we are again," Elizabeth sighed. "Having to choose which monsters to fight. I never thought we'd need to make those choices here, in America, of all places."

"The difference is," Richard turned back to his wife, "this time we're not just eliminating monsters. We're protecting our children from one."

Sarah huddled against the wall, her parents' casual discussion of wartime vampirism somehow more terrifying than the violence she'd just witnessed. The raven called again, its cry a herald of this new, terrible world.

"If we don't act," Richard said, "someone else will. There is a change in the air, and we need to be prepared. This detective might just prove to be useful."

"Or she could expose everything we've built," Elizabeth said.

"In this world of endless distraction and disbelief? No one would ever believe her," Richard replied.

Sarah clutched the USB drive in her pocket, the only solid thing in a world that had suddenly become a nightmare. Whatever was on that drive - whatever connection existed between her family and Burton Holdings - it was the key to understanding what was happening.

But first, she had to survive the night.

And figure out what her brother had become.

40

THE FOURTH ESTATE

I ona Melville burst into the precinct, her face a storm cloud of fury. She slammed her phone down on her desk, the screen still displaying the offending article:

KILLER ON THE LOOSE?
Wealthy Elderly Targeted
Satanic Cult Suspected

THE ARTICLE, published on a local news blog, detailed a series of "suspicious deaths" at York Tower and hinted at similar occurrences in other upscale apartment buildings in the area. It cited "unspecified sources" and an "anonymous tip," speculating wildly about a satanic cult.

"Who leaked this?" Iona demanded, her voice carrying across the bustling office.

Lieutenant Ortega emerged from his office, his face grim. "Melville, in here. Now."

As soon as the door closed behind them, Iona exploded.

"This is completely unacceptable. We need to issue a takedown notice immediately. This article is pure speculation, and it's going to cause mass panic!"

Ortega sighed, rubbing his temples. "Melville, you know we can't do that. Freedom of the press—"

"Don't quote the First Amendment at me," Iona

snapped. "This isn't journalism, it's fear-mongering. And it will compromise our investigation!"

"It's crazy out there," she said, pointing to the room outside where every one of her colleagues was on the phone, probably trying to calm frantic callers. "Every Tom, Dick, and Harry with a grandparent within a five-mile radius of Union Square is calling in. We haven't had this many panicked calls since the whole 'immigrant pet-eating' fiasco last election cycle!"

Ortega held up a hand. "I get it, Melville. We can issue a statement refuting the claims, but we can't force them to take down the article."

Iona paced the small office. "This is going to make our job ten times harder. The real perpetrator, if there even is one, will go to ground. And what about the residents of York Tower? They'll be hounded by the press—or worse, some copycat cultist will start preying on the elderly."

"Which is why you need to focus on the investigation," Ortega said firmly. "Find out if there's any truth to these deaths being connected. We solve this quickly, the story dies."

Iona stopped pacing. "The leak had to come from someone with inside knowledge. There are details we haven't made public."

Ortega nodded. "I'll look into it. In the meantime, tread carefully. The last thing we need is to add fuel to this fire."

As Iona left Ortega's office, she could feel the eyes of the entire precinct on her. The phones kept ringing, a sign of the panic fueled by the tsunami of social media posts generated by the ridiculous article. She grabbed her jacket and headed for the door.

Whoever leaked this information had just made her job harder. But they'd also made a mistake. They'd revealed that they knew more than they should. And she was determined to find out why.

Her grandmother's voice echoed in her memory as she drove toward York Tower. Stories about Old World monsters that thrived on chaos and fear. Creatures that used panic to hide their true activities. About bloodlines that had learned to manipulate modern media just as they'd once manipulated village gossip.

"When the whole town is looking for monsters under their beds," her grandmother had warned, "the real monsters can feed undisturbed."

AS THE MEDIA frenzy outside York Tower reached fever pitch, Rufus St. John found himself at the center of attention - a position he was thoroughly enjoying. With Will out sick, Rufus had free rein to indulge his newfound celebrity status.

"Oh, you know how it is," Rufus said into the phone, his voice dripping with faux modesty. "Just doing my job, keeping everyone safe. But between you and me, Mrs. Lowenstein always did have a thing for those true crime shows. Obsessed she was."

He chuckled, knowing full well that Mrs. Lowenstein had been more interested in her soap operas than anything nefarious. But it made for a good story, and the journalist on the other end of the line was eating it up.

As he hung up, Mr. Kim approached the desk, his eyes wide. "It's a circus out there. Can't you do anything to move them on?"

Rufus tried reducing the size of his grin, but to no avail. He leaned in conspiratorially. "This is just the tip of the iceberg. I've had calls from as far as Australia asking about our 'satanic cult'!"

Mr. Kim shook his head. "It's ridiculous. We all know that they died of old age. There's no cult, satanic or otherwise, here!"

Mrs. Abernathy appeared at the security desk, newspaper in hand.

"Rufus, have you seen these wild stories? Satanic cults in

York Tower?" She tapped the headline. "In all my years here, I've never heard such nonsense."

Rufus shifted uncomfortably under her gaze. "Just tabloid gossip, Mrs. A. You know how they sensationalize everything."

"Indeed," she murmured, her eyes never leaving his face. "Still, there have been an unusually high number of deaths lately. We can't have everyone thinking York Tower is the next Rosemary's Baby."

Just then, the elevator dinged, and out stepped Skylar Reeves. The reclusive movie star looked almost ordinary in jeans, hoodie and a Yankees baseball cap.

"Mr. Reeves," Rufus stammered, surprised. "This is unexpected."

Skylar Reeves offered a wry smile. "Well, when Satan's minions are allegedly running amok in your building, it seemed like a good time to appear. Who knew we were all living amidst a hotbed of occult activity?"

Mr. Kim laughed. "You don't believe all that, do you?"

"Of course not," Skylar replied. "But my PR company thinks it's manna from heaven, given the role I've just been cast in. What do you think, Rufus? You're our man on the inside."

Rufus puffed up at the attention - and a little surprised that the man remembered his name. "Well, I don't want to speculate too much, but I will say this - the police are investigating something more than five dead old people..."

The three men huddled closer, trading theories and tidbits of gossip, ignoring the elderly Mrs. Abernathy.

As they talked, Rufus reveled in the moment. For once, he was at the center of the action, not just a bystander. Part of him felt a twinge of guilt for enjoying it so much, but another part - a larger part - was too caught up in the excitement to care.

Outside, reporters jostled for position. Inside, the living residents of York Tower buzzed with an energy they hadn't experienced in years. And at the heart of it all stood Rufus, basking in the glow of his fifteen minutes of fame, blissfully unaware of the dark underbelly of the media circus.

Iona's phone buzzed as she made her way to her car. Glancing at the screen, she saw a flood of notifications, all related to York Tower. With a sigh, she opened the latest one - a viral *Entertainment Tonight* article:

SKYLAR REEVES TO STAR IN '*REVENANT NIGHTS*' - COINCIDENCE OR CLEVER PR?
In a twist worthy of Hollywood itself, reclusive superstar Skylar Reeves has been announced as the lead in the upcoming supernatural thriller '*Revenant Nights*.' For those unfamiliar with folklore, a revenant is a corpse believed to return from the grave to terrorize the living.
The timing couldn't be more perfect — or suspicious. With rumors swirling about a potential 'satanic cult' targeting wealthy elderly residents in Reeves' own apartment building, York Tower, social media is ablaze with speculation. Is this merely a case of life imitating art, or is there something more sinister at play?
Sources close to the production claim that Reeves, who is also producing the film, has been 'method acting' for months. Could the star's reclusiveness be tied to this role? Or is the convenient timing of this announcement a masterclass in viral marketing?
One thing's for certain — '*Revenant Nights*' just shot to the top of everyone's must-watch list.

Iona groaned. As if the investigation wasn't complicated enough, now she had to contend with Hollywood. Her phone rang.

"Tell me you've seen the article," Ortega asked.

"Just finished reading it," Iona replied, her voice weary. "I did not have this on my investigation bingo card."

"It gets better," Ortega said. "The internet is exploding with conspiracy theories. Half the world thinks Reeves is behind the deaths as some twisted PR stunt. The other half thinks he's actually hunting vampires."

Iona pinched the bridge of her nose. "Fantastic. Because we didn't have enough to deal with already."

"I need you to talk to Reeves," Ortega said. "Find out about this film, including when he was cast. And for the love of God, make sure he's not actually involved in any of this."

"On it," Iona said, starting her car. "But, sir, what about the original leak? This Reeves angle is a distraction."

"I know," Ortega sighed. "But first, handle Reeves, and then we'll regroup."

Driving toward York Tower, Iona's worries about the Reeves connection added a whole layer of complexity to the case. Surely, surely, no one would be so evil as to kill people as a PR stunt for a movie? It defied belief.

As the building loomed into view, swarmed by reporters and curious onlookers, Iona took a deep breath, parked her car and stepped out into the melee. It was time to separate fact from fiction, Hollywood from reality. And maybe get one step closer to the truth.

But as she pushed through the crowd of reporters, Iona couldn't shake the feeling that the real story was being buried beneath the sensationalism. Her grandmother had warned her about creatures that used chaos as cover for their true activities.

"When everyone's looking for the obvious monster," she'd said, "the real predator feeds in peace."

41

BLOOD AND EARTH

Richard Blackwood stood in the driveway of Fir House, the weight of time pressing down on him like a physical force. His mind drifted back to a cold Vermont night in 1793...

Manchester had always been a quiet town, but in the winter of 1793, an eerie stillness had settled over it. It began with the Burton family. Isaac Burton's wife, Rachel, had fallen ill shortly after their wedding. Within months, she was dead. When Isaac remarried, his new bride, Hilda, soon succumbed to the same wasting illness.

Whispers started. At first just murmurs of bad luck, of a curse on the Burton family. But as more townsfolk fell ill, the whispers grew louder. 'Vampire,' they said, in hushed tones behind closed doors.

He'd been barely eighteen when he'd watched fear grip the town. His father, Richard Sr., a respected businessman, tried to quell the growing panic. "There will be a rational explanation," he'd said. But rationality was in short supply as the death toll rose.

The night the town council exhumed Rachel Burton's body was etched into Richard's memory.

The hate on the faces of the townspeople and the cold biting through layers of wool as he and his father joined the group of townsmen at the cemetery.

"Stay behind me," his father had said, so Young Richard

watched from the shadows with his father as the group approached the freshly dug grave. The whispers of "vampire" had grown to a roar, and these upstanding citizens were here to put an end to the terror.

"Almighty God, our eternal Father, we come before You in this dark hour, seeking Your divine protection. Shield us, O Lord, from the forces of evil that threaten our town. By the blood of Your Son Jesus Christ, cleanse this land of the unholy scourge that plagues us," the mayor began, his voice carrying the weight of his role. "We beseech You, Father, to cast out Satan and all his minions. Let Your holy light pierce the shadows where evil lurks. Protect us from the touch of the damned, from those who would rise from the grave to torment the living."

Richard's pulse quickened as he watched the men dig like demons, their faces grim in the torchlight. His father's hand on his shoulder tightened.

The portly minister took over, his mouth disguised by a beard as mammoth, and as white, as the snow on Bromley Mountain.

"Grant us strength, O Lord, to carry out Your will. Guide our hands as we work to purge this evil from our midst. Let the power of Your Holy Spirit surround us, a bulwark against the darkness. In the name of Jesus Christ, our Savior, we pray for deliverance from this ungodly pestilence. May His sacrifice on the cross be our shield, His resurrection, our hope. Amen."

Richard's breath caught in his throat as the shovels struck something solid. As they scraped away the remaining earth, the diggers' faces twisted into a mixture of fear and exhilaration.

The body of Rachel Burton lay there, but it was nothing like the slight woman he remembered. Grotesquely swollen, with the skin stretched tight. Her face, once pretty and kind, was now bloated beyond recognition, a dark, angry red. The shroud they'd buried her in was in tatters, as if she'd been thrashing about in her grave.

Richard had wanted to look away, but couldn't, watching

as the selectman drove his shovel into Rachel Burton's corpse.

Blood gushed from the wound.

Far more than should have been possible for someone so many months dead. The dark liquid had poured out in a malevolent flood.

The cloying sweetness of decay mingled with the metallic tang of fresh blood should have made him gag. But it had done the opposite. A ravenous hunger consumed him, and it was all his father could do to hold him back, as Richard watched in horror as the men dragged the body beyond the village and onto a funeral pyre.

The town clerk announced that the pestilential body would not burn unless its heart was torn out. The magistrate, a man of the law, duly laid open Rachel's chest with repeated blows of the blunted spade, and, thrusting in his hand, he ripped out her accursed heart.

As the heart was torn into pieces and the body consigned to the flames, something changed in Richard's eyes. The ravenous hunger that had consumed Richard was more than morbid fascination. It was a hunger of the blood - primal, dangerous, transformative.

At the edge of the pyre, Isaac Burton stood watching. His eyes scanning the crowd. Richard knew Burton had been systematically eliminating those who had wronged him, including the townspeople who had whispered, who had accused, who had sought to question his behavior. And now, those eyes had settled on young Richard.

And his father saw it too. The way Burton's gaze locked onto Richard. The subtle tensing of Burton's body, like a predator preparing to strike. In that moment, Richard's father understood two things: his son was changing into something dangerous, and Burton intended to claim Richard as his own.

"Go," his father whispered urgently, gripping Richard's shoulder. "Now. Before he sees you fully."

Richard was sent away that very night. Not to protect the

town, but to protect Richard himself from Burton's hungry gaze. The Blackwood legacy of survival had begun.

But Burton had followed.

Back in the present, Richard sighed heavily. The memory of that night had haunted him for centuries. The decision his father had made had brought him wealth and power beyond imagination, but it had also bound them to a darkness they could never escape.

Burton's obsession had twisted into something far more dangerous than simple revenge. He'd spent two centuries building his own empire, his own network of influence, all designed to corner the Blackwood family. The deaths at York Tower weren't random - they were chess moves in a game that had been playing out since that snowy night in Vermont.

Now, with the recent events at York Tower threatening to expose everything, he wondered if history was about to repeat itself. Would they once again face the torch and pitchfork, this time in the glare of modern media?

He stared at his daughter and his son. Sarah, still human, still innocent of what her family truly was. James, now transformed, bearing the weight of their supernatural legacy. The Blackwood legacy must be protected, no matter the cost.

But this time, Richard thought as he looked at his children, they wouldn't be running. They'd been running for over two hundred years, always one step ahead of Burton's relentless pursuit. Always moving, always hiding, always looking over their shoulders.

This time, they would make their stand. In New York, in the city they'd helped build, surrounded by the empire they'd created. Burton wanted to finish what he'd started in Manchester?

Then let him come.

The war that had begun with Rachel's death in a Vermont cemetery would finally end. One way or another.

Richard touched the ancient scar on his neck, a reminder of that first encounter with Burton's fury. He'd been running from this fight for centuries. But now, with his children's lives at stake, he was ready to face the monster that had shaped his entire existence.

Some debts, he realized, could only be paid in blood.

And some wars could only end with one side utterly destroyed.

42

UNRAVELING

Will touched his neck where the bite mark pulsed with each heartbeat. The reflection staring back from his bathroom mirror looked like a stranger - gaunt, hollow-eyed, with skin stretched tight over sharp cheekbones. He'd avoided looking at himself for days, but tonight the mirror demanded his attention.

The bite had changed from an angry red to something darker, more ominous. Thin black lines spread outward like spider webs, mapping the progress of whatever poison was coursing through his veins. His grandmother's voice echoed in his memory, stories she'd told about the old country. About bloodlines marked by ancient curses. About debts that followed families across oceans and through generations.

"Some hungers," she'd whispered, "are passed down like family heirlooms. They wait in the blood until the right moment, the right prey comes along."

Will had dismissed those tales as Old World nonsense. But now, with his reflection wavering like a bad television signal, he wondered if his grandmother had been trying to warn him about something real.

The familiar scents of his city had transformed beyond recognition. Hot dogs from the corner vendor now made his gorge rise, while the tang of blood from the butcher's shop a block away called to him like a dinner bell. Each passing day brought new horrors, including a hunger that food couldn't satisfy.

Desperate to feel normal, Will ducked into a nearby deli. He ordered a pastrami sandwich, extra mustard, the kind of comfort food that had gotten him through tough shifts on the beat. But after just one bite, he doubled over, barely making it to the men's room before his stomach rebelled violently.

His phone buzzed. Rufus' name flashed on the screen.

"Where the hell are you?" Rufus' voice was strained. "This place is a madhouse. The media's crawling all over us, residents are freaking out, and I'm drowning here. Get your ass back to work."

Will managed to agree, though the thought of returning to York Tower filled him with equal parts dread and anticipation. Something was calling him back to that building. Something that had nothing to do with his job or his paycheck.

The next thing Will remembered was standing outside apartment 306 again, with no clear recollection of how he'd gotten there. The blackouts were getting worse, longer gaps in his memory that left him disoriented and terrified. What was he doing during those lost hours? And why did he always end up at the same door?

His reflection in the polished brass door number looked like a corpse - skin pale as parchment, eyes sunken deep in their sockets. He was becoming something else, something his grandmother would have recognized from her darkest stories.

Will pounded on the door with what little strength remained in his skeletal frame. His fists hammered against the sturdy wood, the sound echoing through the empty hallway like gunshots.

"I know you're in there!" he shouted, his voice cracking. "What's happening to me? What did you do?"

The door remained stubbornly closed, but Will's enhanced hearing picked up sounds from within. The soft rustle of feathers. The clicking of tiny claws on brass perches. And beneath it all, the satisfied chirps of creatures feeding.

Will pressed his face against the cool brass surface, his supernatural senses straining for any sign of the apartment's occupants. He could smell them now - the metallic scent of fresh blood, the musty odor of captive birds, and underneath it all, something else. Something cold and ancient that made his new predatory instincts recoil.

Exhausted, Will slumped against the door. Whatever was happening to him, he would have to face it alone.

As Will descended the stairwell, each step an effort, the terrible truth settled over him like a funeral shroud. He wasn't just sick. He wasn't just dying. He was becoming something else. Something that would serve whoever had marked him with that bite.

He fumbled for his phone, typing out a message to Rufus with shaking fingers: "Still feeling rough. Taking another sick day. Sorry."

The lie tasted like ash in his mouth, but it was better than the alternative. Better than returning to work and potentially hurting someone he cared about. Because with each passing hour, Will could feel his humanity slipping away like sand through his fingers.

Outside York Tower, Will hailed a cab, but the driver took one look at his emaciated appearance and drove off without stopping. The next one did the same. Finally, a battered yellow taxi pulled over, the driver squinting at him through thick glasses.

"You okay, buddy? You look like death warmed over."

Will managed a weak smile. "Just getting over the flu."

As the city blurred past the window, Will closed his eyes and tried to remember what it felt like to be human. To care about normal things like baseball scores and whether his bills were paid. But those memories felt like they belonged to someone else, someone who'd died the moment that courier's teeth had pierced his skin.

His grandmother's final warning surfaced from the

depths of his memory: "When the hunger comes, child, when it takes hold of your blood, there's only one choice left. Fight it with everything you have, or become the monster."

Will touched the bite mark one last time, feeling the corruption spreading through his veins like poison. The hunt had already begun. The only question was whether he'd retain enough of himself to choose which side he was on when the war finally reached its bloody conclusion.

The cab pulled up to his building, and Will stumbled out, leaving the driver staring after him with worried eyes. As he climbed the stairs to his apartment, Will made a decision that would change everything.

He wouldn't fight this alone. Tomorrow, he would find Detective Melville and tell her everything. About the courier, about the apartment, about what was happening to him. Maybe she could stop whatever was coming. Maybe she could save the people he was no longer sure he could protect.

But tonight, he would lock his door and pray that whatever he was becoming wouldn't hurt anyone while he slept.

Some battles, his grandmother had taught him, were won by knowing when to ask for help.

Even if that help came from someone who might have to destroy you to save everyone else.

43

RELUCTANT ALLIANCE

The vials of blood sat on his kitchen counter, a smoking gun. With a deep breath, he pressed 'call'.

"Melville," came the sleepy answer.

"Detective, it's Will Taylor from York Tower. We need to talk."

There was a pause. "Mr. Taylor, it's after midnight."

Will swallowed hard. "It's about the deaths at York Tower. And... other things. Things I can't explain over the phone."

Melville's voice sharpened. "Where are you now?"

"My apartment. But I can't... I don't want to do this here." Will glanced at his window, half-expecting to see the courier's face peering in.

"Fine. Meet me at the all-night diner on 9th and 53rd in thirty minutes."

The line went dead. Will stared at his phone, then at the vials. He couldn't leave them here, but carrying them around seemed risky. Finally, he wrapped them carefully in a hand towel and tucked them into an inside pocket of his jacket.

The night air bit into Will's skin as he hurried down the street, every shadow seeming to move. The diner's neon sign flickered, casting an eerie glow on the nearly empty sidewalk.

Inside, the harsh fluorescent lights made Will wince. He

spotted Melville in a corner booth, a steaming cup of coffee in front of her. Her eyes widened slightly as she took in his gaunt appearance.

"You look like hell," she said as he slid into the booth.

"Feel like it too," he muttered.

A thin waitress appeared, a lipstick smear marring one slightly crooked tooth. "Coffee?"

Will nodded, though the thought of ingesting anything made his stomach churn.

Once the waitress left, Melville leaned forward. "Start talking."

Will took a deep breath. "It started with the bite," he began, pulling down his collar to reveal the angry mark on his neck. "At first, I thought it was just a mosquito. But then..."

He told her everything - the courier, the mysterious Room 306, his growing aversion to food, the heightened senses. Melville listened without interrupting, her expression unreadable.

"And then there's this," Will finished, carefully placing the wrapped vials on the table. "They were delivered to my apartment tonight."

Melville's eyes narrowed as she examined the vials. "Do you know what's in them?"

Will nodded grimly. "Blood. I'm sure of it."

"How?"

Will hesitated. "I can... smell it. That's part of what I'm trying to tell you, Detective. Something's happening to me. Something I can't explain."

Melville sat back, her fingers steepled. "Normally, I'd say you were crazy. But..." She reached into her bag and pulled out her phone, showing Will a photo. "I saw these at the Met. Notice anything familiar?"

Will leaned in, his eyes widening. The vials in the photo were nearly identical to the ones on the table. "What are they?"

"Blood reliquaries, supposedly from Romania. Over 500 years old." Melville put her phone away. "I've got the lab results on those stoppers we found at York Tower. Traces of degraded blood."

"What are you saying?"

Melville's voice dropped to a near-whisper. "That either we're both going crazy, or there's something going on at York Tower that defies logical explanation."

Will slumped in his seat. "So, you believe me?"

"I believe that you believe it," Melville said carefully. "And I believe that we need to investigate further. Together."

"Together?" Will echoed, surprised.

Melville nodded. "You've got inside access to the building, and... whatever's happening to you might be key to understanding all this. But Taylor, if I find out you're involved in these deaths..."

"I'm not," Will said quickly. "I swear. Detective, I think I'm being turned into a weapon. Against the Blackwoods."

Melville leaned forward. "What do you mean?"

Will touched his neck where the bite mark pulsed. "My grandmother used to tell stories about the old country. About a sea captain named Isaac Burton who lost everything because of love gone wrong. About how he swore revenge against the Blackwood family and has been hunting them for over two hundred years."

"Two hundred years?" Melville's skepticism was clear.

"She said Burton followed the Blackwoods from a place called Manchester, Vermont, all the way to New York. That he was patient as death itself, building his own empire while tracking theirs. Waiting for the right moment to strike." Will's voice dropped. "I think that moment is now. And I think he's using me to get to them."

"You think this Burton is behind the deaths at York Tower?"

"I think Burton is behind everything," Will said. "The courier who bit me works for him. The vials, the mysterious apartment, the targeting of elderly residents - it's all designed to frame the Blackwoods while Burton destroys them from the shadows."

Melville felt a chill that had nothing to do with the night air. "So the Blackwoods aren't the killers?"

"No," Will said. "They're the victims. They've been running from this maniac for centuries, trying to build a normal life while he hunts them like animals.'

"Then we have a deal," Melville said, standing and leaving a few bills on the table. "I'll take those vials. And get some rest. Tomorrow we start hunting the real monster."

As they prepared to part ways, Will caught Melville's arm. "Detective, if I'm right about this, if Burton really has been planning this for centuries, then everyone connected to the Blackwood family is in danger. Including anyone who gets close to the investigation."

"Including you?"

"Especially me," Will said grimly. "I think I'm supposed to be his final weapon against them. The insider who destroys everything they've built."

The street lamps flickered as they parted ways, casting long shadows that seemed to reach out with grasping fingers. In the distance, a lone figure watched silently before melting into the darkness.

As Will made his way home, he couldn't shake the feeling that telling Melville the truth had set something in motion that couldn't be stopped. His grandmother's warnings echoed in his mind: "Some monsters wear the faces of victims while they hunt the innocent."

But for the first time since the nightmare began, Will didn't feel completely alone. Melville believed him, or at least believed that something was terribly wrong. And more importantly, she understood that the Blackwoods weren't the enemy.

44

THE BLACKWOOD CONNECTION

The morning sun did little to dispel the unease that had settled over Will since his late-night meeting with Detective Melville. He squinted against the light as they approached the imposing Blackwood Real Estate Development building.

"Remember," Melville murmured as they entered the sleek lobby, "we're here for a routine follow-up. Nothing more."

Will nodded, trying to ignore the way his heightened senses were overwhelmed by the mix of expensive perfumes and cleaning products. The same receptionist appraised them with indifference.

"Detective Melville and William Taylor to see Richard Blackwood," Melville announced, flashing her badge.

Moments later, they were ushered into Richard Blackwood's opulent office. The man himself rose from behind an expansive desk, his tailored suit a stark contrast to Will's ill-fitting clothes, which were now several sizes too big for him.

"Detective Melville, and Will, now that's a surprise," Blackwood smiled, though Will caught something wary in his eyes. "To what do I owe this visit? Shouldn't you be behind the desk at York Tower, Will?"

Melville took the lead.

"I have some follow-up questions about York Tower, Mr.

Blackwood. And Mr. Taylor is here because of his familiarity with the building."

As Melville began her questions, Will's attention wandered. His gaze swept the room, taking in the family portraits, the leather furnishings. The scent of old paper and antiques was undercut by something that made Will's mouth water despite his revulsion. His eyes were drawn to the crystal decanters behind Blackwood's desk.

He was so distracted that he almost missed the door opening. A woman entered, her resemblance to James unmistakable. Sarah Blackwood, Will remembered her from his original recruitment interview. Richard's daughter.

Sarah hesitated when she saw the visitors, her eyes widening as they landed on Will's emaciated form.

"I'm sorry," she said smoothly, "I didn't realize you had company."

"It's fine, Sarah," Blackwood replied. "Detective Melville and Will were just leaving."

But as Sarah turned to go, she knocked a stack of files from a side table. Papers scattered across the floor, and she immediately bent to gather them.

"I'm so clumsy," she laughed, waving away offers of help. "Please, don't let me interrupt."

Will watched as Sarah efficiently collected the papers, but not before she had slipped an envelope into Melville's open bag. The movement was so swift and subtle that Will wasn't sure he'd really seen it.

As they left the office, Melville's hand brushed her bag, a silent acknowledgment. They waited until they were well clear of the building before ducking into a nearby coffee shop.

"Did you see that?" Will asked in a low voice as they claimed a corner table.

Melville nodded, carefully extracting the envelope from her bag. "Let's see what Ms. Blackwood thought we needed to know."

Property records, contracts, and copies of old wills

emerged from the envelope. As they pored over the papers, a disturbing picture emerged.

"Look at this," Will said, pointing to a series of bequests. "All these elderly residents leaving their fortunes to something called Burton Holdings upon their deaths. And it goes back decades."

Melville frowned, her finger tracing dates and names. "You're right. And most of these are from residents of Blackwood properties, including York Tower. But why would so many people leave their estates to some holding company instead of their families?"

Will's blood ran cold as the pieces clicked together. "Burton Holdings. Isaac Burton. He's been systematically stealing from the Blackwood tenants for decades, making it look like the Blackwoods are the ones profiting from these deaths."

"So the recent deaths might not be isolated incidents," Melville said slowly. "They could be part of a long-standing operation to frame the Blackwood family."

"Think about it," Will continued, his voice urgent. "Burton has been patient, building a case against the Blackwoods one death at a time. Making them look like predators who profit from their tenants' deaths. But really, he's the one who's been killing people and stealing their money."

Melville felt a jolt of understanding. "That's why Sarah slipped us these documents. She's discovered that someone has been parasitically attached to her family's business for decades."

"The Blackwoods are being set up," Will said grimly. "Burton's not just hunting them for revenge - he's systematically destroying their reputation, their business, everything they've built. When this all comes out, they'll be ruined."

They exchanged a look.

"We need to talk to Sarah Blackwood," Melville said. "She knows more than she's letting on. But why did she give us this information? What's her angle?"

"Maybe she's finally figured out that her family is in danger," Will suggested. "That someone's been using their business to commit crimes while making them look guilty."

As they sat in the coffee shop, surrounded by the normal sounds of city life, Will knew they were seeing only the tip of the iceberg.

If Burton had been planning this for centuries, if he'd spent decades building a case against the Blackwoods while committing crimes in their name, then the scope of his revenge was far greater than anyone imagined.

"There's something else," Will said quietly. "If Burton's been doing this for decades, stealing from elderly residents and framing the Blackwoods, then how many people has he killed? How many families have lost their loved ones to his revenge plot?"

Melville's face paled as the full implications hit her. "We're not just looking at a few suspicious deaths. We could be looking at decades of systematic murder, all designed to destroy one family."

The weight of Burton's patient, methodical evil settled over them like a dark cloud. This wasn't just about ancient grudges or supernatural revenge. This was about a monster who had spent centuries perfecting the art of destroying lives while remaining completely invisible.

With growing horror, Will realized that he was supposed to be Burton's final weapon in this war. The insider who would deliver the killing blow to the Blackwood family.

45

TRUE IDENTITY

Will nodded, but the dizziness hit him like a freight train. The once comforting aromas of the coffee shop twisted his stomach into knots. He gripped the table, his knuckles white, fighting to keep himself grounded.

"Taylor?" Melville's voice cut through the haze. "Are you okay?"

He tried responding, but the words caught in his throat. Darkness clawed at his vision, dragging him under.

When he came to, Karl Middleton was standing in the doorway, his usual confident demeanor replaced by something far more urgent. He moved swiftly, his eyes scanning the room like a man expecting trouble.

"We need to talk," Karl said, his voice low. "But not here."

Melville exchanged a wary glance with Will, but she followed as Karl led them outside. The street offered no comfort; the chilly air bit at Will's skin, and the shadows seemed sharper somehow, as if the world itself were on edge.

Karl stopped beneath a flickering streetlamp, turning to face them. His voice dropped to a conspiratorial whisper. "The documents you found? They're proof of something much larger."

"Burton Holdings has been systematically targeting elderly residents in Blackwood properties for decades."

Melville crossed her arms. "Systematically how?"

"They've perfected a method," Karl said, leaning in, "of manipulating elderly tenants into leaving their estates to Burton Holdings. But it's not just manipulation. It's murder, made to look like natural causes."

He pulled out a sheaf of papers from his coat, holding them out to Melville. "Look at the patterns. Multiple residents dying within short periods, always with convenient estate transfers to Burton Holdings. Medical reports, sudden deaths, all tied back to Isaac Burton's operation. It's not coincidence - it's methodical."

Will rubbed his temples, a pounding ache blooming behind his eyes. He tried to focus, but the implications felt too massive, too impossible. "You're suggesting what, exactly?"

Karl's jaw tightened. "It's not just financial exploitation. Burton's been accelerating the process. The high death rates in Blackwood properties aren't accidents - they're deliberate murders designed to frame the Blackwood family."

Melville's tone was sharp, cutting through the growing unease. "You're saying Burton's been killing people for decades?"

Karl nodded grimly. "Murder, yes. But it's more than that. It's a highly organized, multi-generational operation of systematic elder abuse and property acquisition. And York Tower? That's his crown jewel. It's where he's concentrated his efforts for the final phase."

"What about Sarah Blackwood?" Will said, recalling the mysterious envelope slipped into Melville's bag.

Karl hesitated, his expression softening slightly. "She may be trying to expose Burton's infiltration of her family's business. But if that's true, it means she's in as much danger as anyone."

Melville's skepticism sharpened. "You've got a lot of accusations here. You'd better have proof."

Karl reached into his coat and pulled out a USB drive. "Financial records. Medical reports. Death certificates. A money trail that ties it all together. It's all here."

Will's vision blurred momentarily, his head swimming. He steadied himself against the lamppost. "Even if this is true, what does it mean for us?"

Karl's voice was grave. "It means Burton knows you're investigating, and he won't hesitate to silence you. You're both in danger."

Melville's frown deepened, her arms folding tighter. "So let me get this straight. Burton's been running an elaborate elder abuse and murder scheme for decades, framing the Blackwood family, and no one's noticed until now?"

Karl's gaze remained fixed. "Normally, he's careful. But something has changed. He's grown bolder, more urgent. And that's why we have a chance to stop him now."

Will swallowed hard. The weight of Karl's words pressed down on him like a rock. "This is insane. A multi-generational conspiracy? You really expect us to believe this?"

Karl's frustration flared. "I don't care if you believe me. But think about everything that's happened - the deaths, the financial records, the way you've been targeted. None of it is coincidence."

Melville scoffed, but her voice wavered. "What do you think this is, some kind of gothic horror story?"

Karl stepped closer, his voice dropping to a near-whisper. "This isn't about money anymore. Burton's tied to something much older. Something that's been operating for centuries. He's not entirely natural."

Melville tensed, her skepticism wavering. "Older how?"

Karl's eyes darkened. "I've been hunting Burton for years. He's relentless at taking what he wants. They are relentless at taking what they want. Burton wanted you, Will..." He paused. "You're not just sick. You're changing. If we don't stop it, you'll become one of them."

The words hit Will like a hammer. His mouth went dry. "What are you talking about?"

Karl's gaze bore into him. "You've felt it, haven't you? The hunger? The sensitivity to everything around you? The changes in your body. Burton did this to you. And if we don't act fast, it'll be too late."

Melville shook her head, but her confidence faltered. "This is insane."

Karl's expression hardened. "You want proof? Fine. Come with me to York Tower. I'll show you what's hiding in plain sight."

Will hesitated, glancing at Melville. Her skepticism was warring with the flicker of doubt in her eyes.

"I don't trust him," she said. "But there's a kernel of truth in what he says, I'm sure of it. And we can't ignore that."

Will took a deep breath. He turned to Karl, his voice steady despite the tremor in his hands. "Show us."

Karl's grim smile returned. "You're not going to like what you find. But it's the only way you'll believe me." He glanced toward the looming silhouette of York Tower in the distance. "Are you ready to see the truth?"

As they walked toward the building, Karl began to explain what his grandfather had told him about Manchester, Vermont. About how Isaac Burton had been a sea captain who'd lost his wife Rachel to Richard Blackwood. About how Burton's grief had twisted into something monstrous, driving him to hunt the Blackwood family across centuries.

"Burton doesn't just want revenge," Karl said as they approached York Tower. "He wants to prove that love can't survive what we become. That the Blackwoods' happiness was built on his suffering. This whole operation, all these deaths, it's not just about money or property. It's about destroying everything the Blackwoods have built together."

"You're talking about a man who's been alive for over two hundred years," Melville said, her skepticism returning.

"I'm talking about something that used to be a man," Karl corrected. "Something that's spent centuries perfecting the art of revenge. And now he's finally ready to end it."

Whatever the truth was, whatever Karl was about to show them, Will knew there was no turning back.

46

SOUVENIRS

Will, Iona, and Karl hurried through the lobby of York Tower, barely sparing a glance at Rufus. The security guard rose from his desk, his face twisting in confusion and anger.

"Hey! Where the hell have you been?" Rufus called after them. "What's going on?"

Will didn't stop. He couldn't. The words burned on his tongue, unspoken, as he led the group to the elevators. "Stay downstairs, Rufus," he barked, cutting through the man's protests without looking back.

Behind him, Iona cast a fleeting glance over her shoulder. "Shouldn't we tell him something?" she whispered.

Karl answered instead. "No. He's safer not knowing."

The elevator door opened and they stepped inside, the silence between them growing heavier as they ascended to the third floor.

The hallway outside apartment 306 was eerily quiet, the dull hum of fluorescent lights casting long shadows across the floor. Will led the way, gripping the master key in his hand. Behind him, Iona pulled her shirt up over her nose, the stench of death thick in the air.

"I can't believe I'm doing this. I should have called this in," she muttered, her voice muffled through the fabric.

Karl, walking calmly behind them, seemed unaffected

by the stench. "You get used to it," he said in response to Will's stare.

Used to it? The strangest part was that the stench didn't bother Will. Not like it did Iona. He could smell it - the decay, the rot - but it wasn't repulsive. It smelled like dinner.

He shook off the thought, focusing instead on the door ahead. He could hear Rufus' voice crackling over his earpiece, but he cut him off with a terse command.

"Stay out of this, Rufus. Stay downstairs. I'll handle it."

Rufus' protest died in the static, and Will unlocked the door.

The three of them stepped into the dimly lit room. The first thing that hit them was the oppressive stillness, followed quickly by the overwhelming scent of blood. The air was thick with it. The curtains were drawn, casting the room in heavy shadows, but even in the gloom, they could see the outline of a bed in the corner.

There, shackled to the bed frame, was Tom Forrester.

Will's breath caught in his throat as he recognized the man - though recognize felt like a stretch. Tom, who had once been a vibrant, lean figure always dressed in sleek cycling gear, was now a hollowed husk. His skin was gray, ashen, and tight against his bones. His once-fit body was withered, like it had been drained of life itself. His business shirt, now stained with dark patches of dried blood, clung to his sunken frame.

"What the hell...," Iona whispered, lowering her shirt in disbelief. She moved cautiously toward the bed, but Karl stopped her with a firm hand on her arm.

"Don't get too close," he warned, his voice low. "He's barely alive, but that doesn't mean he's harmless."

Tom's chest rose and fell in shallow, ragged breaths, and his eyes, half-lidded and dull, flickered with the faintest glimmer of consciousness. Will knelt beside him, staring at the man who had once been so full of energy, always talking about his next triathlon or cycling event. Now, Tom's life hung by a thread.

"What happened to him?" Will asked, though he already knew the answer.

Karl stepped forward, his gaze hardening. "This is what Burton does. He drains them slowly, keeps them alive just long enough to feed, then tosses them aside when they're no longer useful."

"Jesus Christ..." Iona breathed, taking a step back, the weight of the situation finally sinking in.

"He doesn't feed every night, just enough to keep his victims on the brink."

Will felt a surge of rage building in his chest. He had known Tom, passed him in the halls, shared casual conversations about cycling routes and the *Tour de France*. Tom had just been another tenant at York Tower, going about his life. And now this.

"We have to get him out of here," Will said, his voice tight with anger.

Karl shook his head. "It's too late for him. He's too far gone."

"What the hell do you mean, 'too late'?" Will snapped, his voice rising. "He's still breathing, isn't he?"

Karl's face remained impassive. "That's not living. He's already his. Even if we took him out of here, the damage is done. He won't recover."

"There has to be something we can do," Will said, his voice cracking.

Karl met his gaze. "The only thing we can do is stop Burton. If we don't, more people will end up like him."

Will glanced down at Tom again, taking in the papery, gray skin marked by the puncture wounds. He believed Karl, but none of the other dead tenants had been found like this. Apart from Marion Bruce. But even her death was nothing like what was being done to Forrester.

"How many more are there?" Will asked, barely above a whisper.

Karl's voice was low, grim. "In this building?"

Will felt the air sucked out of his lungs.

Then Karl gestured toward a nearby shelf, one that at first glance seemed unremarkable.

Will knew, with absolute certainty, even as he stepped closer to look, that he recognized everything on display. They were all items belonging to the dead residents of York Tower.

Will's fingers hovered over a delicate sterling silver pen, its weight unmistakable. It had belonged to Marion Bruce. He remembered how Marion used the pen to sign for her book deliveries, of which there were many. She'd explained to him once that the pen had been a gift from her favorite store, The Strand, to thank her for her loyalty.

Next was a small architectural sketchbook, with gold embossed initials on the bottom right-hand corner - J.M. - Jacob Marsden. He'd once shown it to Will in the lobby, on his way back from delivering a lecture at Columbia University. Will's hand hovered over the cover, his mind replaying their last conversation, a lighthearted argument about who would win the World Series that year.

Then there was a pair of tiny, well-worn ballet slippers. Eleanor Lowenstein kept them on display under a glass dome in her apartment, a relic from her days at Juilliard.

A miniature model ship caught Will's eye next. That obviously belonged to Robert Chang. No one examining his collection would ever have missed one model, not from the hundreds that decorated the man's apartment.

And then there was Elgar Dunblane's pipe. A vintage pipe that was never far from Dunblane's puckered mouth, but always unlit. Will and Rufus had joked about it being more an affectation than an addiction to tobacco.

Will's breath caught. "So, Mr. Chang, Mr. Dunblane, Mr. Marsden, Mrs. Lowenstein, and Mrs. Bruce," he murmured, piecing it together.

Karl's expression darkened. "They were all targets. This isn't just about feeding. It's about dominating the building."

"They never stood a chance." Will whispered.

But it was more than just trophies, Will realized. This was Burton's way of claiming victory over the Blackwood family. Each item represented not just a life taken, but a strike against everything the Blackwoods had built. Their tenants, their reputation, their legacy - all of it being systematically destroyed.

"Burton's been collecting proof," Will said, understanding dawning. "Not just killing people, but gathering evidence to frame the Blackwoods. Making it look like they're the ones profiting from these deaths."

Karl nodded grimly. "He's spent decades building a case against them. When this all comes out, when these trophies are discovered, it'll destroy the Blackwood family completely."

The lights flickered and died, plunging the room into darkness. The hum of the building's electricity cut out, leaving them in eerie silence.

Karl's voice cut through the darkness, tense and urgent. "We need to move. Now."

But before they could react, Will let out a strangled gasp. In the dim light from Iona's phone, they could see him doubled over, clutching his stomach.

"Will?" Iona stepped toward him.

Karl's hand gripped her arm. "Wait," he said, but it was too late.

Will's head snapped up, his eyes wild and unfocused. In the shadows, they gleamed with an unnatural light. A low growl escaped his throat as he straightened up, his gaze fixed on Iona.

"Oh God," Iona breathed, taking a step back. "Will?"

Will lunged at her, his teeth bared.

Iona gasped.

Karl grabbed Will from behind and they struggled, Karl's strength only just enough to hold Will back as Iona stumbled away.

"Will, stop!" Karl forced him to the ground. "This isn't you!"

Will thrashed violently, but Karl's grip held firm. Then, as quickly as it had started, Will stopped. His body sagged against Karl's.

"I'm... I'm sorry," Will gasped, his voice cracking with desperation. "This isn't me."

Karl's grip loosened against his body. "We know, Will. We know."

The room fell silent except for the sound of Tom Forrester's labored breathing. In the darkness, surrounded by the trophies of Burton's decades-long campaign of revenge, they finally understood the true scope of what they were facing.

This wasn't just about a few mysterious deaths. It was about a monster who had spent over two centuries perfecting the art of destroying everything the Blackwood family held dear.

And Will Taylor was supposed to be his masterpiece - the final weapon in a war that had begun with love and betrayal in a small Vermont town.

But Burton had made one mistake. He'd underestimated the power of human connection, the bonds that could survive even supernatural corruption.

Will wasn't just Burton's weapon anymore. He was their best chance of stopping the monster once and for all.

The question was whether he could hold onto enough of his humanity to see it through.

47

THE PRICE OF POWER

Matthew Peart hadn't always been a man consumed by the shadows of York Tower and its enigmatic residents. Once, he'd dreamed of becoming something more.

As he sat there, swirling his expensive scotch in a Waterford crystal tumbler, he was reminded of a very similar night fifteen years ago when everything changed.

December 23, 2009. The Blackwood Group's annual Christmas party.

He could still smell the pine garlands and mulled wine, still hear Sinatra crooning through hidden speakers. The boardroom had looked magical, with Manhattan's lights spread out below like scattered diamonds. He'd spent weeks rehearsing what he'd say to Sarah, planned every detail down to the Jean-Georges reservation.

"You're like a brother to me, Matthew." Her laugh had sliced through his carefully rehearsed words, not cruel but light, dismissive - as though his feelings were a harmless child's folly, something to be brushed aside with a smile. *Brother.* She'd relegated him to a corner he couldn't escape.

He'd fled the party, wandering through the winter streets until reaching the bar of the St. Regis.

The St. Regis' old King Cole Bar, where the wealthy and powerful had been drowning their sorrows for a century.

He'd ordered a scotch that night - the most expensive on the menu, because wasn't that what successful men did?

"An excellent choice."

The voice beside him was cultured, precise. A man sat there - tall, elegant in an old-fashioned way. His suit reminded Peart of the portrait of Alexander Hamilton by John Trumbull, in the Metropolitan Museum of Art. In that portrait, Hamilton's suit was a masterful composition of dark, finely tailored wool, the sharp lapels framing a crisp white cravat, while a pale waistcoat lent a touch of understated elegance to the somber attire - a fitting uniform for a man who carried the weight of a nation's future on his shoulders. This stranger seemed to emulate Hamilton's attire with absolute precision.

"I saw what happened." The stranger's accent was impossible to place. "With Ms. Blackwood."

Peart's face burned. "I don't know what you're talking about."

"The Blackwoods have always been cruel that way. So caught up in their own importance, they forget others might have... aspirations."

"Who are you?"

"Someone who recognizes potential. Real potential, not the kind they measure in family names and trust funds." The man studied his own drink. "Tell me, Mr. Peart, how long have you worked for them? Handling their special cases, their discreet arrangements?"

Peart swallowed hard. "What do you mean?"

"The elderly residents who die so conveniently. You're not blind, Mr. Peart. You've seen the patterns."

"How do you-"

"I can offer you power. Real power. Not just signing documents and following orders. The kind of power that would make Sarah Blackwood see you in quite a different light."

"Who are you?"

The stranger's smile was gentle, fatherly. "My name is Isaac Burton. And I believe we can help each other."

Matthew stared at the man, the offer of power hovering like a whispered promise. For a moment, he thought of the boy he'd been - idealistic, determined, naive. But that boy hadn't survived his father's expectations, Sarah's laugh or the Blackwoods' indifference. He raised his glass, his voice steady. "What do I have to do?"

Outside the bar's windows, snow fell on Manhattan. And in that quiet corner of the King Cole Bar, Matthew Peart made a choice that would change everything.

But Burton hadn't told him the whole truth that night. Hadn't explained that the power he offered came with a price. That serving Isaac Burton meant becoming complicit in something far darker than corporate espionage or financial manipulation.

Burton had told him stories that night, as the snow fell and the scotch flowed. Stories about Old World justice and New World opportunities. About a family that had stolen what rightfully belonged to others. About how the Blackwoods had built their empire on betrayal and blood.

"They took everything from me," Burton had said, his voice carrying the weight of centuries. "My wife's love. My future. My very soul. And in return, they've lived in luxury while I've wandered the earth seeking justice."

Peart had listened, mesmerized by the man's passion, his eloquence, his obvious pain. Burton painted a picture of the Blackwood family as monsters hiding behind a veneer of respectability. Creatures who fed on the weak and vulnerable while maintaining their facade of wealthy philanthropy.

"But you," Burton had said, his eyes gleaming in the dim light, "you could be the instrument of their downfall. You have access. You could expose them for what they really are."

Now, fifteen years later, Peart drained his scotch, thinking of Marion Bruce's recent death. Another "heart attack" to add to his files. Outside his window, York Tower's ravens gathered. Soon, Burton's promises would be fulfilled. Soon, Sarah would understand what real power looked like.

But as Peart sat in his expensive apartment, surrounded by the fruits of his collaboration with Burton, he couldn't shake a growing unease. The deaths were coming faster now, more violent. Tom Forrester's disappearance had been particularly brutal. And the way Burton looked at him lately, as if Peart were just another piece to be moved around the board...

He pushed the thought away. Burton needed him. Without Peart's legal expertise, his access to the Blackwood files, the whole operation would collapse. He was indispensable.

Wasn't he?

Outside his window, a raven landed on the fire escape, its black eyes seeming to stare directly at him. For a moment, Peart felt like the bird could see straight through him, could see all his secrets and schemes and petty jealousies.

Then the raven cawed once and flew away, leaving Peart alone with his expensive scotch and his expensive apartment and the growing certainty that he'd made a deal with something far more dangerous than he'd ever imagined.

But it was too late to back out now. Burton's plan was in motion, and Matthew Peart was committed to seeing it through to its bloody conclusion.

Even if that conclusion might include his own destruction.

After all, Burton had never promised that Matthew would survive to see the Blackwood family's downfall.

Just that he would be instrumental in causing it.

And she would never laugh at him again.

48

RACE AGAINST TIME

Rufus stood behind the security desk, glaring at the radio in his hand. Will had just cut him off - again. For weeks, his old friend had been distant, shutting him out of whatever mess he was tangled up in. They'd faced down some of the toughest criminals in the city - and some of the dumbest, but they'd always done it together. Now, whatever Will was up to, he'd dismissed Rufus like he was some rookie guard, not his long-time partner. That wasn't right, and Rufus was well and truly steamed.

It was bad enough that Will had canceled their golf days. Rufus had shrugged it off at first, figuring Will was just under the weather. But now, seeing the way he was wasting away, looking sick as a dog, and still refusing help - it was infuriating. What was so damned important that Will couldn't just ask for a hand? Even worse, Will seemed to be spending more time with that detective. Rufus could damn well see there was something going on between them. Maybe not an affair, but who the hell knew?

The thought twisted in Rufus' gut. An affair in the empty apartments?

Rufus gripped the desk's edge until his knuckles whitened. He'd tried to confront Will about it earlier, but all he got was a brush-off. Will had never been one for secrecy, so why now? Rufus had half a mind to march up there and demand answers.

But like a bad rash, Peart reappeared, his nose wrinkling like he'd stepped into a garbage heap. "Rufus, are you going to do something about that stench, or just stand there glaring at the walls?"

Rufus barely held back an eye-roll. "What smell?"

"The third floor - again! It's unbearable. I'm trying to live in a civilized building, not some cheap motel. I can't even sleep."

Before Rufus could snap back, Mrs. Johnson shuffled into the lobby, her frail frame barely upright. She looked awful - worse than usual. Her skin had a waxy sheen, and her movements were slow, almost mechanical. Rufus' anger faltered. She was a widow, living alone since her daughter had abandoned her to move to Idaho - the country's Potato Capital.

"Mrs. Johnson, can I help?" Rufus asked, stepping around the desk.

Mrs. Johnson gave a weak smile. "Are there any packages for me?"

Packages? The woman was a shopping powerhouse, but she didn't order stuff online, not like the rest of the residents. "No, there's nothing. Look, we got a call from your daughter. She's on her way back from Boise. She's been worried about you not answering your phone."

"My daughter? Yes... that's right. My phone hasn't rung," Mrs. Johnson murmured, though something in her voice sounded off. "Perhaps you could check it?"

"Of course. I should wait until Will gets back to reception."

"Mr. Peart can be trusted," she suggested. "My daughter's call..."

And Rufus didn't have a comeback.

"Please, I miss young Sally."

Rufus held out his arm and flinched as she latched on with a strength he hadn't expected. Her grandmother's stories came flooding back - tales from the old country about creatures that grew stronger as they fed. About how the recently turned were often the most dangerous because they hadn't learned to control their new abilities.

She leaned on him as they headed toward the elevator. But there was something about her that made the hairs on Rufus' neck prickle. Something that reminded him of the stories his own grandmother had told about Old World monsters that followed families to America.

Peart, standing a few feet away, looked impatient. "Look, I'm happy to look after things here, but..."

Rufus shot him a glare, but before he could respond, the elevator doors slid open. He helped Mrs. Johnson inside, making sure she was steady against the burnished rail that ran around the three walls.

"I'll be back in a second. Just rest in there, okay?" he said, stepping out of the box, realizing he'd left his master key at the desk.

At that moment, the lights flickered as another electrical surge raced through the building. The elevator doors slid shut with a muffled clang, and the lobby was thrown into darkness. For a heartbeat, everything was silent. The usual hum of the building's machinery cut off. Rufus' heart pounded in his chest.

Peart's panicked voice cut through the gloom. "Rufus! What's happening?"

Rufus' eyes struggled to adjust to the dimness, and he fumbled for his flashlight on the desk. He found it, the beam cutting a narrow swath through the blackness. He swung it toward the elevator, but all he could see was the shadowy outline of the closed doors.

An eerie wail from the elevator seemed to reverberate through the building, echoing off the walls. Rufus took a hesitant step toward the elevator, the beam of his flashlight trembling. Somewhere in the bowels of the building, the hum of the backup generator kicking in joined the screams from the elevator. The emergency lights flickered to life, casting an eerie, low-level illumination over the lobby.

"Mrs. Johnson!" Rufus called out, his voice cracking. He

moved toward the elevator, but the emergency lights were barely enough to show his own feet. He could hear Peart muttering about the situation, but Rufus' focus was on the elevator.

A loud crash came from within the elevator. Rufus jumped, his flashlight swinging.

Rufus jabbed at his radio, his voice tight with urgency, "Will, come in! I need you here right now - Mrs. Johnson's stuck in the elevator, and I need your help."

Peart's voice was almost hysterical. "Do something! Get her out of there. The building's falling apart!"

"Shut up!" Rufus snapped, trying to keep his own nerves in check. "I'm thinking."

He tried to pry open the elevator doors, but they were stuck. The sound of frantic scratching and muffled thuds from inside the elevator only added to his growing fear. Rufus grunted with effort, trying to wedge his fingers into the gap, but the doors wouldn't budge.

"Hold on, Mrs. Johnson!" Rufus yelled, pressing his ear against the door, hoping to hear any sign of her. "For crying out loud, Peart, come and give me a hand, will you?"

Then the elevator jolted, and together Rufus and Peart pushed at the ancient doors. The doors creaked open enough for Rufus to shine his torch through the gap.

"Hold on, Mrs. Johnson, we've almost got you out," Rufus said.

But inside, the elevator was empty.

The metallic scent of blood hung in the air, mixed with something else - something that reminded Rufus of his grandmother's warnings about creatures that could disappear at will. About how the newly turned were often the most unpredictable, driven by hungers they didn't understand.

"Where is she?" Peart whispered, his earlier bravado gone.

Rufus shined his flashlight around the elevator car, looking for any sign of Mrs. Johnson. The walls were scratched, as if something with claws had been trying to get out. Or in. Dark stains marked the elevator floor, too dark to be anything innocent.

"She couldn't have just vanished," Rufus said, but even as he spoke the words, he knew they weren't true. True monsters could do exactly that.

The power flickered back on, and the normal hum of the building resumed. But normalcy felt like a lie now. Something had happened in that elevator, something that defied explanation.

"We need to call the police," Peart said, his voice shaking.

"And tell them what?" Rufus asked. "That a sweet old lady disappeared from a stuck elevator? They'll think we're crazy."

But as they stood there in the restored light of the lobby, both men knew that crazy was starting to seem like the most reasonable explanation for what was happening at York Tower.

Mrs. Johnson was gone.

Something told Rufus she hadn't gone far.

And he was about to discover that sometimes monsters wore the faces of people you trusted most.

49

SHADOWS IN THE STAIRWELL

Rufus stared into the empty elevator, his mind reeling. He fumbled for his radio, his fingers clumsy with terror.

"Will! What the hell is going on? Where are you?" He barked into the device. "Get down here now, damn it!"

The radio crackled, emitting a high-pitched tone that made Rufus wince. No response came through the static.

"Screw this," Rufus muttered, clipping the radio back onto his belt. He turned to Peart, hovering nearby, his face pale as moonlight.

"Stay here," Rufus ordered. "Mrs. Johnson has to be on another floor. The elevator must have gone up or down."

As Rufus moved toward the stairwell, he hesitated. Find Mrs. Johnson or Will? The choice tore at him, but in the end, friendship won out. Will not answering the radio might mean he's in trouble, and Rufus wasn't about to let his partner down.

Inside the stairwell, Rufus went up first. He'd only descend to the parking garage after he'd checked all the other floors. That place gave him the creeps, especially after finding Tom's bike abandoned there.

As Rufus began his ascent, the emergency lights flickered, casting writhing shadows on the walls like something alive.

Each step echoed in the confined space, the sound bouncing back at him from the darkness above.

He made it to the first floor and stepped out into the empty foyer. "Will?" Rufus yelled out, his voice bouncing back. "Mrs. Johnson?"

A couple of doors opened, and faces lit with cellphone torches peered out. "What's going on?" a disembodied voice asked.

"The power's gone out, nothing to worry about, just trying to get maintenance out to fix it," Rufus blathered. "Have you seen Will?"

A chorus of "no's" followed by the closing of doors and the clicking of locks.

Rufus returned to the stairwell, the light from his own torch dimming ever so slightly. As he grabbed the flashlight, he remembered that it needed new batteries. Why hadn't he replaced them the last time the electricity played up?

Somewhere below him, a door opened and closed.

Rufus paused, straining to hear. "Hello?" he called again. "Peart?"

No response came, but he could have sworn he heard footsteps, slow and deliberate, beginning to climb.

The air in the stairwell grew colder with each step Rufus climbed. His breath came out in visible puffs, despite the temperature outside, making each step harder than the last.

"Will!" he shouted again, desperation creeping into his voice. "Mrs. Johnson! Anyone?"

As Rufus reached the fire door for the second floor, he paused. This was Mrs. Johnson's floor. Maybe she had somehow made it back to her apartment? He pushed open the stairwell door.

The hallway was dark, save for the emergency lights. Rufus' flashlight barely pushed through the gloom as he made his way toward Mrs. Johnson's apartment. Her door stood ajar.

"Mrs. Johnson?" he called out, pushing the door open. The beam of his flashlight swept across the living room, revealing an eerily still and silent space.

The furniture stood undisturbed. What caught Rufus' attention was the unusual emptiness of the room. No signs of life, no personal touches that usually marked Mrs. Johnson's presence.

His eyes were drawn to a dark, viscous trail leading from the living room to the bedroom. His police instincts bristled at the sight, but he pushed away the alarming thoughts it evoked. It couldn't be what he feared. Not here. Not Mrs. Johnson.

With trembling hands, Rufus followed the trail, his flashlight beam dancing erratically as he moved. The bedroom door was closed. He reached out, his hand hovering over the doorknob. Did he really want to see what was on the other side?

A sudden noise from the living room made him whirl around.

"Who's there?" Rufus called out, his voice cracking.

Silence was his only answer.

Rufus backed away from the bedroom door, his heart pounding. Whatever was going on in there, he didn't want to face it on his own, regardless of the fact that the woman was in her 80s.

He hurried back to the stairwell, and as he yanked open the stairwell door, he could have sworn he heard a soft chuckle coming from Mrs. Johnson's apartment.

As he rounded the landing between the second and third floors, Rufus collided with a figure coming down. He let out a startled yelp, stumbling backwards.

"Mrs. Pike?" he gasped, recognizing the woman.

Mrs. Pike stood there, swaying. Her usually immaculate appearance was disheveled, her hair wild and her eyes unfocused. An unnatural grin split her face.

"Oh, Rufus," she giggled, the sound setting Rufus' teeth on edge. "Isn't this wonderful? I wish the whole city was like this. I'm going outside to check."

"Where are your children?" Rufus asked, dread settling in his stomach like a stone.

She laughed again, poking him hard in the softness of

his gut. "They're upstairs, sleeping. It's so much easier when they're asleep."

Before Rufus could stop her, she slipped past him, continuing down the stairs. Her movements were too fluid, too graceful for someone who should be panicked by the power outage.

"Wait!" Rufus called after her, but she was already gone, her laughter fading.

Then he heard it - her voice, drifting up from below. She seemed to be talking to someone, her tone sickeningly sweet.

"Hello, darling," her voice crooned. "Isn't it exciting?"

Rufus strained to hear the response, but could only make out a low murmur. If that was Peart she was talking to, he'd be furious. The guy was meant to be manning the front desk.

The stairwell felt smaller and the shadows deeper. Rufus' heart pounded as he forced himself to keep climbing. He really needed to lose weight, although not as much as Will. He'd gone too far. The footsteps behind him seemed closer now, matching his pace.

"Will, is that you?" he called out again, his voice cracking. "This isn't funny anymore, buddy."

The emergency lights flickered once, twice, then went out completely. And then his flashlight failed, plunging him into total darkness. He could hear his own ragged breathing, and then the soft scrape of shoe leather behind him.

"Will? Reply damn you! Will!" Still no answer.

He spun around, his eyes wide. "Who's there?" he demanded, trying to keep the fear out of his voice, his finger still pressing down on the radio's talk button.

A cold breath touched the back of his neck, carrying with it the scent of old earth and older hungers. His grandmother's stories flooded back - warnings about creatures that hunted in the dark, that fed on fear and blood and the trust of those who loved them.

Rufus' flashlight beam cut through the darkness of the

third floor hallway. Every shadow seemed wrong somehow, twisted. The backup generators should have kicked in by now.

"Mrs. Johnson?" he called out. "June?"

His radio crackled. Static.

"Will? You there?" More static.

The beam of his flashlight caught movement at the end of the hallway. A familiar figure stood there, illuminated in the harsh light.

"Sally?"

She turned, and for a moment, Rufus felt that familiar flutter in his stomach. The same feeling he'd had every time he'd seen her over the past nine months.

"Sally?" Rufus called again, moving cautiously forward. "What are you doing here? You should have told me you were coming—"

"Have you seen my mother?" Her voice trembled.

Rufus felt his chest tighten. They'd just been texting for weeks about a coffee date he'd finally got the guts to ask her about. A coffee date he hadn't yet found the guts to tell Will about...

"Sally, listen to me," Rufus said, moving closer. "Something's going on in the building. You need to get out—"

A shadow detached itself from the darkness behind Sally. Rufus' flashlight beam caught June Johnson's face, but it wasn't the face he remembered from Sunday's cheerful goodbye. Her eyes were wrong, her mouth twisted into something inhuman.

"Mom?" Sally turned, and Rufus saw the moment of recognition turn to horror on her face. "Mom, what's going on?"

"Sally, get behind me!" Rufus lunged forward, but June moved with impossible speed.

The flashlight clattered to the floor, spinning wildly, its beam turning the hallway into a nightmare carousel of light and shadow. Each flash revealing a fresh horror - June's face twisting into something inhuman; her fingers curving into claws; her mouth stretched too wide; her teeth gleaming unnaturally sharp.

"Mom, please!" Sally's voice cracked with desperation. "It's me!"

In the dancing beam of light, Rufus caught a glimpse of June's eyes. For a fraction of a second, he saw something there -- a flicker of recognition, perhaps even horror at what she had become. But it vanished as quickly as it appeared, replaced by an emptiness that was worse than any monster's malice. This wasn't just June's body transformed; it was the complete extinction of decades of maternal love, replaced by pure, primal hunger.

The next flash caught Sally's face, showing the absolute devastation there as she watched the woman who had raised her, transform into something from a nightmare.

Tears streamed down her cheeks, but her eyes remained fixed on her mother's face, searching desperately for any sign of the woman she knew.

"June!" Rufus shouted, drawing her attention. "This isn't you!"

But the thing that had been June Johnson responded with a sound no human throat could make - a hiss that seemed to echo from the depths of a grave. She moved like a spider, her joints bending in ways that made Rufus' stomach lurch. The flashlight's beam caught her moving across the wall, defying gravity, her head twisted completely backward to keep her eyes fixed on her daughter.

"Run!" he shouted at Sally. "Get out of the building! Now!"

The spinning light caught Sally's hesitation, although this - whatever it was - was not her mother. Then Mrs. Johnson launched herself forward with explosive force. Rufus barely managed to intercept her, feeling muscle and sinew far stronger than the woman's tiny frame should have contained. This wasn't just inhuman strength. It was the complete abandonment of any restraint a mother might show toward her child, severing of the most fundamental of bonds.

He could feel June's claws raking at him as he held her back, listening to the sound of Sally's footsteps finally retreating. The flashlight's beam had slowed its spin, offering longer glimpses of June's transformation. Her skin had taken on a corpse-like pallor, her veins dark and prominent. But it was her expression that truly haunted him - a complete absence of the warmth, the kindness, the fundamental June-ness that had defined her. The woman who had spent Sunday afternoons dancing the tango in the park, who brought cookies to the security desk during the holidays, who beamed with pride whenever she spoke of her daughter - she was gone, leaving only this hollow vessel of violence.

As his strength wavered, a lifetime of memories crowded in -- his dad teaching him how to track deer, his first days on the force, and finally, long calls with Sally and her descriptions of Idaho sunrises.

He'd never told Will that he was tired of the city, tired of the concrete and noise, ready for a change. That Sally had awakened something in him he thought he'd lost when his dad died.

That sometimes the bravest thing you can do is admit you need something different...

June uttered one inhuman snarl of frustration as she twisted from his weakening grip. The snarl was followed by a sharp pain deep in his neck. Rufus' last thoughts were of endless country vistas, of coffee dates that would never happen, and of Will - his best friend, always by his side. Brothers from another mother.

Then the darkness took him, and the retired cop who loved hotdogs with mustard, and baseball on the big screen, cold beers and golf, was gone. Replaced by something else. Something which hungered for one thing, and one thing only. Blood.

Outside of York Tower, in the blackest of nights, a single raven's cry shattered the city.

A cry of triumph.

50

GRIEF

"Did you hear that?" Will asked, his breath coming in gasps.

Iona and Karl stared at him.

"Rufus? Can you hear me?"

Nothing.

"Rufus, stop screwing around and answer the radio."

"It's too late," said Karl, his voice tense.

"Like hell it is!" Will said. "Rufus?" He searched the building for a familiar voice, his senses stretched to their limit, but there was none.

The only response on the radio was static, with an absolute absence of human noise.

"Where is he?" Will stared at Karl, expecting him to answer.

"He's gone. I could hear... You soon learn what it sounds like," Karl replied, his face grim.

"It?" Iona asked, her brow furrowed.

Karl shook his head. "The sound death makes when it's not natural. When something ancient claims what it believes it's owed."

"We have to find him," Will insisted, pushing himself up from the chair he'd been slumped in.

Karl moved to block the door of apartment 306. "Will, I'm telling you, it's too late."

"Our priority is stopping Burton before he completes his

revenge. We need to leave. Now," Karl said, his tone brooking no argument. "The longer we stay here, the more danger we're in."

Will stumbled, his legs barely supporting him. As he steadied himself against the shelf, he spotted Marion Bruce's sterling silver pen. Without thinking, he pocketed it, a small piece of normalcy in this nightmare.

"We can't leave without Rufus," Will said.

Iona moved to support Will. "I agree. We need to find him first."

Karl's frustration was palpable. "You don't understand. Every second we stay here—"

"We're not leaving him," Iona cut him off, her tone final.

Karl looked between them, then sighed. "Fine. But we do this quick, and at the first sign of trouble, we're out. Got it?"

Will nodded and tried ignoring the pulse in Iona's neck as she and Karl moved to either side of him, supporting his weight as they made their way out of the apartment.

The foyer and opposite hallway yawned before them, a maw of inky blackness that swallowed their meager cell phone lights. With an unspoken mutual agreement, they made their way to the stairwell, avoiding the open doors of the elevators.

The walls of the narrow stairwell pressed in on them. Shadows danced at the edge of their vision, teasing and taunting. More than once, Iona swore she saw something move behind them, only to find nothing when she flashed her light toward the inky blackness.

As they finally reached the lobby, a figure loomed out of the darkness, brandishing what looked like a weapon.

"Stop right there. I'm armed." The voice was high-pitched, edged with hysteria.

"Peart?" Will's voice was a hoarse rasp, barely recognizable.

The figure lowered its weapon slightly, revealing Peart's sweat-slicked face, his eyes wide with relief. "Oh, thank Christ," he breathed. With his knuckles still white around the fire extinguisher, he continued, "I thought... I thought you were one of them."

"One of what?" Karl demanded, his tone sharp.

Peart's eyes darted around the lobby, as if expecting something to leap out of the shadows at any moment. "The... homeless. The woman who attacked me. She must have snuck into the building somehow."

Peart missed the look of judgment on Karl's face as he continued to complain. "You should have seen her. She must have been high on something. Drugs, like angel dust."

"What is this? Studio 54?" Iona said, her mouth tight. "That hasn't been a thing since the 70s."

As they got closer, Karl noticed a smear of blood on Peart's cheek. "You're bleeding," he said, taking a step backwards.

Peart touched his cheek, looking at the red smear on his fingers with surprise. "It's not mine," he said, his voice shaky. "It's hers. I swiped at the crazy woman with the sign-in folder before I grabbed this," he gestured with the extinguisher.

Karl's eyes narrowed, scanning the lobby. "We need to move. Now."

"But Rufus—" Will started.

"Is not here," Karl finished firmly. "And we won't be either if we don't leave right now."

"What about me? That woman could come back at any time," Peart whined.

"We need to get out. Now," Karl hissed, ignoring Peart, his eyes scanning the surrounding darkness.

As they moved toward the exit, Will cast one last, anguished look back into the building's depths. "Rufus," he whispered, his voice breaking. "I'm sorry."

The group stumbled into The Night Owl Cafe and Will collapsed into a booth, his face ashen. Iona slid in next to him, while Karl and Peart took the opposite bench.

After ordering coffees, an uncomfortable silence fell over the table. Iona, seizing the opportunity, turned to Peart.

"Mr. Peart, you've been handling the Blackwoods' real

estate for some time now, right? What can you tell us about York Tower's ownership?"

Peart looked uncertain. "I... I don't know. After what happened tonight..." He shuddered. "Look, I think I'm going to stay at a colleague's house tonight. I hope that by the time I return to the building, additional security measures will be in place." He stood up abruptly. "I can't discuss this anymore right now. I need some time to process everything."

As Peart left, the remaining trio sat in tense silence. Will's condition was visibly deteriorating, his skin taking on a sickly pallor.

Karl reached into his pocket and pulled out a small vial. He glanced around before tipping its contents into Will's coffee.

Will stared at the dark liquid. "Is that... blood?" he asked, his voice barely above a whisper.

Karl nodded grimly. "It was, once. There's enough humanity in it still to quench your thirst."

Iona watched in shocked silence as Will, after a moment's hesitation, drained the cup.

"This will be hard to understand, Will." Karl said solemnly, "but you can only fully recover once your 'sire' dies."

"Sire?" Will echoed, confusion filling his voice.

"The original vampire who turned you," Karl explained.

"So, what's our next move?"

Karl leaned in, his voice low. "We need to stop Burton and identify which one of the Blackwoods was responsible for turning you."

"No," Will said firmly, his voice stronger after the blood. "You've got it backwards. Burton's the one who bit me. Burton's the one who's been hunting the Blackwood family for over two centuries. The Blackwoods aren't our enemies - they're Burton's victims."

Karl's expression shifted, understanding dawning. "You're saying Burton is your sire?"

"I'm saying Burton is behind everything," Will said. "He's

been planning this for centuries, and now he's in the endgame."

The weight of Rufus' death settled over them like a funeral shroud. Will's oldest friend, his partner, the man who'd taught him to shoot straight and keep his head down. Gone. Transformed into one of Burton's weapons in this ancient war.

"Rufus was just collateral damage," Will said, his voice hollow. "Burton's turning everyone connected to the Blackwoods into his servants. Mrs. Johnson, Mrs. Pike, probably half the building by now."

"Then we stop him," Iona said firmly. "Before he destroys anyone else."

Karl nodded, but his expression was grim. "Burton's had over two hundred years to plan this. He's not going to be easy to stop."

Will touched Marion Bruce's pen in his pocket, drawing strength from the small connection to normalcy. "Then we'd better get started."

51

SHADOWS IN THE NIGHT

The blood-laced coffee sat heavy in Will's stomach, but with it came a surge of energy that felt both foreign and familiar. His senses, already heightened, pulsed with each heartbeat in the cafe. The elderly man two booths over had a slow, steady rhythm. The server behind the counter, younger, faster. And Iona beside him - he forced himself to stop listening.

"We need to go back," Will said, his voice stronger. He gripped the edge of the table, and the silver pen in his pocket seemed to burn against his thigh through the fabric. "Rufus could still be alive."

"Will—" Karl started.

"Don't tell me it's too late," Will snapped, his eyes fixing on Karl with an intensity that made the other man lean back slightly. "You keep saying that, but you don't know."

Karl was quiet for a moment, studying Will's face. Then he sighed, running a hand through his hair. "You want to know how I know? Fine. Let me tell you about Manchester."

Iona leaned forward, her coffee forgotten. "Manchester?"

"Vermont," Karl clarified, his voice dropping. "Everything everyone thinks a New England town should be."

"The perfect place to raise a family. The perfect place to hide monsters, too," his laugh was bitter.

Will had to force himself to listen to Karl's words,

because at least they drowned out the heartbeats thumping in his temples.

"I was a florist there," Karl continued. "Good at my job. I got to work every day with a woman I loved - my wife, Sophie. We had a daughter, Emma." His voice caught slightly. "We lived in one of those developments that looks good on paper. Blackwood Estates."

Iona shrugged.

"Yeah," Karl nodded, seeing their reaction. "I wouldn't expect you to recognize the name, but they're a big deal in New England. They were expanding back then, buying up property all over. The houses were nice, prices were good. Perfect for young families."

Karl's fingers traced the rim of his coffee cup. "Started with missing pets. Then old Mrs. Henderson disappeared. Everyone figured she'd gone to live with her daughter in Florida. Then the Patels' teenage son vanished. People said he'd run away. Then..."

He stopped, his jaw working. "Emma started talking about someone who'd visit her window at night. Sophie and I thought it was just an imaginary friend. Until the day I came home early from my shift and found Sophie... and Emma..."

Will's enhanced senses picked up Karl's elevated heartbeat, the slight tremor in his hands.

"They weren't quite dead," Karl said, his voice hollow. "But they weren't alive either. Not really. They were changing. Like you are now, Will. I didn't understand then. Tried to help them, to save them. That's when Richard Blackwood showed up at my door. Said he could help. Said he knew what was happening."

"What did he do?" Iona asked softly.

"He killed them." Karl's voice was flat. "Said it was a mercy. Said once the change starts, there's only one way to stop it. I tried to fight him, but he was too strong. Too fast. But he didn't kill me. That's when I learned about vampires, and that's when I became a hunter."

Will felt the silver pen burning stronger now, as if responding to his rising anger. "The Blackwoods... they're all vampires?"

Karl shook his head. "The Blackwoods have dozens of other children all around the country, not just James and Sarah. Some are what they call 'custodians.' They maintain properties, manage the feeding grounds. Keep everything looking legitimate. But they all serve someone older."

"Do you know who?" Iona asked.

Karl sighed. "I've spent years training, learning. Found others like me. We've tracked their operations across the country. But the original sire... he's different. Older. More powerful. And he has a special interest in York Tower."

"Why?" Will asked, but even as he spoke, a wave of weakness hit him. The borrowed strength from the blood was fading fast.

"Why not," Karl shrugged. "It's a vertical feeding ground, with hundreds of potential victims, all in one place. Perfect cover too - wealthy older residents, 'natural' deaths, grieving families too rich to ask too many questions. But I don't think that's the reason. I think there's something more to it. And I also think that knowing what that is, will be the key to all of this."

"And Rufus?" Will pushed himself up from the table, swaying.

"Will, listen to me," Karl said. "I've seen this before. The way they operate. If Rufus is still in that building, he's either dead or changing. And if he's changing, the kindest thing we can do is—"

"Don't you dare say it's mercy," Will growled, his hands in fists.

"The sun will be up in a few hours," Karl said. "That's when we make our move. But right now, you can barely stand. And I'm not losing anyone else to those monsters. Not tonight."

Will slumped back into his seat, the truth of Karl's words hitting him as hard as his growing weakness. The silver pen burned in his pocket, a constant reminder of what he was becoming. Of what Rufus might also become.

"Tell us more about the sire," Iona said, her detective's instincts kicking in. "What do you know about him?"

"Not enough. He's careful. Changes his appearance, his identity. But he's never far from his investments." Karl's expression darkened and he looked at Will meaningfully. "He's starting something new."

"What do you mean?" Will asked, though part of him already knew the answer.

"Most times, the transformation is quick. Violent. But you... he's taking his time with you. Making it slow. Making it last. I've seen nothing like it."

Will felt for the pen again. "Why me?"

Karl placed his hands on Will's bony shoulders. "That's what we need to find out. But not now. Not until sunrise."

Will wanted to argue, but the weakness was overwhelming now. The heartbeats were becoming too loud again, too tempting. He closed his eyes, trying to block them out.

"Rest," Karl said. "You'll need your strength for what's coming."

The pen in Will's pocket was a painful reminder of everything he stood to lose - and everything Rufus might have already lost.

But as Will's consciousness faded, carried away on a tide of supernatural hunger and human exhaustion, one terrible thought echoed in his mind: What if Rufus wasn't dead? What if he was somewhere in York Tower right now, experiencing the same agonizing transformation that was consuming Will?

What if his best friend was becoming Burton's weapon against him?

The thought was more terrifying than death itself. Because it meant that when they finally faced Burton, Will might have to choose between saving the Blackwood family and destroying the man who'd been like a brother to him.

The ancient war that had begun in Manchester,

Vermont, was forcing him to become something he'd sworn never to be: a man who might have to kill his best friend to save strangers.

But first, he had to survive the night. And hope that when morning came, there would still be enough of Will Taylor left to make that choice.

52

O CAPTAIN! MY CAPTAIN!

The elevator chimed and Matthew Peart stepped into York Tower's penthouse, bouncing with his usual nervous energy.

"What are you doing here, Matthew?" Richard's voice was dangerously quiet.

"Just some last minute papers to file. End of month stuff."

"How long have you been his agent?" Richard asked.

Peart adjusted his cuffs, a small man's gesture of self-importance. "Whose agent? What are you talking about, Mr. Blackwood?"

"Stop playing games." Elizabeth cut in. "We know about Burton."

"All perfectly legal," Peart interrupted, his tone condescending. "Every 'i' dotted, every 't' crossed. Really, Elizabeth, you should trust your legal team more."

Sarah looked at her parents. "Someone tell me what's going on?"

"Your father," Peart said, examining his manicured nails, "is about to spin you some tragic tale about being a reluctant monster. Aren't you, *Richard*? About how you've tried so hard to be civilized?"

"I never asked for this life," Richard snarled. "I've done what I had to do to survive, to protect my family. But I never became like him. Like Burton."

Peart's laugh was sharp. "No? Tell that to the delightfully young Miss Tessa Burrell in Vermont. I'll never forget watching her dance that first time. Which really was also the last time, wasn't it? Or the Downing boy in Boston? Did you know he wanted to be a professional ice hockey player for the Boston Bruins? No? I didn't think so. He had such talent. Or shall we discuss the recent departures from York Tower?"

"That's different," Richard's voice shook. "We never... we took only what we needed. We weren't predatory about it."

"Predatory?" Sarah whispered. "What do you mean?"

"Oh, this is delicious," Peart smirked. "She doesn't know, does she? About Daddy's special diet? About what really happens to all those wealthy residents who die in your buildings?"

Elizabeth moved to Sarah's side, but Sarah pulled away.

"Tell her, Richard," Peart's smile widened. "Tell her about the family legacy. About why you're so particular about your tenant selection. Oh, your father thought I didn't know. As if it takes a genius to work it out - the careful screening, the mysterious deaths, the way none of you age..."

Richard's face was haunted. "We're not what you think we are, Sarah. What we've built, what we are... I tried to protect you from it. Tried to give you a normal life."

Peart's laugh was hollow. "Really, Richard? You still don't get it? I've been in your organization for fifteen years. Every document, every contract, every property deal - they all lead back to him. You think you've built an empire?" His voice dripped with contempt. "You've built your own cage."

"And you're nothing but Burton's lapdog," Richard snarled.

"*I* made me. Not Burton. Yale Law, top of my class, an unparalleled résumé. Which made me the perfect infiltrator." Peart's voice had lost its whine, replaced by something older, colder. "You Blackwoods, so proud of your wealth, your status. Did you really think you'd carved out your own little empire on your own, without him knowing? Without his involvement?"

The lights in the penthouse flickered.

Peart's smirk melted into something else entirely. For the first time, his carefully maintained facade cracked, replaced by an expression of almost religious reverence.

"He's here," he whispered.

The darkness was absolute. Even the city lights seemed to die, as if something was drawing all illumination into itself. Sarah felt her mother's hand find hers in the dark, squeezing tight.

"Richard," a voice cut through the blackness. "Look how well you've done with my gift."

The voice was cultured, precise - the accent you'd expect from an old European court, now extinct everywhere except in period dramas. But there was something beneath it, something that belonged to narrow streets and dark ports. Something that had sailed across oceans carrying ancient grudges and older hungers.

A match flared. In its weak light stood a man, tall and elegant in an old-fashioned way, holding the flame as if he'd been lighting candles his whole life. His face was sharp, unaged since he'd stood at the helm of his ship, watching Lisbon burn. Since he'd buried Maria. His wife. The only woman who had ever loved him.

"Burton." Richard's voice was barely a whisper.

"Captain Burton, if you please." The match went out. Another sparked immediately. "I miss when people showed proper respect."

"What do you want?"

"Want?" Burton's laugh was like steel on stone. "I made you, Richard. Through Rachel, *our* beloved Rachel, I gave you everything you are. Your strength. Your wealth. Indeed, your very existence." The match illuminated his smile. "And how did you repay me? By stealing her from me."

"She was mine—"

"No. She married me. My wife. Not yours to take." The words cut through the darkness like a blade. "Everything you built, everything you are, came from the gift of her blood. My blood." Burton's eyes found Sarah in the darkness. "And now I'll take something of yours. Something precious. Just as you took something precious from me."

Elizabeth's grip on Sarah's hand tightened. "No."

The flame faltered, then vanished.

"Who's Rachel?" Sarah's voice trembled in the darkness.

"Someone from your father's past," Elizabeth answered quickly. Too quickly.

"That's not an answer." Sarah flinched at her mother's touch. "What's going on? Who is he? What does he mean about blood?"

Burton's chuckle drifted across the blackness, but it was Peart's voice that answered, carrying none of its usual whine. "Oh, you want answers now? How different from that night at the Christmas party." His footsteps echoed as he moved across the room. "Do you remember, Sarah? When I asked you to dinner? You laughed. Actually laughed."

"Peart, please—" Elizabeth started.

"Don't 'Peart' me anymore, Elizabeth," he snapped. "I've finished with being your obedient little lawyer. I'm no longer the man you pat on the head and dismiss as you sit on your Italian leather designer couches, sipping French champagne from designer crystal glasses I've procured for you. Me. Doing your bidding without question for fifteen years." Another match flared, illuminating his face from below, twisting his features. "Captain, might I make a request? A small reward for years of faithful service?"

Sarah's stomach turned at the way Peart looked at her, naked hunger in his beady eyes.

"The girl?" Burton's voice held amusement. "You aim high for a servant, Peart."

"She needs to learn her place." The lawyer's eyes gleamed in the match light. "Like her father. The mighty Blackwoods, looking down their noses at everyone. Remember how you sneered at me, Sarah? 'But, you're like a brother to me.' A brother?" He spat the word. 'I want her to remember that moment every single time she looks at me. Every time I—"

"Enough." Burton's voice interrupted Peart. "You forget yourself."

Sarah's fear drained away, replaced by pure contempt. "You think I'd consider you even if you were the last man on earth? A tiny troll with a face like a pinched ass and a voice that could crack windows?"

The darkness couldn't hide Peart's sharp intake of breath.

"Look at you," she continued, her voice dripping with disdain. "Five-foot-nothing in expensive lifts, with your manicured nails and a beauty regime the Kardashians would envy. Strutting around the office like Napoleon with an addiction to Sephora. At least Napoleon had presence," Sarah added. "All you have is a whine that makes dogs cover their ears and cologne that announces your arrival five minutes before you get there, and hides the utter stink of how much of an ass-licker you are."

"You'll regret—" Peart started, his voice rising to that glass-breaking pitch.

"What? I'll regret not settling for a man who looks like he was assembled from spare parts at a Ken doll factory?"

A low chuckle cut through the tension. Burton. "The girl has spirit," he said. "Rather like Rachel." His voice hardened. "But spirit can be broken." Burton struck another match, gliding around the room. "Spirit made Rachel fight too, at first." The match caught a candle, bringing a steady flame to the darkness. "There was such fire in her. Even after I turned her." Another candle lit. "You'll be pleased to know that she never forgave me for marrying her. All she wanted was you. I couldn't let that happen, now could I? So, I taught her a lesson, one she took to the grave with her."

He paused by the window. "You thought you were clever, Richard, running from Manchester. As if I hadn't watched a thousand families try to escape over the centuries. But you were different. You had her blood in you. My blood."

The candlelight cast long shadows as Burton continued his circuit of the room. "I gave you time. Let you build your little empire. Let you think you'd escaped. And I watched as you did exactly what I knew you would - create more feeding grounds, more hunting territories. Following the pattern I created centuries ago."

"The developments," Sarah whispered. "All those properties..."

Burton smiled. "Quiet communities. Wealthy residents. Deaths that raise no suspicions. Your father learned well, even as he tried to deny what he is." Another candle flared to life.

"Just as Rachel denied what she was after I made her. Just as Hilda did, for a time. Although that is one regret I have. In those early days, my appetite sometimes got away from me," Burton continued.

Elizabeth stepped forward. "You're wrong about Richard. About all of us."

"Am I?" Burton's laugh held no humor. "Tell me, Elizabeth, how many residents of York Tower have... passed on this month? How many convenient heart attacks? How many 'natural causes'?"

Sarah looked at her mother, seeing the truth in Elizabeth's face before she turned away.

"But your father," Burton continued, lighting the final candle, "he thought he could be civilized about it. Thought he could contain it. Control it. Just like Rachel did. Every one of my children thinks they can fight what they are. It's ever so entertaining to watch them struggle with the loss of their humanity. Some I encourage, others I leave to forge their own paths, and make their own families. But none have been as successful as you."

His smile in the candlelight was terrible to behold.

"Now you love something, so it's time for another lesson."

53

A PLAN

The Night Owl Cafe felt wrong. Too normal, mundane, with its flickering neon and late-night regulars. Will slumped in the booth while Karl pulled another vial from his jacket.

"Drink." Karl's voice was low, barely audible over the clatter of coffee cups.

Will's hands shook as he took the vial. "How many do you have?"

"Not enough." Karl watched the street through the window, his face tight. "Not for all of us, anyway."

"We need backup," Iona said, her detective's mind already working on the problem. "There has to be someone we can call."

Karl's laugh was bitter. "You'd think so, wouldn't you? Who were you thinking of? The Ghostbusters? Sorry, lady, but that's just in the movies." He turned from the window. "There used to be more of us. Hunters. We had networks, safe houses. Then last month, six of our best disappeared in Boston. Two weeks ago, our Chicago chapter went dark. It's like someone's picking us off, one by one."

"Burton?" Will asked between sips.

"Has to be. His servants are everywhere in every city. Rich bastards with their towers and their developments, feeding on people like..." He caught himself, glancing at Will.

"Like cattle," Will finished.

Iona pulled out her phone. "I'm calling it in. We need tactical support, firearms, the bigger the better—"

"Right." Karl's voice dripped sarcasm. "And what exactly are you going to tell them? That York Tower is run by vampires? That one of your officers is turning into one? I'm sure that will go down great with Internal Affairs. And guns won't do anything. But the silver pen in Will's pocket—"

"How do you know about that?" Will gasped.

"We have evidence. The deaths, the documents—" Iona interrupted.

"What documents? The ones that show the Blackwoods are masters of executing cut-throat business deals? Face it, Detective. We're on our own."

The silence that followed was broken only by the clink of Will's empty vial against the table.

"There has to be a way," Iona insisted. "Something we can use against them. Something to fight back with."

Karl observed Will. "How're you feeling?"

"Like my insides are trying to become my outsides." Will managed a weak smile. "But I can think straight now. And I can..." He hesitated. "I can feel them. In the building. It's like radio static in my head. They're all there, I think."

Karl stared at him, a contemplative look on his face. "You can feel them? That's a new one to me," Karl said slowly, drawing out every syllable, as if he were tasting the words. "If we can get close enoug—"

A raven's cry cut through the chatter. They all looked up. The sound felt wrong. Unnaturally joyful.

"We need to move," Karl said. "Now."

"Why?" Iona asked. "What was that?"

"A warning. Or a celebration." Karl looked scared. "Either way, we're running out of time."

The sidewalk outside was empty except for their small group.

The neon from the cafe window painted the wet pavement in sickly reds and blues.

"I know someone," Karl said finally. "Charlotte."

"The florist?" Will asked. Even in his weakened state, he remembered the girl who delivered arrangements to York Tower.

"She's not just a florist." Karl pulled out his phone. "She has a particular talent for making things that vampires don't like."

"Your florist is a witch?" Skepticism dripped from Iona's voice.

"I didn't say that." Karl punched in a number. "But she knows things. Ancient things. Ways of fighting them that don't involve guns or—" He stopped as someone answered. "Char? Yeah, it's happening. Tonight. We need everything you've got."

Will leaned against a lamppost, feeling the city spin around him. Through the static in his head, he could sense movement in York Tower. Something was changing. Something was wrong.

"She'll meet us," Karl said, hanging up. "But we need to hurry. She says the ravens are gathering."

"What does that mean?" Iona asked.

A sound overhead made them all look up. Three ravens perched on the cafe's neon sign, their black eyes reflecting the artificial light like tiny red stars.

"It means," Karl said, "we're not the only ones making plans."

Charlotte's shop sat in the shadow of St. Patrick's Cathedral, its windows dark except for the small apartment above. Will checked his phone again as they approached. Still nothing from Rufus.

The back door opened before Karl could knock. Charlotte stood there, her usual florist's apron replaced by something that looked more like a tool belt, filled with small vials and wooden implements.

"You look awful," she said to Will before leading them through the shop, past buckets of lilies that made Will's nose burn. The fresh-cut flowers and arrangement tables had been pushed aside, revealing a workspace that looked more like an armory than a florist's studio.

"Holy water," she said, handing each of them tiny vials. "From St. Patrick's itself. The monsignor there owes me a favor. Don't ask."

"And these?" Iona picked up a thin wooden stake.

"*Lignum vitae*," Charlotte said, checking each stake before handing them out. "Hardest wood in the world. The Spanish called it the Wood of Life. Ironic, considering what we use it for."

"Right." Iona's voice dripped with sarcasm. "And where are my silver bullets?"

"Those are for werewolves." Charlotte explained blankly.

Iona started to laugh, then stopped. Her face went through several expressions before settling on bewilderment. "Wait. Werewolves are real too?"

"Let me guess, you were Team Jacob," Will said, trying to smile despite the pain.

"Shut up," Iona said, staring at her stake with new respect. "I guess *Team Jacob* was the better choice then..."

"Focus," Karl snapped. "Will, anything from Rufus?"

Will checked his phone again. "Nothing."

"He might just be busy," Iona said, without conviction.

The ravens' cry pierced the night again, closer this time. Charlotte moved to the window, her face grim. "Whatever's happening at York Tower, it's starting soon."

"Wait." Will's voice was strained. "There's something else. Someone else is there."

He pressed his fingers to his temples. "With the Blackwoods, but not all of them are there. James Blackwood is missing."

"How can you possibly know that?" Karl demanded.

"I can feel them. Like... like radio stations. Each one is different. But James... his signal's somewhere else." Will's eyes were unfocused. "He's moving fast. He's tracking someone. Hunting, I think."

Charlotte's mouth opened. She turned to Karl, who nodded.

"It must be Burton," Karl explained to the group. "For the

connection to be this precise. Will's not just sensing them, he's linked to their network somehow."

"Who's James tracking?" Iona asked.

Will's face paled as horror dawned.

"What?" Iona demanded.

"The boys. Your son and Amanda Pike's boy. Young blood..." Will swallowed. "The strongest blood there is. And he's so angry..."

Iona was already pulling out her phone, fingers shaking.

"We need to split up," Karl said, but Charlotte cut him off.

"No, that's exactly what Burton wants. We need to stick to the plan. Get to York Tower, stop him at the source."

"My son is out there!" Iona's voice rose.

"And my partner's in York Tower," Will said. "What's left of him."

The ravens cried out again, their calls forming a horrible chorus above the city streets.

"We need to make a choice," Karl said. "Now."

Will's vision blurred as the weight of the decision crashed over him. Through the supernatural connection burning in his veins, he could feel Burton's presence like a malignant tumor at the heart of York Tower. Could sense the ancient hatred that had driven the sea captain across centuries, from the smoking ruins of Manchester, Vermont to the marble halls of Manhattan.

Burton wasn't just killing the Blackwood family's tenants anymore. He was turning them. Building an army of the recently dead to destroy everything Richard and Elizabeth had built. And somewhere in that building, Rufus was either dead or becoming one of Burton's weapons.

But the boys were out there too. Finn and Ethan, two kids who'd stumbled into the crossfire of a war that had been raging since before their great-great-grandparents were born.

"Together," Will said finally, his voice cutting through the chaos. "We do this together, or we all die separately. But first..." He looked at Iona. "We save the boys. Because if we don't, there won't be anyone left to save by the time we reach Burton."

54

MERCY

James Blackwood heard it first - the wet, tearing sound that echoed in the stairwell. Then the smell hit him with such intensity he nearly doubled over. Copper-rich and overwhelming, the scent of blood was still new to him, still shocking in its power. Just days after his father had turned him, every sensation remained raw, undiluted.

He took the stairs three at a time, his newfound strength surprising him. The world moved differently, as if everything had slowed down while he'd somehow sped up. He followed the sounds of feeding, trying to control his own hunger as it rose unbidden.

He found them between the third and fourth floors. June Johnson, the woman who'd spent Sunday afternoons practicing ballroom dancing in the rec room, was now something else. Her fingers, curved into claws, held Rufus' shoulders as she tore into his throat. Blood ran down the security guard's uniform in dark rivers, and James fought the urge to join her feeding. His father hadn't prepared him for this - the raw, primal need that came with seeing fresh blood.

"Mrs.—!" James reached for her, but she moved with a speed that matched his own new abilities.

She vaulted over the railing, disappearing into the darkness below, leaving only the echo of her inhuman snarl.

James blinked, still adjusting to how his enhanced vision could pierce the shadows.

Rufus lay crumpled against the wall. His eyes found James, recognition and horror fighting for space in his fading gaze. The smell of his blood was intoxicating. James clenched his fists to maintain control.

"S-Sally?" The word bubbled out with blood.

"She got away." James knelt beside him, knowing there was nothing he could do. The damage was too extensive, the blood loss too severe. His father had barely explained turning someone, but James knew Rufus was too far gone. The knowledge came to him like muscle memory, though he didn't understand how.

"Good." Rufus' hand twitched, trying to reach his phone.

"I'm sorry," James said, his hands moving to Rufus' neck. "The only mercy I can give you now is a quick end." He hoped he had the strength to do this cleanly - another skill his hasty transformation hadn't prepared him for.

Something like gratitude flickered in Rufus' eyes. James made it as swift as he could, praying his inexperience wouldn't cause additional suffering. He held the body until the last warmth faded, until what had been Rufus was truly gone.

A sound from below made James lift his head. His enhanced senses, still overwhelming in their intensity, caught fragments on the night air - Sally's perfume, already fading into the distance. But there was something else. Something younger, fresher. Two distinct scents that made his new predator instincts surge.

Boys. Young ones.

He moved to the window, his heightened vision easily penetrating the pre-dawn darkness. In the shadows of a construction site across the way, he caught movement. Two small figures on what they probably thought was a grand adventure in the dark.

He caught June's scent, moving fast, and moving toward them. The intensity of her hunger was like a physical force.

Ethan Pike and Finn Melville. Amanda's boy and the

detective's son. And the ravenous June Johnson was hunting them.

James stood, letting Rufus' body slip to the floor. He had to stop her. Had to reach them first. Though how he'd control both June's bloodlust and his own, he did not know.

James paused at the window, his mind racing faster than his human thoughts ever had. Someone had turned June Johnson, and it wasn't anyone from his family. His father might be ruthless in business, might feed when necessary, but he'd never turn someone so recklessly, so completely. This was different. Savage. Uncontrolled.

The transformation reminded him of stories his grandfather had told, back when James was still human enough to dismiss them as family folklore. Tales of a sea captain from Vermont who'd lost everything to love turned sour. Who'd spent centuries perfecting the art of turning grief into weapons.

Isaac Burton. The name whispered through James' enhanced consciousness like a curse.

Part of him wanted to return to his family in the penthouse, but he pushed the thought aside. He was still struggling to grasp his parents' true age, the weight of their immortality - although he was confident that they could handle themselves. The Blackwoods had been handling themselves for centuries, but his sister, Sarah, was a different matter. He pushed that worry aside. One problem at a time.

The boys had no chance against June. None. He knew this without a shadow of doubt. Why? Because he felt it now himself, raw and demanding. June Johnson might look like someone's grandmother, white-haired with age spots dancing up her wrists, all frail and harmless in her cardigan and sensible shoes, but she was running on pure instinct now. And those instincts were screaming for blood. The easier the better.

There was something more disturbing about June's transformation.

Burton's technique was different from his father's

careful, controlled turning. This was weaponizing grief and hunger into something unstoppable.

He caught their scent again in the wind, his nostrils flaring at the promise of young, vital blood. He pushed down the hunger, disgusted by his own response. Ethan and Finn. And they didn't know they were being hunted.

James made his choice. His sister and parents would have to wait. First, he had to save those boys - from Mrs. Johnson, and possibly from himself.

Because if Burton was turning the building's residents into weapons, then this wasn't just about the Blackwood family anymore. This was about stopping a monster who'd learned to weaponize love itself.

The war that had begun with Rachel's death in a Vermont cemetery was spreading beyond the Blackwoods. Now innocent children were in the crossfire.

And James Blackwood, newest vampire in a family of centuries-old predators, was the only thing standing between Burton's revenge and two boys who'd never asked to be part of an ancient war.

As James prepared to leap from the window, he realized that some choices defined not just who you were, but who you could become.

And he'd rather die human than live as Burton's kind of monster.

55

———

FIRST LOVE

Elizabeth watched the men circle each other, these two ancient predators in modern dress. Richard in his tailored suit, Burton in his captain's coat, that somehow didn't look out of place, even now. The candles threw their shadows long against the penthouse walls.

"You led them," Richard's voice was raw. "Whipped them into a frenzy. The brave Captain Burton, leading the good people of Manchester against the demons in their midst."

Burton's smile was gentle, almost fond. "Of course I did. They needed someone to trust. Someone to follow." He moved to the window, his reflection ghostlike against the city lights. "And who better than their protector? The man who'd guide them to dig up those poor women's graves, to desecrate the bodies of the demons who'd been terrorizing their little town."

"Rachel's body." Richard's hands clenched. "You encouraged them to mutilate Rachel's body. You cheered them on."

Elizabeth felt the old ache in her chest. It wasn't jealousy. She'd made peace with Rachel's ghost long ago.

Richard had told her everything about Rachel.

Her grace, her kindness, how Burton had turned her. And how she'd tried to save her beloved from the same fate, only to die for it.

"Hilda's body too," Burton nodded. "Though she was just

a bonus, really. A loose end to tie up." He turned from the window. "I had to make them believe the horror lay within their own cemetery. Not in their harbor. Not in their brave captain's house."

Sarah made a small sound, but Elizabeth couldn't comfort her daughter. Not now. Not with Burton's eyes on them all.

"I'll never forgive you," Richard hissed. 'Not for what you did to her body. Not for making me watch."

Elizabeth's chest tightened at her husband's pain. Centuries of grief compressed into those few words. She knew about Rachel, had always known. But hearing the raw agony in Richard's voice made it fresh again, made it—

She stopped breathing.

A new scent seeped into the penthouse. Blood. Fresh blood. And with it, a scent she'd know anywhere - James. Her son.

Her nostrils flared, her heart racing, as her most basic instincts warred with her most primal fear. The blood wasn't James', but it was on him. And there was something else with it, something wrong. Something newly turned.

Burton's smile widened, as if he could taste her fear.

"A mother's love," Burton's voice was silk over steel. "So delicious, and so predictable." His eyes slid toward Sarah's. "You're right to be afraid, Elizabeth. After all, Rachel was about Sarah's age, if I remember correctly."

Elizabeth kept her face neutral. Let him gloat. Let him misread her terror. Every instinct screamed that James was in danger, that something was wrong. But Burton's focus on Sarah might give James a chance, whatever trouble he'd found.

"Although Rachel," Burton continued, passing his palm through the candle flame with deliberate slowness, "Rachel at least knew what she was getting into. Your daughter's been rather... sheltered, hasn't she? Such a shame to learn about her family's true nature under these circumstances."

Elizabeth resisted the urge to reach for her daughter's hand. The blood scent was stronger now. It wasn't James' blood, but it was on him. And there was another scent, a wrongness... She knew that scent. Someone had been turned. Recently and violently. And for the first time in decades, Elizabeth Blackwood was truly afraid.

"It's been at least a quarter century since I last had a wife," Burton mused, his eyes lingering on Sarah. "Far too long, wouldn't you say?"

"But sir—" Peart's voice cracked. "You promised—"

Burton silenced him with a look that could have frozen hell. Peart shrank back into the shadows, his earlier bravado fizzling away to nothing.

Elizabeth's fingers tightened around Sarah's hand, willing her daughter to stay quiet. Now wasn't the time for the girl's usual sharp tongue. Not with Burton's attention fixed so firmly on her. Elizabeth could smell James' departure now, the scent of blood growing fainter as he moved away from the building. She had to keep Burton's attention here, away from that telling smell.

"You bastard," she spat, launching herself forward until Richard caught her arm. "You won't touch her. I won't let you—"

"The lady doth protest too much, methinks," Burton smiled. "Though I appreciate the theatrical effort, Elizabeth. Truly. Such maternal devotion." He moved closer, inhaling deeply. "But one might wonder what you're trying so hard to distract me from."

Elizabeth's heart stuttered, but she pressed on, becoming more hysterical, more dramatic. Anything to keep his attention. She had faith in Richard. Between them, they might save Sarah. Perhaps. As long as James didn't return to the penthouse.

"I'll die before I let you near her," Elizabeth screamed, letting her voice edge toward hysteria.

Burton just laughed.

"But you promised." Peart's whine cut through Elizabeth's theatrics. "After fifteen years of service. You said—"

"You're interrupting," Burton's voice held infinite patience.

"No!" Peart stepped forward, his small frame vibrating with rage. "I've waited too long, done too much. You promised me I could have Sarah. And power. You promised—"

The movement was too fast to follow. One moment Peart was standing, the next Burton's hand was through his chest, holding something that pulsed once, twice, and then stopped.

"I find," Burton said conversationally, letting Peart's body crumple to the floor, "that promises, like people, have a limited shelf life."

Elizabeth pulled her daughter closer, feeling her shake. Even Richard took a step back. None of them had seen it coming. None of them had known Burton was that fast. Or that strong.

The smell of Peart's blood joined the cocktail of scents in the room, and Elizabeth realized with growing horror that Burton wasn't just playing with them. He was demonstrating his power. Showing them exactly how helpless they were.

But more than that, he was enjoying himself. The patient sea captain who'd spent centuries planning his revenge was finally getting to savor every moment of the Blackwood family's terror.

And somewhere in the building below, something else was hunting. Something that carried James' scent but moved with Burton's savage hunger.

56

MORNING HAS BROKEN

The streets around York Tower held that peculiar emptiness that comes just before dawn, when even New York's insomniacs have given up and gone home. James moved through the shadows, still marveling at how differently the world appeared through his new senses. Just days after his father had turned him, every sensation remained overwhelming - the texture of brick against his fingertips, the whisper of rats in the sewers below, and most startlingly, two distinct scent trails that cut through the pre-dawn air: June Johnson's raw hunger and the bright, vital smell of young boys that made his own hunger surge.

He could hear them up ahead, their whispered excitement carrying to his enhanced hearing with unsettling clarity. Each heartbeat was a drum in his ears, and he had to concentrate to focus on their actual words.

"Careful," Ethan was saying. "It probably costs more than both our allowances for a year."

"How'd you even get it?" Finn's voice was full of admiration.

"Mr. Chang's door was open. I've been watching the place, you know, *detecting*."

Ethan mimicked the hard-boiled detectives from his books.

"Like Sherlock Holmes, but better. I've been keeping notes on everyone in the building."

"What notes?"

"Well," Ethan said theatrically, "Mrs. Bruce on six used to get these weird deliveries every Tuesday. Little wooden boxes. And Mr. Marsden? He had this secret compartment behind his bookshelf. Found that when they were clearing out his place."

"No way!"

"Way. Got this from there." Ethan fished in his pocket with his free hand, producing a silver pocket watch.

James flinched involuntarily at the sight of silver.

"And Mrs. Henderson's cat brooch she told everyone had been stolen from her apartment? It wasn't missing."

"You didn't steal it, did you?"

"Found it under the radiator in the lobby outside her apartment. Mom says I shouldn't take stuff, but it's not stealing if no one wants it anymore, right? Like Mr. Chang's ships. They're just sitting there while his family argues over what to do with all his models."

"What else have you found?" Finn's voice sounded full of admiration.

Then James caught another scent in the wind, and his newly heightened senses nearly overwhelmed him with its intensity - June Johnson.

The old woman was paralleling his path, moving through the alleys on the other side of the street. *Hunting.* The boys had no idea they were being stalked from both sides of the street, one hunter trying to save them while fighting his own predatory instincts, one giving in completely to the hunger.

The model ship they carried was a beautiful thing. His enhanced vision picked out every detail. All brass and polished wood, a toy that wasn't really a toy at all. The kind that called to young boys like a siren's song. Worth sneaking out for, James supposed. Worth risking everything to sail it on the park pond while the city slept.

James cursed. His father hadn't prepared him for this - how to stop another vampire without giving in to his own darkness.

"We'll be back before anyone wakes up," Ethan was saying. "Mom sleeps forever these days."

"I don't know..." Finn sounded nervous. "Maybe we should go back. It feels weird out here."

Mrs. Johnson's scent shifted, and James staggered from the wave of bloodlust that rolled off her like a heat haze of need. He could feel what she was feeling, recognize it from his own overwhelming hunger of the past few days - the thundering sound of young hearts beating, the intoxicating smell of blood so close to the surface, the promise of strength and life that could be taken so easily. He swallowed hard against his own rising need.

The boys walked on, completely unaware, the stolen ship held between them like pirate treasure. Their footsteps echoed on the empty path, heading toward the pond. Toward the shadows where June waited. James flexed his hands, trying to prepare himself for whatever would come next, though how he'd control both June's bloodlust and his own remained a terrifying mystery.

Burton wasn't just turning people anymore. He was weaponizing them. Taking everything pure - a grandmother's love, a mother's protection - and twisting it into instruments of destruction. June Johnson had probably baked cookies for these boys at some point. Had smiled at them in the lobby, asked about their schoolwork.

Now she was hunting them like prey.

James understood with crystalline clarity that this was Burton's true genius. Not just the physical transformation, but the psychological destruction. Turning love into hunger. Trust into betrayal. Safety into terror.

The boys would never be the same, even if he saved them. They'd learn tonight that the world contained monsters. That the kind old lady from the second floor could become something that wanted to drain them dry.

And in the distance, the sky lightened.

Soon he'd have to deal with another aspect of his transformation he barely understood.

The ancient war was corrupting everything it touched. Even the children.

James picked up his pace, racing against time, against his own hunger, and against the horrifying possibility that he might be too late to save anyone. Including himself.

57

CHOICES

The predawn light cast long shadows across York Tower's entrance. Karl handed Will the final ampule of blood.

"Last one," he whispered. "Make it count."

This time, Will knocked back the blood without hesitation. It hit his system like an electric shock, flooding his veins with borrowed strength and terrible clarity.

Iona touched his arm. "I can't," she said, her voice a whisper. "I understand everything you've said, about stopping them, and saving others, but..." She looked at each of them. "Finn is my son."

Karl shook his head. "We need you. Without enough force—"

"Which way?" She cut him off, turning to Will. "You can sense them. James Blackwood. The boys. Which way?"

Will felt the pull, the different signatures in his head like radio stations bleeding through static.

"Central Park. By the pond at Cherry Hill."

"Iona, wait," Karl called as she turned. "You can't take on James Blackwood alone. He's too strong. He'll turn you like Burton plans to turn those boys."

"If you had children, you'd understand."

"The sire is the key," Karl shouted after her.

Without looking back, she increased her pace and disappeared into the pre-dawn darkness.

Will's eyes glazed over for a moment. "James... James isn't alone out there."

"Of course he isn't," Karl spat. "He's got his whole damned family behind him. And unless we get in there and take out Burton—"

Will barely heard him. The heavy glass doors of York Tower loomed before them, the reception desk beyond conspicuously empty. That was wrong. Someone should always be behind the desk. Rufus had been such a stickler for the rules when he'd worked out the rosters every month. They had joked that spreadsheets were his superpower.

Rufus.

The smell hit him as they crossed the threshold. Death. Blood. Rufus' blood. The scent of everything he'd lost punched through him like a physical blow.

He staggered, catching himself on the door. Rufus was dead. The knowledge settled into his bones with terrible certainty. His friend, his partner, the man who'd got him through his divorce, who'd taught him to shoot straight at the academy, and who'd dreamed of one day hitting a hole-in-one. Will could only pray that there was a decent golf course in heaven.

But through the supernatural connection burning in his veins, Will sensed something worse than death. Rufus' essence was still there, still in the building, but transformed. Twisted. No longer the man who'd worried about Will's weight loss and planned fishing trips they'd never take.

Burton had turned his best friend into a weapon. Another piece on the chessboard of his centuries-long revenge.

And then none of it mattered. Not the Blackwoods, not Karl's mission, not even avenging Rufus. All that mattered was stopping another death. Stopping a young boy from losing his future and stopping a mother from experiencing this same crushing loss.

"Will, don't—" Karl started, but Will had already slammed through the doors back out onto the street.

His feet barely seemed to touch the ground as he ran,

desperation carrying him toward Iona. Behind him, he heard Karl curse, and Charlotte's alarm.

But he didn't stop. He couldn't. Not while there was still someone left to save.

Through the static in his head, Will could feel the supernatural forces converging on Central Park. Burton's hunger, ancient and patient. James' confusion and barely controlled bloodlust. And underneath it all, the pure terror of two children who had no idea they'd wandered into the crossfire of a war that had been raging since before their country was even founded.

Will ran faster, his supernatural strength carrying him through the darkness toward the sound of young voices and the scent of ancient evil. The war that had begun in Manchester, Vermont, was about to claim its youngest victims.

Unless he could reach them first.

The hunt was on. And this time, Will Taylor was determined to be the hunter, not the prey.

Even if it killed what was left of his humanity.

He would not let the children die.

Not on his watch.

Not while there was still breath in his body and fight in his soul.

58

FINE DINING

Peart's body lay crumpled on the penthouse floor in a pool of blood. Richard had moved to Sarah's other side, bracketing his daughter between himself and Elizabeth.

"Such a shame about Matthew," Burton said, adjusting his cuffs casually, as if he'd just swatted a fly. 'Though hardly a loss. There are always more lawyers. They breed like rats in this city."

He moved to the floor-to-ceiling windows, gazing out over the terrace where ravens perched like dark omens against the lightening sky. "But this..." he gestured at York Tower, at the city beyond, "this is impressive. You've developed quite the operation. Like a carefully curated wine cellar, but for discerning palates."

Sarah stiffened between her parents, the casual way Burton discussed human lives chilling her to the bone.

"The Hendersons were like aged prosciutto - well-preserved, full of character." Burton's voice took on the affected tone of a sommelier describing vintage wines. "The Marsdens? More of a smoky pastrami, wouldn't you say, Richard? And poor Mr. Chang..." He smiled, the expression predatory in the candlelight. "A delightfully exotic addition to the menu. Like finding that rare imported delicacy at Dean & DeLuca that you simply must try."

"They were people," Sarah whispered, her voice breaking.

"They were inventory." Burton turned from the window, his eyes reflecting the candle flames like a beast's. "But managed so... elegantly. Clean apartments, discreet disposal, legitimate paperwork. A perfect system. Though perhaps a touch too perfect. Too controlled." His eyes found Richard's. "Too civilized."

Ravens gathered on the terrace, their black forms stark against the dawn sky. More arrived with each passing minute, settling on the expensive outdoor furniture, on the edges of the infinity pool, on the carefully maintained container garden. Their presence felt like a gathering storm, an army of darkness responding to their master's call.

"You see," Burton continued, "that's always been your problem, Richard. You try so hard to maintain appearances. To be respectable." He gestured around the opulent penthouse. "All this? It's just window dressing. Like putting a beautiful display case around what we really are."

The ravens watched through the glass, their eyes reflecting the penthouse lights like tiny crimson stars. Sarah felt their gaze like a physical weight, pressing down on her with the force of centuries-old malice.

"But now," Burton smiled, revealing teeth that seemed too sharp in the flickering light, "we strip away the pretense." He held out his hand toward Richard, palm up, like a gentleman requesting a dance. "Give me the girl."

Elizabeth's fingers tightened around Sarah's arm like a vise.

"After all," Burton's smile widened, showing more of those impossible teeth, "we both know how this ends. I take what you think is yours, and keep what's mine. That's how it worked with Rachel." His voice dropped to a whisper that somehow carried across the room like a death sentence. "That's how it's always worked."

Outside, the ravens began to call - not the harsh caws Sarah remembered from nature documentaries, but something else. Something that sounded almost like laughter. As if they were celebrating a victory.

The candlelight guttered as Burton took a step closer, and Sarah realized that she was looking at her own death. Not just death. Something worse. Something that would turn her into the kind of monster that discussed human beings like menu items.

The ravens' laughter grew louder, echoing off the glass like the sound of breaking bones.

Or like the sound of hope dying.

59

BIRDS OF A FEATHER

The model ship caught the breeze perfectly, its minuscule brass fittings gleaming in the wintry light. Tiny waves lapped at its hull as it cut through the pond at Cherry Hill, leaving ripples in its wake.

"Look at it go!" Ethan's voice carried across the water. "It's like the America's Cup racing!"

The boys ran along the path, keeping pace with their prize. A leaf-blower started up somewhere in the distance, mixing with a distant siren and the crescendo of morning birdsong. The city was waking.

"Over there!" Finn pointed to where the wind was pushing the ship toward the far bank. "We can catch it at the bend!"

They ran faster, their sneakers slapping against the path, faces split with grins that only stolen adventures can bring. An icy breeze picked up, catching the ship's tiny sails, making it skip across the water's surface like something alive.

Then June stepped onto the path ahead of them.

The birdsong stopped. Just stopped. As if someone had flipped a switch, leaving only the distant drone of the leaf-blower and their own tortured breathing.

The boys froze.

In the dawn light June's skin looked like wax that had been left too close to a heater. Her clothes hung wrong on her frame, as if her bones had shifted beneath them. She looked like a Halloween decoration that had been left out too long in the rain.

"Mrs. Johnson?" Ethan's voice cracked. "Are you okay?"

Behind them, the model ship hit the bank with a soft bump.

"Step away from them."

James Blackwood's voice cut through the silence as he emerged from the shadows. The path was still dark, the rising sun not yet high enough to breach the canopy of trees.

The boys stood between the two figures.

"Who are they?" Finn whispered. "Do you know them?"

"The old lady is Mrs. Johnson. From the second floor," Ethan replied. "He's James Blackwood. His family owns the building."

"What's wrong with her face?"

June's head snapped around at an unnatural speed, like a puppet with broken strings. Her laugh started low, then rose to something that might have once been feminine. A laugh which might have once belonged to the woman who brought still warm cookies to tenant meetings. Now it was just wrong.

When she smiled, her teeth gleamed - too many, too sharp. "The prodigal son," she said, her voice rasping like dead leaves. "Come to play hero?"

James took another step forward. "This isn't you, Mrs. Johnson. They're little boys, with their lives ahead of them."

Her laugh came again, higher this time, more hysterical. "Not me? But I've never felt more myself. So alive.' Her eyes fixed on the boys. "And so hungry."

"What's happening?" Finn's voice trembled. "Ethan?"

The woman lunged at the boys with inhuman speed. James reacted instantly, shoving them both into the pond before meeting her charge. Their collision echoed like thunder across the water.

Iona rounded the corner at a dead run, Will right behind her. She took in the scene with a cop's practiced eye

- two boys in the water, James Blackwood wrestling with...
June Johnson. Sally's mom?

Something was wrong with June. Terribly wrong. Every instinct Iona had screamed that June was the threat here, not James, but that didn't make sense. Karl had been so certain about the Blackwoods.

"It's Mrs. Johnson!" Will's voice cracked. "She's been turned!"

"It's not James," Iona breathed, watching the impossible fight before her.

James' head snapped toward them at the sound of their voices. That moment of distraction was all June needed. She struck like a snake, tearing into his neck with newfound strength. Blood sprayed across the path.

In the pond, Finn was struggling to keep Ethan's head above water. "Help! He can't swim!"

Iona's gun was in her hand before she registered drawing it. The report was deafening in the morning quiet. June jerked back from James, blood smearing her wrinkled face. For a moment, Iona caught a glimpse of Sally in those ancient features - something in the set of the jaw, the curve of the cheek. But there was nothing of the doting mother left in those hungry eyes.

June bolted into the shadows, leaving James bleeding on the path.

Will reached him first, hands pressing against the wound. But the blood kept coming, hot and red and completely overwhelming. Will's pupils dilated, his breathing growing ragged.

"Don't," Iona pleaded. "Will, please."

The boys' screams echoed across the water. Ethan was flailing wildly now, dragging Finn under with him. Iona didn't hesitate - she dove into the pond.

Will remained frozen, staring at his blood-soaked hands. Slowly, trembling, he raised one finger to his lips.

"No..." James' voice was barely a whisper. "Don't..."

Will paused. Then tasted his first drop of fresh blood.

The flavor exploded across his senses like lightning

through his veins. Not the preserved, diluted essence Karl had been feeding him, but pure life force, warm and intoxicating. Every cell in his body screamed for more. The hunger that had been gnawing at him for days roared to life, demanding satisfaction.

Will's hand moved toward James' neck, where the blood flowed freely. Where the warmth promised strength and clarity and an end to the constant ache of transformation.

But as his fingers touched the wound, Will saw something in James' eyes. Not fear. Not even resignation. Hope. The kind of hope that said James still believed Will could choose to be human.

Could choose to be better than the monster Burton was creating.

The ancient war was offering Will everything he'd ever wanted - power, strength, an end to uncertainty and pain. All he had to do was feed. All he had to do was become what Burton intended.

All he had to do was stop being Will Taylor.

The boys were still screaming in the water behind him. Iona was fighting to save them both. And James Blackwood, vampire heir to a centuries-old dynasty, was trusting Will to make the right choice.

To prove that some bonds were stronger than blood.

That some choices mattered more than hunger.

Will's hand trembled as he pressed it harder against James' wound, staunching the flow instead of feeding from it.

"Hold on," he whispered. "Help is coming."

Burton hadn't counted on Will Taylor still remembered who he used to be.

And Will wasn't ready to let that man die.

Not yet.

60

BLOOD IS THICKER

Elizabeth's legs gave out. "James," she whispered, the name tearing from her throat like a physical wound. Sarah watched her mother crumple, and her father stagger back as if struck.

Burton's laugh filled the penthouse, echoing off the marble floors and glass like the sound of breaking glass. "Ah, the joys of family bonds." His eyes glittered with malicious delight as he watched them suffer. "Do you feel it, Richard? The way the blood screams when one of our line dies? Exquisite."

Sarah's hands trembled. James. Her brother. Dead. A week ago, her biggest concern had been the company's quarterly reports. Now she stood in a room with vampires - her own parents among them. The revelation still felt surreal, like a fever dream she couldn't shake.

Memories flooded through her of James smuggling candy into her sickbed when she was seven, his pockets full of chocolate and his eyes twinkling with conspiracy. The time he'd confronted her boyfriend on the steps of their brownstone, his voice tight with protective fury. Lecturing her about taking night classes, hovering like a mother hen whenever she stayed late at the office.

Always hovering. Always protecting. They'd fought constantly about her independence, her career, her life choices. But James was her brother. Her flesh and blood.

The one constant in her life who'd been both her greatest protector and the biggest pain in the ass.

Even after she'd watched him change, even after he'd tried to explain what their father had done to him, he was still just James to her. The brother who'd taught her to ride a bike and helped her with calculus and threatened to break the legs of anyone who hurt her.

Burton's laughter drowned out her mother's sobs. Sarah felt something crack inside her - not a supernatural bond like her parents shared (she was still human, still normal, still sane, wasn't she?), but something deeper. More primal. And in that place where grief and rage collided, where disbelief gave way to terrible clarity, she became something else entirely.

With a scream comprising a lifetime of sisterly love and frustration, she launched herself at Burton. Through the red haze of her fury, she was dimly aware of movement in the stairwell. Footsteps climbing upward - heavy boots on metal stairs, labored breathing. Hunters coming to kill her family. Something above them, radiating a hunger Sarah had only just learned to recognize from her father's hurried, desperate lessons about their kind.

But those threats felt distant now. Burton's smile, her parents' pain, James' absence - it all crystallized into a single point of burning fury. Her brother was dead, and his killer stood before her, laughing.

Sarah didn't stop to consider her frailty, that the supernatural strength coursing through Burton made him capable of snapping her like a twig. James had died protecting someone, she was certain of it. He would never have gone down otherwise. Now it was her turn to protect what remained of her family, vampire or not.

She flung herself at the monster before her with everything she had. Her humanity became her weapon. Because while vampires thought in centuries, humans lived and loved and raged in the moment. And in this moment, Sarah Blackwood - still human, still mortal, still trying to process that vampires were real - was nothing but rage incarnate.

Her small fists connected with Burton's chest, and for a heartbeat, she saw surprise flicker across his ancient features. Not because she could hurt him - she couldn't - but because she had dared to try.

"You killed him!" she screamed, pounding against his chest like waves against a seawall. "You killed my brother!"

Burton caught her wrists with casual ease, his grip like iron manacles. "Your brother," he said conversationally, "died trying to save children who meant nothing to him. How perfectly... human."

"He was worth a hundred of you," Sarah spat.

"Perhaps," Burton agreed. "But he's still dead. And you, my dear, are still very much alive." His grip tightened until Sarah gasped. "For now."

Through the penthouse windows, more ravens arrived, their dark forms blotting out the dawn sky. They pressed against the glass like living shadows, their cries growing louder and more urgent. Sarah could swear she heard something like words in their calls - ancient words in a language that predated civilization.

"You see," Burton continued, his voice taking on the cadence of a professor lecturing to particularly slow students, "James died because he thought he could choose to be better than what he was. Because he believed love could triumph over nature." His smile was hideous. "How delightfully naive."

"Let her go," Richard's voice was deadly quiet.

"Or what?" Burton laughed. "You'll kill me? You've had two centuries to try, Richard. What makes you think you can succeed now?"

Elizabeth struggled to her feet, her face streaked with tears. "Because now we have nothing left to lose."

The temperature in the penthouse plummeted. Frost began forming on the windows, creeping across the glass like grasping fingers. The candles flickered and dimmed, their flames struggling against an unnatural wind.

Burton's smile faltered for the first time.

"You think grief makes you stronger?" he asked, but Sarah caught the uncertainty in his voice. "It only makes you desperate."

"Maybe," Elizabeth said, her voice like winter wind. "But desperate people do desperate things."

The footsteps in the stairwell were getting closer. And somewhere in the building below, Sarah could sense other presences - ancient, hungry things that had been sleeping and were now awakening. Her father's face had gone stone-cold, and even her mother looked like something carved from ice.

Sarah realized with growing horror that Burton's greatest mistake hadn't been killing James.

It had been doing it in front of his family.

Because the Blackwoods might have spent centuries running from their nature, but they were still vampires.

Vampires, Sarah was learning, did not forgive, or forget.

And they would not let their children s murders go unavenged.

61

IN DAWN'S CLEAR LIGHT

James' blood seared Will's tongue, a molten hunger drowning everything else until—

"Help me!" Iona's desperate cry pierced the fog of bloodlust. "I can't hold them both!"

Through red-tinted vision, Will saw Ethan thrashing in the pond, dragging Finn under with him. Iona fought to keep both boys' heads above water, her jeans dragging her down like an anchor, her dark hair plastered against her face as she struggled to keep them afloat. Will stared at his blood-covered hands, James' taste still burning through him, each heartbeat pushing the hunger deeper into his veins. The need. The power. The—

"WILL! Don't you *dare* lose yourself now!"

Something in Iona's voice reached past the monster clawing inside him, found the human core that remained.

Will plunged into the pond. The shock of cold water cleared his head as James' blood washed away in crimson swirls. He reached Ethan in three desperate strokes, wrapping an arm around the boy's chest. The child's terrified heartbeat pounded against Will's arm as he pulled him clear, freeing Iona to focus on Finn.

The sun crested the tree line, and Will felt each ray like a judgment. Morning light flooded Cherry Hill, bringing with it a sudden chorus of birdsong, as if nature itself had been holding its breath through the night's horrors. Behind them, James' body smoldered where the sunlight touched it; his remains crumbled and collapsed, leaving nothing but a pile of gray ash that could have passed for the remnants of an illicit campfire.

The leaf-blower's whine grew louder, shattering the moment. Its operator rounded the bend, unknowingly scattering James' ashes to the wind before freezing at the sight before him - two adults and two children floundering in the early morning pond.

"Hey!" The machine sputtered to silence. "You folks okay?"

"Help us out," Iona gasped between chattering teeth. "The boys can't—"

The gardener rushed forward, boots crunching on the gravel path as he helped drag them to safety. They collapsed in a shivering heap as water pooled beneath them on the sun-warmed stones. Ethan clung to Will's arm, his small fingers digging in with desperate strength.

"There was a woman," Iona said between ragged breaths, her cop instincts kicking in even now. "In her 70s. White hair. Cardigan. If you see her—"

"She won't be back," Will cut in, his voice as hollow as he felt. "Not in the daylight. Not after what James did to protect these boys."

Will gently disentangled himself from Ethan's grip and pushed himself up. His soaked clothes weighed him down, but rage drove him forward now - not the supernatural hunger that had consumed him moments before, but human fury. Pure, righteous anger at what Burton had done to James, to Rufus, to innocent children who'd just wanted to sail a toy boat.

He ran, each squelching step carrying him away from the pond, away from James' scattered ashes, away from what he'd almost done. The taste of vampire blood still burned on his tongue, but it was overshadowed now by something stronger.

The need for justice.

Burton thought he could turn Will into a weapon? Fine. Will would be a weapon. But not the kind Burton expected.

He would be the instrument of the sea captain's destruction, because some monsters needed to be stopped, no matter the cost.

As he ran through the empty streets toward York Tower, Will wasn't afraid of what he was becoming. He was going to use it.

And Isaac Burton was about to learn that turning Will Taylor into a monster had been the biggest mistake of his very long life.

Because this monster remembered who he used to be.

And he was coming home.

62

———

GOING UP

Amanda Pike's pale, emaciated fingers hovered over the polished brass handle. She could smell them beyond the door. Creatures, the like of which she was beginning to know all too well. The smell of their hunger was becoming all too familiar. The three Blackwood scents hit her like signatures - Richard and Elizabeth's controlled, aged blood, and their daughter Sarah's human pulse singing with youth and fear. And then Burton's scent - her sire, the one who'd cursed her with this terrible, twisted, burning hunger.

But the Blackwoods didn't matter. They were just rich parasites playing at being predators. Only preying on the elderly and infirm, but never killing for fun. They fed for sustenance. Not like Burton.

Her fingers closed around the door handle. Such a mundane thing, cool brass against her skin. How strange that something so ordinary could be the gateway to such horror.

Behind her, two floors down, she could hear the labored breathing of strangers climbing the stairs. Hunters, by the smell of them. She could have sworn she knew their scents fractionally. They thought they were being quiet, but to her new senses, they might as well have been stamping up the stairs.

Amanda smiled, her lips pulling back to reveal teeth that were no longer entirely human. Let them come. They'd be too late to stop what needed to be done. Burton had to die. For Ethan and Zoe. For every parent who'd ever had to protect their child from monsters, both real and imagined.

The maternal rage that had been simmering in her chest since her transformation exploded into white-hot fury. Burton had turned her into this thing, this mockery of motherhood. Had made her hunger for her own children's blood. Had corrupted the most sacred bond in existence - the love between mother and child.

He would pay for that. Even if it meant her own destruction.

Amanda turned the handle, silent as death itself, while eight floors below, death had already visited.

Will burst through the lobby doors, pond water streaming off him. His reflection caught his eye - a stranger staring back, wild-eyed and dripping, nothing like the confident security officer who'd started his shift what felt like a lifetime ago. Before everything went wrong. Before Rufus...

The elevator's familiar space felt wrong now. Everything looked normal - brass railings gleaming, carpet freshly vacuumed - except for those tiny drops of blood by the button panel. Rufus' blood. He knew it as surely as he knew the weight of failure pressing against his chest.

"You're overthinking again, rookie," Rufus would have said, the way he had a hundred times. But Rufus wasn't here to say it. Wasn't here to complain about the puddles forming beneath Will's feet on his pristine carpet, or to argue with the cleaning company about their standards. And there'd be no more terrible coffees in the break room while trading stories about the building's eccentric residents.

Will's hand shook as he swiped his access card. The penthouse button lit up, and the doors slid closed with their usual quiet precision. Just another morning at York Tower. Except for those drops of blood that no one else would notice. Except for the empty desk in the lobby where Rufus should have been sitting, doing his impossible crosswords, and pretending not to watch Will's back.

The elevator began its smooth ascent. Will counted the floors, each number bringing him closer to whatever waited above. To the truth about the Tower. To the reason his friend had died protecting the building's tenants while Will had been chasing shadows in the park. To Burton, and the Blackwoods, and all the secrets that had been hiding behind York Tower's polished facade.

Seven floors to go. Six. Five.

Will checked his holster, though he already knew the gun would be useless. Rufus had tried to tell him that morning, tried to explain about Burton, about the impossible things happening above him. But Will hadn't listened. Hadn't wanted to believe.

Four floors. Three.

He thought of Rufus' last radio call. The fear in his voice when he'd mentioned Mrs. Johnson.

Two floors.

Will squared his shoulders, feeling the preserved blood burning in his veins, giving him strength for what was to come. Whatever was waiting for him, he wouldn't let Rufus' death be for nothing.

One floor to go.

The elevator slowed its ascent, and Will braced himself. For the truth. For justice, or vengeance, or whatever came next.

The elevator chimed.

And as the doors slid open, Will Taylor stepped into hell itself.

The penthouse reeked of blood and terror. Candles flickered in the pre-dawn darkness, casting writhing shadows on marble walls. In the center of the room, Isaac Burton held Sarah Blackwood like a trophy, while her parents flanked him like predators themselves.

And scattered across the expensive Italian marble, Matthew Peart's body lay in a spreading pool of crimson.

"Ah," Burton said, his voice carrying centuries of patient malice. "Our final guest has arrived."

Will's hand moved to the silver pen in his pocket, Marion Bruce's last gift burning against his palm.

Isaac Burton's long reign of terror was about to end.

63

CHAOS

Amanda slipped into the penthouse, her heart hammering against her ribs as her eyes found Burton by the terrace. Dawn's flattering light made him look almost human. The blood bond tugged at her veins, demanding submission, but one thought burned brighter than Burton's call: "Where is Ethan?" She gently closed the door behind her - to stop herself from running, if nothing else.

Burton turned, and the mild amusement in his expression made her want to scream.

"Your boy?" Burton's voice slid through her veins like ice. "You'll have to be more specific. Everyone seems to be losing their sons."

Richard Blackwood moved like lightning.

Amanda pressed herself against the wall, her body swaying toward Burton even as her maternal instincts screamed to find Ethan.

"Elizabeth, take Sarah. Run!" Richard grappled with Burton, sending them careening into a wall of books. Leather-bound volumes rained down around them as ravens exploded from the terrace, their wings beating against the glass, drowning Sarah's screams as Elizabeth pulled her behind an ornate silk screen - and the penthouse door burst open.

Karl and Charlotte charged in with their stakes raised.

"Blackwoods!" Karl snarled, raising his stake. "End them all!"

Amanda swayed between Burton and the door, her face contorted as the blood bond sang in her veins, conflict infusing every fiber of her body. To protect her own son - or submit to her sire.

The elevator chimed and Will burst out, water dripping from his clothes. The penthouse door was wide open and a tableau of madness presented itself. And among it all, he saw Karl moving toward the silk screen where Elizabeth and Sarah huddled, murder in his eyes. "No!" He yelled, grabbing Karl's arm. "They're not the enemy!"

"They're vampires! Monsters!"

A crystal chandelier swayed overhead as Burton and Richard slammed into another wall. Will positioned himself between Karl and the two women. "Karl, listen to me - James' blood... I can feel it. Burton is-"

Karl threw Will aside with a cry from the Crusades. Charlotte pressed her stake to Amanda's throat. "Nobody leaves alive."

"Please," Elizabeth begged from behind the screen. "My daughter isn't a threat..."

"RUN!" Richard's voice boomed.

Ravens beat against the windows as Burton's laugh echoed like a funeral bell.

"This isn't what you think." Will's blood pounded in his ears - the urge to lunge at Karl's neck - the power surging through his veins - the desire to keep what remained of his soul. "You're fighting the wrong enemy."

Karl edged toward the screen, centuries of vampire hunting doctrine burning in his eyes. "The girl has to die. The taint runs in their blood."

"Sarah isn't one of them!" Will dragged him back. "Amanda's only half-turned. We can save them!"

Burton caught Richard's fist mid-swing. "Save them? A blood bond can't be broken."

Will felt the preserved blood coursing through his veins, fighting Burton's influence - and the pieces clicked together.

"The blood in Karl's vials..." The realization hit him like a thunderbolt. "It was Rachel's, preserved from Manchester. That's why I can resist Burton - I've been drinking the blood of his first creation, his first betrayal."

Burton's amusement vanished. Richard froze mid-swing. The ravens' wings matched Will's pounding heart as the truth crystallized.

"You're wrong," Richard gasped. "Burton killed her. She turned me."

Burton inhaled deeply, eyes bright with recognition. "Ah, Manchester, Vermont. That lovely little house in Blackwood Estates." His smile widened as Karl went rigid. "Your daughter - Emma, wasn't it? Such a sweet child. And your wife Sophie... they made a delightful amuse-bouche."

"You..." Karl's voice shook. "It was you?"

"Emma tasted of strawberry lip gloss and summer nights. Sophie had just washed her hair - lavender shampoo, I believe."

Karl's stake clattered to the floor. Will watched the truth shatter him - all these years hunting the Blackwoods, when the real monster had been someone else entirely.

"Amanda!" Will maintained his position in front of the women. "Your son is safe! He's with Detective Melville, in the park!"

Amanda's eyes cleared. "Ethan?"

"James tried to save him. James Blackwood was protecting the boys when-"

"Lies!" Charlotte's stake pressed harder into the woman's neck. "Why would a vampire save a human child?"

"Because not all monsters are the same! The Blackwoods only fed to survive, but Burton... Burton feeds for pleasure!"

Burton straightened, releasing Richard's throat, his face a study in cold fury. "A fascinating theory. Shame you won't live to prove it."

The chandelier gave way. As everyone looked up at the falling crystal, Charlotte's stake flashed forward, plunging through Amanda's neck.

Amanda's scream cut through the chaos like a blade -

not just pain, but pure maternal rage. Her eyes found Burton's as her life bled out onto Italian marble.

"My children..." she whispered, her voice carrying across the penthouse like a curse. "You turned me... against my children..."

Burton's smile faltered as Amanda's body crumpled to the floor.

"Yes," he said softly, but there was something like uncertainty in his voice now. "I did."

Will's hand closed around the silver pen in his pocket, Marion Bruce's final gift burning against his palm. The preserved blood in his veins sang with righteous fury - not just his own anger, but Rachel's rage, carried across centuries. She'd loved Richard Blackwood. Had died trying to protect him from Burton's jealousy.

And now her blood would finally have its revenge.

"This ends now," Will growled, the pen sliding into his hand.

64

THE PRICE OF VICTORY

For a heartbeat, no one moved.

Amanda's body slumped to the floor, her final breath carrying a mother's curse. Karl's eyes darted between Richard and the screen where Elizabeth still shielded Sarah. Centuries of misplaced vengeance focused into one moment as he charged toward mother and daughter, stake raised.

Richard moved instantly, shoving Sarah behind him, leaving Elizabeth exposed for just a fraction of a second. It was enough. Karl's stake found her heart.

"No!" Richard roared, shattering the windows as Elizabeth crumbled to ash.

Will's hand closed around the silver pen in his pocket. In the same moment that Elizabeth died, he launched himself at Burton, driving the silver point toward the vampire's heart.

Burton twisted. The pen skidded off a rib, sinking deep but not deep enough. Burton's howl of pain rattled the chandelier crystals still scattered across the floor. Blood - old, dark blood - spread across his pristine shirt.

Sarah's sob caught in her throat as her mother turned into a pillar of ash beside her. And as her hands tried to gather three hundred years of existence, her mother's form crumbled into dust.

Ravens poured in through the windows, their wings beating against the walls, their beaks snapping at anything that moved. The morning light caught their feathers, turning the chaos into a storm of black glass.

Burton stumbled back, the pen still protruding from his chest. His smile was gone, replaced by something ancient and terrible. "This isn't over." His voice carried over the ravens' screams. "It's never over."

He fell backward through the broken window. By the time Will reached it, Burton was gone, leaving only bloody handprints on the wall.

Richard froze, his face twisted in grief and fury, staring at where his wife had last stood. Karl backed away, stake still raised but hands shaking, the zealot's certainty finally broken.

Karl dropped his stake, the clatter lost in the ravens' chaos. "All these years..." His voice cracked. "I've been hunting the wrong monster?"

"She was protecting our daughter," Richard's words came out between sobs. "She wasn't even fighting back."

Sarah's hands were gray with her mother's ashes. "Dad?" Her voice was small, childlike. "Dad, I can't... I can't keep her together. She's blowing away."

Charlotte pressed herself against the door, her stake slick with Amanda's blood. Everything she'd been taught, everything she'd believed about the Blackwoods, crumbling like the ash that swirled around them.

Outside, the ghostly sound of sirens floated up to them.

"Richard." Will's voice was soft but firm. "The sirens. You need to go."

But Richard couldn't take his eyes off the settling ash, off his daughter's desperate attempts to gather what remained of her mother. Three centuries of love, reduced to dust.

The ravens' wings beat a funeral march as the first rays of the morning sun finally struck the penthouse floor.

Will knelt beside Sarah, his voice gentle. "I'm sorry about your mother. She died protecting you."

Sarah looked up at him, tears streaking through the ash on her face. "She called me her greatest treasure."

"Because you are," Will said simply.

Richard finally stirred, moving to kneel beside his daughter. Together, they gathered what they could of Elizabeth's remains, though most had already scattered on the wind that rushed through the broken windows.

"She's gone," Sarah whispered.

"No," Richard said, his voice stronger now. "She's free. For the first time in centuries, she's free."

The sirens were getting closer. Karl looked toward the stairwell, then back at the Blackwoods. "I need to tell them something. About what happened here."

"Tell them the truth," Will said. "That you stopped the real monster."

"What about Burton?"

Will touched the spot where the pen had found its mark. "He's wounded. Badly. Silver does that to his kind. And now he knows we're coming for him."

"We?" Richard asked.

"The war isn't over," Will said. "But now we know who we're really fighting."

As the police poured into the building below, the survivors of the penthouse battle looked out over a city that would never know how close it had come to an ancient evil claiming final victory.

Burton was gone, but not defeated. The Blackwood family was shattered, but not destroyed. And Will Taylor had discovered that some monsters could choose to be human.

The price of victory had been paid in blood and ash and broken families.

But it had been paid. And sometimes, that was enough.

Outside the broken windows, the ravens took flight, disappearing into the dawn sky like shadows fleeing the light. Their master was wounded, perhaps dying.

But wounded was not dead.

Will looked out over the city he'd sworn to protect, feeling the weight of his transformation settling over him like armor.

He would be ready if Burton returned.

They all would.

EPILOGUE

The New York Times called it the 'York Tower Murders'. The Post was less subtle: 'Mother's Deadly Rampage'.

Despite the sensational headlines, the case was closed within weeks. Detective Melville's report was concise and convincing - Amanda Pike, suffering a severe postpartum psychotic break exacerbated by her husband's prolonged absences, had been responsible for the deaths at York Tower. Her own death was ruled self-inflicted after what was described as a *violent confrontation with building security.*

The disappearances of Elizabeth and James Blackwood were noted, but not dwelled upon. Society columns speculated they had fled to Europe after the scandal, too ashamed to face New York society. Richard Blackwood's official statement expressed deep regret over the tragic events at his property, and announced his temporary withdrawal from public life to care for his daughter, Sarah, who had witnessed everything.

The Times didn't mention the USB drive Sarah had slipped to Detective Melville, or the evidence it contained of Burton Holdings' decades-long financial manipulation of elderly residents across Blackwood properties.

Rufus St John was hailed as a hero. His funeral drew hundreds, including Mayor Adams, who praised his sacrifice in protecting York Tower's residents. Will leaned against the wall at the back of the church, away from the sunlight streaming through stained glass windows, thinking about the holes-in-one that would never be scored and fishing trips that would never happen.

Sally Johnson spoke at the service, her voice breaking as she described the security guard who'd become like family to her. She never mentioned finding her mother's body in the stairwell, or the mercy Will had shown in ensuring June's suffering ended quickly. Some truths were too dark for public consumption.

The vials of Rachel's blood had done their work. Will's transformation had stabilized, leaving him with enhanced senses and strength, but his humanity intact.

He'd told no one about the additional vials he'd found in apartment 306, not even Iona. He'd cleared those out before the crime scene team arrived. The preserved blood of Burton's first victim had become Will's anchor to his human soul.

Karl and Charlotte had disappeared after the funerals, their hunter network dissolved. If they were rebuilding somewhere, tracking Burton across the globe, no one in New York knew about it. The war had moved on, but Will doubted it was over.

Melville's son Finn had nightmares about the park, but the therapist said that was normal for a child who'd nearly drowned. Finn never talked about seeing James turn to ash, or the attack by June Johnson. But sometimes, when he thought no one was looking, he'd touch the spot on his neck where phantom teeth had almost found their mark.

Iona kept her gun closer now, loaded with the silver bullets Karl had left behind. Bullets she hoped never to fire, but knew she might have to. The official story was clean, but she remembered the truth. Some stories were too dangerous to tell, but too important to forget.

York Tower stood empty, its residents fleeing from the building's dark history. The apartments remained unsold.

Even in New York's cutthroat real estate market, some bargains were too good to be true.

Window washers refused to work there after reporting constant attacks from ravens. The birds had claimed the building as their own, their calls echoing through empty hallways. They were waiting for something. Or someone.

Richard and Sarah Blackwood had indeed left the country, but not in shame. They'd gone hunting. Richard's grief had crystallized into cold purpose, and Sarah's humanity had become their greatest weapon against creatures who'd forgotten what it meant to love.

The case was closed, and the city moved on.

But in the shadows between skyscrapers, Will Taylor walked his beat with new purpose. His enhanced senses picked up things others missed - the scent of old blood, the whisper of supernatural movement, the subtle wrongness that preceded an ancient evil's arrival.

Burton was still out there. As patient as death itself, building new plans in dark places. The silver pen had hurt him, but silver wounds healed eventually. And when they did, he would return.

Will was ready for him.

In the end, some wars never truly end. They just wait for the next generation to pick up the weapons their predecessors had dropped.

Will Taylor, security guard turned reluctant hunter, understood that.

He also understood that some things were worth fighting for: Justice. Truth. The simple right of children to sail toy boats on park ponds without being hunted by monsters.

As he walked through the sleeping city, silver pen burning in his pocket like a promise, Will smiled.

Let Burton come. Let him bring his ravens and his ancient grudges and his centuries of hate.

Will Taylor would be waiting.

The End...

If you enjoyed reading about vampires hidden in plain sight, perhaps you might also enjoy a ghost story. Described as the "Antiques Roadshow if Stephen King was the host..." Kirsten McKenzie's gothic ghost story *Painted*, brings you the same sort of chills as those felt by Will, outside apartment 306 of York Tower.

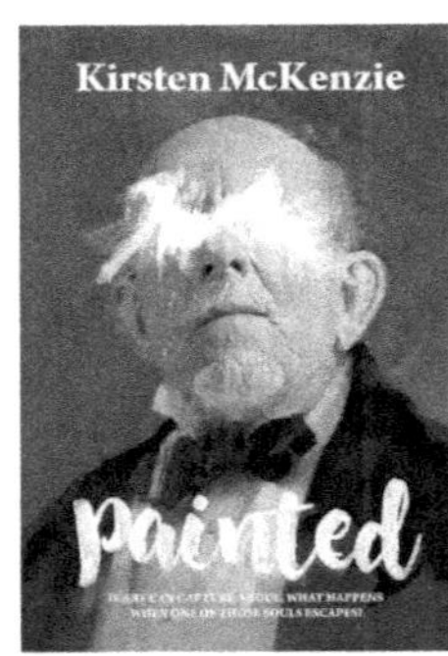

REVIEW

Dear Reader,

Thank you for daring to tread the halls of York Tower.

If you enjoyed creeping through the chilly corridors of the *Vampires of York Tower*, could you please leave a review or a rating on your preferred digital platform?

Reviews are essential to authors.

Thank you

Kirsten McKenzie x

BOOK CLUB DISCUSSION QUESTIONS

1. What was your favorite part of *the Vampires of York Tower*?
2. Did you race to the end, or was it more of a slow burn?
3. Would you want to live in York Tower?
4. Would you want to read another book by this author?
5. What surprised you most about the characters in this book?
6. Where do you want to retire to, in a perfect world?
7. Are there lingering questions from the book that you're still thinking about?
8. Who deserved to die, and who should have lived?
9. What do you think happens after the official ending?
10. Did the book make you squeamish in any way? How?

ACKNOWLEDGMENTS

The idea for this book blossomed as I was in an anesthetic fug after ten hours of surgery. As the nurses woke me continuously to check my wounds and to administer more pain relief, I left increasingly weird voice notes for myself. Thank you to the nurses at Mercy Ascot. They are the true heroes we all deserve. Especially in our darkest moments.

I've always loved reading, and watching, vampire fiction, and zombie fiction, much to my family's dismay! There's something about the undead which fascinates. I also really loved the series 'Only Murders in the Building'. A marriage, of sorts, between the two seemed inevitable. So here we are.

Thank you to my dear friend Emma Oakey for her editorial assistance. And to my brilliant beta readers for their invaluable assistance in ironing out the kinks - Terry Masters, Ken Briggs and David Cox. You are all legends.

As always, I wouldn't have managed to finish this one without the assistance of Andrene Low. What on earth would I do without you???

Finally, thank you to my wonderful family, Fletcher, Sasha, and Jetta. And to the cat, Lulu. You all make life way more interesting than my books!

Kirsten xxx

ABOUT THE AUTHOR

Kirsten McKenzie spent 14 years fighting international crime as a Customs Officer in England and New Zealand before joining the family antique business. Now a full-time author, she writes time travel trilogies and thrillers from her home in New Zealand, where she lives with her husband, two daughters, and a rescue cat.

Her historical time travel trilogy, *The Old Curiosity Shop* series, has been called "*Antiques Roadshow* gone viral". Her latest collaboration is the Cheviot Hills Time Travel series with author Shawn Inmon. Book #1 is titled *The Deadly Life of Diana Penn*, with book #2 - *The Helpful Life of Gris Morley*, out in early 2026.

Kirsten's bestselling gothic thriller *Painted* almost made it to Netflix. Her latest thriller, *The Vampires of York Tower*, adds a dark twist to her body of work.

When not writing, she organises author events and speaks at literary festivals worldwide.

Join her newsletter at:
www.kirstenmckenzie.com/newsletter